TANDEM BOOKS LIMITED

The Edge of Battle

Barrie Pitt

After the November attack the English Army had
been forced back over their own tracks by
Rommel's Panzers in a brilliant counter offensive
which came to a breathless, grinding halt in the
dustbowls between Tmimmi and Gazala.

Rommel's lifeblood was petrol and the Afrika
Corps had cached their remaining precious
supplies in the surrounding wadies and desert hills.

Moving out from Siwa and up from Kuffra came a
small silent group of gallant British soldiers whose
job was to infiltrate, seek out and destroy this
lifeblood of an immensely powerful modern army.

This brilliant and exciting book is the story of two
men who chose to serve and of how they lived and
fought to the death in one of the decisive battles of
the war.

D1340576

The Edge of Battle

Barrie Pitt

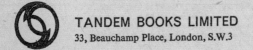

TANDEM BOOKS LIMITED
33, Beauchamp Place, London, S.W.3

First Tandem Edition 1965
Copyright © Barrie Pitt

Made and printed in Great Britain by
C. Nicholls & Company Ltd

PART ONE

Chapter 1

ALAN LOCKYER lay on his back, hands behind his neck, knees raised, in the classic attitude of the cartoonist's tramp, khaki cap-comforter in place of the battered billycock, eyes half-closed against the blue brilliance of the Cyrenaican sky above him. Were it not for a desire to savour to the full this delicious content, he would have allowed himself to drift off into sleep: as it was, he remained on the edge of wakefulness, his thoughts wandering across the border into dreams and back again, as awareness and a slight sense of duty tugged against the warm indolence and comfort of his position.

He was happy. Happier – and he knew it – than he had ever been in his life before, happier – and he suspected it – than he was ever likely to be again, but with a sureness of instinct which had only come to him of late he wasted no time in sadness for past or future, but lived joyously in the present.

He was twenty-two and in perfect health. At no expense to himself he had been transported from a dull and pompous suburbia, set – so his memory told him – in the confines of a tight stiff collar and under grey and weeping skies, to the warm, gently-pulsing, open beauty of the Jebel Ahkdar. Below him, forty feet away and dropping ten, ran the Martuba By-pass: thirty-five miles west along it, lay Slonta, and here, like a latter-day satrap, waited General Piatti for the results of his latest offer of 5,000 lire for information leading to Alan's capture.

It was not a very large sum. In actual fact it was worth little more than the paper it was printed on and moreover it must be admitted that Alan was not particularly specified, being merely one of the group whose individual nuisance value had been assessed at that figure: but it all added up to a feeling of satisfaction. Not only was he living a life of carefree, almost idyllic indolence, but he was acquiring considerable merit at the same time, and as far as the danger of anyone qualifying for the reward was concerned, Alan had been out long enough to realise that this was almost non-existent. Almost – not quite. Just – almost. And the slight element of risk gave his unexacting duties a piquancy which salved his conscience and justified his content. He sighed happily, and settled his shoulders further into the gritty soil under him.

Somewhere away in the distance, an engine muttered, labouring its vehicle over the battered road surface, its growing persistence penetrating the honey haze around Alan's mind and dragging him fully awake. He rolled over and looked down at the road. Beside him behind the clumped bushes, lay his friend and partner in the clandestine duties of the day. Together they waited, watching the point where the road first came into their view around a steep and wooded bluff.

"Starting early this afternoon, aren't they?" observed Alan. "Only three o'clock! Il Duce must be getting anxious!"

"Rommel's getting anxious you mean," answered his companion. "So'd I be if I had to rely on a shower of wops for supplies. What with Musso lookin' after his lines of communication, and those perishin' horse flies they breed around Gazala, I don't reckon he's sitting all that pretty!"

"Sooner be in his shoes at the moment than Cunningham's though," said Alan reflectively, "Look out, Jim – here they come."

Flat to the ground, peering through the sparse cover, the two men watched the corner. Eventually, a fifteen hundredweight truck came into sight and grumbled fussily past, it's engine worn, its body scarred, nondescript boxes piled in the back.

"Naafi Stores!" muttered Jim, marking a dust-covered exercise book in the appropriate column. "What a way to win the war – sitting behind a bush, counting Ities driving past with fags for the Afrika Korps!"

"Driving by in our trucks, too!" agreed Alan cheerfully. "Never mind, James, my lad, you don't want to let it get you down. It's better than sitting in the transit camp, whichever way you look at it – and all this might be of some use to someone, sometime. How do you think G.H.Q. would know what they're up against without the reports His Nibs sends in?"

"They could probably read it in the Egyptian Daily Mail!" said Jim gloomily, " – always supposing they've got chaps there who can read. Sometimes I doubt it!"

"No spirit in which to win the war, Jim," said Alan reprovingly, " – you must remember we are intrepid spies. And here – if I am not mistaken – come that fine body of enemy troops, Graziano's Glee-Boys."

To the rather desperately sung strains of "Giovanezza, Giovanezza . . ." a lorry swept by crammed with dishevelled youths ranging from the age of eleven up to sixteen. The emblem of the Fascist Youth was painted on the truck bonnet and its significance caused Alan's brows to come level and Jim's mouth to tighten in severe disapproval.

"Why the blazes don't they send those kids home?" asked Jim.

"He's not going to get his victory march through Alexandria now, and he must know it. What about the kid's parents and their schooling?"

"I doubt whether either of them count for much compared to old Musso's feelings, Jim. They were sent out to pull his processional chariot – and I don't think he'll let them back while he can kid the Ities that there's any hope of 'em doing it. In the meantime, they probably come in useful for odd jobs. We used the Boy Scouts in the last war."

"That was at home," said Jim, " – and we certainly didn't let 'em go around shooting prisoners of war – "

"Here's something, Jim. This looks better!"

Three German troopcarriers, their cargoes sitting with the peculiar uniformity which only the Teuton can impress upon their rankers, hummed powerfully by, dust clouds swirling in the air behind them. Their evident worth as a foe dispersed some of the repugnance that sight of the regimented children always aroused in British troops, and Jim duly marked their passage in the exercise book. When he looked up, however, his snub nose was wrinkling in another form of distaste. "Phew!" he said. "You can smell 'em even from here. What the blazes is it? Something they eat, or what?"

"I don't know," answered Alan, his nostrils still holding the faint, sepulchral odour. "It was the same in the last war. I read somewhere that when our chaps took their trenches, they couldn't live in the dug-out for the first few days. Remember in Belgium, the first time we smelled it? I thought it was Diesel oil then, but it's not. It's just Jerry!"

"It's a stink, anyway," said Jim. "What's the matter?"

Alan had twisted around suddenly and was staring after the departed troop carriers. He lay, alert but curiously relaxed, grey-blue eyes half-hooded, long, narrow face unworried.

"They've stopped just around the corner," he announced. "Let us advance strategically to the rear!"

Picking up messtins, waterbottles, exercise book and weapons, they scrambled to their feet and beat a rapid retreat over the hill-crest behind them, pausing only to drag an overcoat over the place where they had been lying. It would pass a casual inspection.

Down the back of the hill they ran, Lockyer leading, long legs covering the ground easily and confidently. Behind him, Jim Bannerman dodged neatly between the rocks and bushes, his more compact, tighter-knit frame a brisk contrast to Locket's tall ungainliness. They ran over the top of the next rise and then stopped, dropping beside the end of a low stone wall which ran down, further behind them again, to end above a stone water cistern built deep into the ground.

"Reckon we're far enough back, Alan?" asked Bannerman. "We'll be bitched if they come this far – it's pretty open behind us."

"They won't," answered Lockyer. "They'll search the top and the road slope – that's all, and unless some of 'em have actually been shot up by the parashots or the Long Range Desert Group, they won't do even that very thoroughly."

Speculatively, Alan's eyes roamed along the crest of the hill over which they had just run, watching for the first signs of the Germans. In due course they appeared, minuscule, khaki, purposefully scurrying. The searching forms appeared and disappeared over the ridge, sometimes heads, sometimes torsos, occasionally full bodies, bobbing up and down over the hill-crest like tiny Aunt Sallies.

"Could you hit 'em from here, Jim, do you reckon?"

Jim scanned the broken and scrub-dotted slopes which separated them from the prospective target, his lips moving in silent computations.

"Best part of half a mile," said he at last. "It'd be pretty dicey. If three of 'em stood together for more than ten seconds, I'd reckon to put a shot into the group – maybe two – but I couldn't guarantee to hit one by himself, especially if he was moving." He squinted along the barrel of his rifle, then laid it flat again. "I'd scare the daylights out of him, though" he added. "He wouldn't hang around!"

Alan stored this information with other carefully-garnered military lore.

"What could you do with a Bren up here?"

"Not much more than keep 'em off the crest." Jim, a regular, was the source of true military knowledge in the partnership, contributing to its efficiency from prewar experience in Palestine. Yet, despite this – despite also Jim's authority of rank, for he was a Corporal – it was Alan who led. His was the imagination, the ability to plan – and there was neither conscious superiority on his part nor hidden rancour in Jim's acceptance of a relationship which had now become natural to both of them. Alan now drew back below the hilltop and scrambled to his feet.

"Let's get along towards the place where they stopped the trucks," he said. "The road may break back around that corner as far as the end of this ridge. If it does, we can watch 'em from there, and check the rest of the traffic as well."

He slung his rifle, glanced quickly across the slope behind them, and moved off, hands in his overcoat pockets, head forward, eyes sweeping the foreground. Jim followed – the strong arm man, the guardian, the bodyservant. Occasionally one of them would move higher up the slope to keep check on the whereabouts and activity of the German patrols.

From a point almost a mile along the ridge, they saw the road again, now three hundred yards distant, its rutted surface curving away both sides to vanish behind dun-coloured bluffs. They could keep a temporary watch here, but it was a poor position compared to the one they had just left.

"The trucks must be around that corner somewhere," said Alan, pointing away to the left. "Between a quarter and half a mile. Pity we can't get nearer."

They lay behind rocks on the wide and now rather shallow crest, Alan marking the book as traffic roared, coughed or purred its way past, journeying up either to the front at Gazala or to the hastily re-constructed bases at Bomba or Tmimmi. They had been there almost an hour when three troop-carriers went past.

"That them, do you think?" asked Jim.

Alan squinted after the heavy trucks, black-rimmed thumbnail tapping against front teeth. At last he nodded.

"I reckon so."

There was silence for a while, and a question-mark hung in the shimmering air. Then Alan pushed himself up off the ground and slung his rifle again.

"Let's get back – but watch out." he said, and moved off. Instead of returning the way they had come, however, he led off across the ridge, parallel and within sight of the road, curving with it until they came to the steep end of the first ridge. Twice on the journey they dropped flat, once when a lone staff car hummed by, once for a pair of stuttering motor-cycles. Afternoon haze and the drivers' concentration on the road gave them an invisibility upon which fair risks could be taken.

At the foot of the slope, Alan paused.

"Jerry came up the other side of this. He must have first stopped just around that corner there." The ridge rose thirty yards away and the road bent away behind it. "If we're wrong, and that was three other troop-carriers – then they're still here. Freeze if you hear anything."

Cautiously they climbed towards the top, their hands and faces now coated with a thin sheen replaced as fast as the heat and the dry air evaporated it. For the first time since coming to the Jebel, Alan felt the dryness of throat and the faint, bitter taste around the edge of his tongue which by now he could recognise: it was allied, by association, with the sounds of Stukas, the peculiar 'phoop' of falling mortar bombs, and the insidious odour which had been the subject of their previous discussion. He held his rifle in one hand and wiped the palm of the other on his overcoat. The action was duplicated and repetitive.

At the top they lay down, peering and cautious, but with steadying pulse-beats. Then Alan rose and ran over the top in a crouching run. Behind him, Jim waited, rifle poised and attendant – the cover, the background, the reserve of strength. Seconds later, Alan came back still wary and preoccupied.

"O.K." he muttered. "It was them all right. But keep it quiet and stay off the skyline."

He stared back along the line of the road, then slowly quartered the scene around them. Sweat still shone on his forehead.

"Come on," he grunted, and led a little way down the back of the ridge, then along toward the place where they had first retreated across it keeping the crest between them and the road. As he walked along, some of the doubt left his eyes and a faint smile lifted the ends of a mouth a little too wide, a little too well-shaped.

When they were still seventy yards short of the crossing point, he stopped and lay down, his head just below the crest, making no attempt to move forward or up. Jim dropped unquestioningly beside him and together they waited, one for events, the other for instructions. Occasionally Alan wiped away the sweat, but he never turned to look back at Jim.

From well away in the distance came once more the growing hum of approaching traffic. Alan's head lifted, mouth slightly open, his ears catching and following the sounds. Two lorries rumbled and groaned their way nearer, changed down noisily for a rise around the far corner, changed up as they approached the bend and swung around into the stretch covered by the normal road-watch position. Alan counted five, giving the lorries time to travel about one third of the way along the stretch.

"Now!" he croaked, and pulled himself up towards the crest. Jim followed, taking in the slope, the road, the vehicles, the men and the weapons they carried, in one swift, all-embracing glance. Then he looked at Alan and on past him along his pointing arm.

"I thought so! Look at the bastards!" said Alan, triumphant satisfaction giving the words an almost visible rim.

Beyond the acacia bushes behind which they had themselves hidden from the road – but the other side now, to watch upwards to the hill crest, lay two light-grey and khaki forms, silver and cream against the drab background. The heads of the two Germans were turned away for the moment as they watched their own transport, already a welcome relief in the monotony of their boring, and to them unnecessary, ambush duty.

The lorries roared on past and Alan slid back below the crest, rolled over and sat up. Above him, Jim lay watching the Germans, rifle-butt supporting his chin.

"What now?" he asked softly. "Any point in giving 'em the works?"

Alan shook his head.

"Not likely! Leave 'em where they are. When they're picked up tonight they'll report no sign of anyone, and the place will be left alone for us to carry on. Might be an idea to switch somewhere else for a day or so, though. I wonder what His Nibs will have to say about it when we tell him?"

"Nothing much," answered Jim, a momentary gloom darkening his voice. "He'll turn pale, swallow his fag, and then ask us what to do."

There was no answer from Alan, who had not as yet made up his own mind about their commanding officer, and who, in any case did not judge from the traditions and practice which had moulded Jim's ideas. He rested his elbows on his knees and, hunching forward, supported his chin in his cupped hands, while he considered the possible explanations of the German search of the area.

Betrayal by one of the local Senussi he considered unlikely and in this he was correct, though not necessarily for the right reasons. Like many another man in a similar position, Alan was unable to restrain faith and hope from influencing his mental processes, and the strain of living in the Jebel, a scant hundred miles behind the enemy front line, would have been intolerable without implicit faith in the goodwill and integrity of the Bedouin tribesmen – sturdy individualists all, who were in fact far more actuated by hatred of the Italians than by love for the British.

However, there were other reasons than treachery for this sudden pin-point of the road-watch position.

"Rommel must know we keep checks by now," reasoned Alan, "All he's done is to order occasional searches of likely areas. He can read maps just as well as the bright boys in Cairo."

He examined his conclusions for weaknesses, found none, and accepted them.

"Not to worry!" he decided, easing his buttocks on the striated limestone and lying back. "We're all right, Jack!"

Euphoria again enveloped him in its comforts of physical warmth, laziness and self-satisfaction – for he was still surprised and gratified by this development within himself of talent which he had not known he possessed.

Above him, Jim watched the Germans, the road, the traffic, occasionally glancing down at the spreadeagled figure below him. His thoughts too, were concerned with their recent activities and this clear, probing ability of Alan's, which had once again taken and kept them out of trouble.

"I wonder how he does it?" he asked himself for the thousandth time, unenviously, for he was a simple person, uncomplicated by jealousy or malice, who had long accepted the wide divergence of human talents and character, and if he was always – through a spirit of loyalty – prepared to vote Socialist, he had never taken the doctrine of equality as anything but a political shibboleth.

Occasionally, during the next three hours, one of the four figures on the hillside moved; occasionally traffic swirled by in its accompanying dust-clouds to be dully watched by bored and cursing Teutons, and faithfully recorded in the exercise book by Jim. Then shortly after six o'clock, a light truck drew up, the members of the abortive ambuscade ran joyfully back to the road and were driven off in a chorus of heavily-playful recriminations and mock sympathy.

Alan and Jim watched their departure with mordant satisfaction.

"They want to try doing it for weeks on end," said Alan with some of the complacency of an old soldier. "That'd burn away some of their fat."

"They couldn't," asnwered Jim. "Not those two anyway. They don't know what it's all about yet – they haven't started losing."

He glanced at his watch.

"Back to the cave, chum. Another day gone: roll on the boat."

They tidied away all trace of their occupation of the area, searched the bushes where the Germans had lain but found nothing of use or importance, then made their way back over the ridge into the broken hills where outlaws and rebel shieks had hidden since the Italians first invaded the land. They walked fast and their coats were buttoned up – it was early enough in the year for an evening chill, and the nights were very cold.

The cave was long, once bent, in section oviform conveniently flattened at the bottom into a level but uneven floor. Giant blue shadows patched the grooved and inward-sloping walls, the blank, unwavering glare from the lamps robbing the scene of depth and giving it the strident appearance of a Bralac poster. The lamps hissed gently.

In the angle of the bend, a thin, middle-aged man, awkward of body but aesthetic of head and feature, sat on an upturned crate reading his way through reports piled on a packing-case table in front of him. Occasionally, he consulted a map. Often, he tore the papers he had read into pieces, placing the pad of irregular dockets in a tin beside him, to be burned later.

Charles Codrington St. Xavier Rutledge, ('His Nibs'), scholar of Charterhouse and Balliol, erstwhile marine engineer and Egyptologist of surprising success, now Major (Temp. Act.) on the General List, was in an unenviable position. Unlike the men under his command, his responsibilities were heavy and the resultant strain on his nervous system, continuous and exacting.

Moreover, he could entertain no hopes of an early relief, for he was in the Jebel as a permanency – at any rate until the British won the Benghasi Handicap on a less uneasy and untenable footing. Not for him the raider's glory, the coloured beret, the spreading wings of blue and silver, the swagger, the panache. When the campaign was over, Rutledge, if he still lived, would receive a decorous D.S.O., and resume once again the office routine, the endless sifting of information, from which the present emergency and his peculiar local knowledge had plucked him.

In the meantime, he sat unhappily but efficiently at the centre of a network of straightforward and relatively scrupulous espionage, accepting the reports of his agents and military associates, digesting and forwarding them in succint precis to Cairo.

Now he picked up a torn, discoloured slip of paper, compared the reference on it with a point on the map, destroyed the paper and sat back. For some minutes he sat in thought, thin, nicotine-stained fingers cracking each other's joints in deplored but uncontrollable habit. Then he turned and called softly into the branched depths of the cave: a rustle, a soft padding, and a young Arab appeared, graceful as a bronze tulip. At a liquid sentence from Rutledge, the camouflage nets across the entrance were pulled aside to show the silvered night beyond, and the boy vanished like a shadow.

Ten minutes later, Jim Bannerman marched into the cave, followed by Alan. Sa'ad Ali slid behind them back into the recesses of the cave, and the regular Corporal, reporting to his officer, came smartly to attention and saluted.

"You sent for us, sir?"

Rutledge regarded him with slight apprehension – mingled with annoyance that he should still be awed by the outward briskness of the parade-ground. He cleared his throat.

"Um – yes, Corporal. I did – uh – about this business of the – uh – roadwatch today." Rutledge swallowed and glanced up. "What had we better do about it?"

"Up to you, sir," answered Jim, woodenly.

"Yes," Rutledge looked crestfallen. "Yes – but, er – What do you think, Lockyer?"

"Could we leave the roadwatch a day or so, sir?" asked Alan. "After all, we're only a check on two others, and there's never been a great discrepancy between all our figures."

"That's true." From his voice one would think the point had never occurred to Rutledge. "We could take you away, of course. That is –" – and Alan could have sworn that Rutledge winked, "– if you wouldn't mind?"

Jim flushed slightly, and cleared his throat.

"No, sir. We wouldn't mind!" replied Alan, quickly.

"Good! Good! Then I think we might – er – do that. All right, Corporal?"

"Oh. Yes sir," answered Jim, grimly.

"But what shall we do with you in the meantime?"

Rutledge looked sorrowfully at the pair opposite him, spaniel's eyes in a tired, academic face. "I've – er – got a job here which needs – er – looking into."

The space above his desk became a momentary turmoil of maps, stilled when Jim suddenly leaned forward and tethered the furling edges.

"Oh – thank you, Corporal, thank you! Now look, you see this area here?"

His thin fingers sketched a nervous but nevertheless clearly-defined circle.

"We're in the middle. Here, look – and there's the road, crossing above us. Well, Cairo thinks Rommel's got a big fuel or arms dump somewhere around and they want us to find it for them. Where do you think it might be, Corporal. Or you, Lockyer?"

Alan looked down at the square of brown, wriggling contour lines, speckled here and there with the royal blue dots of wadis and mud-flats, patched with green. The faint, warm excitement which had first come to him years before during a geography lesson at school, of knowing, of understanding completely and fully the significance of each line and symbol and figure, rose again through him, to his eyes, his tongue, the palms of his hands. Smoothly, on the journey from the map to his mind, his brain translated the writhing, coloured maze into the hillocks and dips it represented, while his imagination clothed the land in scrub or trees, leaving it bare where it fell away to the desert in the south: soon the picture of the area lay like a sand-table in his mind.

Rutledge from observation and Jim from experience could both accept the facts of Alan's talent: Rutledge watched with deep interest, Jim with loyal pride.

"How certain is it that there's something here?" asked Alan, eyes still caressing the map.

"Pretty certain, but not completely so. Reports on supplies coming out of Benghasi don't tally with what we know Rommel has close up behind him. If the stuff has left port but hasn't arrived at Gazala, then it's somewhere between, dumped for a rapid retreat, or waiting to be rushed up if he advances again. It's very reasonable that he should form a dump somewhere around here."

The voice was firm now, persuading and unhesitant.

Automatically, Alan's eyes dropped to the southern boundaries of their area, where the foothills sloped away into the desert. Out there, he knew, lay many a carefully camouflaged supply dump of our own – petrol for the vehicles of the Long Range Desert Group, food, explosive and ammunition for the parashots – the bearded, unorthodox, intransigent – not to say bloody-minded – marauders of the Special Air Service.

If we could do it, so could Rommel.

"Try up this way a bit."

The suggestion was hardly audible, but the thin fingers, pointing across the contour lines, persuaded Alan's eyes and mind northwards. They paused along the line of hills between the Coast Road and the Southern Bye-pass.

"Guidano Corba looks a likely place, sir," said Alan at last, naming one of the Italian farming settlements.

All three men stared at the intersection of lines marking the main road junction and the cross-hatching which sprouted like a fuzz around it. Cigarette smoke drifted across the map.

"Road junction, of course," mused Rutledge waving the blue clouds away. "Any other reasons?"

Alan gazed dumbly at the map, suddenly aware of the impossibility of putting into words the conflux of feeling and intuition, of vaguely-perceived reasons for his suggestion. The ground flowed that way: it seemed fitting that there, in the basin in a double ridge, should be concentrated reserve supplies for a front line stretched south from the coast, a hundred miles away. But give chapter and verse for it he could not, and bitterly, Alan recognised that in two or three hours' time, he would probably be able to produce excellent reasons, supported by unanswerable logic.

But not now.

It was always like this, in the presence of Authority – even an Authority as loosely-held as Rutledge's.

"Difficult to say, sir," he eventually managed. "Where else do you think?"

He looked up sullenly to find Rutledge examining him with an air in which detachment and sympathy struggled for mastery, but before either of them could speak again, Jim's ever-present loyalty brought him crashing in to Alan's support.

"If Jerry's got a dump anywhere here, sir," he interjected defiantly, "– he'll have it on a road, won't he? So that he can get at it easily. Guidano Corba's as good a place as any!"

"Oh yes!" agreed Rutledge hastily. "I should say you're most probably right. So you'd like to have a look around there, would you? What do you think you'll find, petrol or arms? Rather a long way back for ammunition . . ."

"It'd be just right for petrol though," maintained Jim stoutly.

Rutledge was now secure behind his air of helpless eagerness.

"Of course it would!" – as though the idea had just burst upon him. "Excellent! Uh – so you'll have a look around that area for oil drums, eh? I think you'll probably prove to be right, y'know Lockyer – it seems just the place. Corporal Bannerman, you'll be able to give us an idea how much explosive will be needed, and the number of men – uh – and so on?"

"Won't the R.A.F. bomb it, sir?" asked Jim, surprised.

"I think not," said Rutledge, shaking his head. "This will be – uh – our party. With some help of, course. I expect the L.R.D.G. will bring in some of these – uh – parashot chaps to give us a hand. That's if we find anything of course. When will you be starting out? Tomorrow?"

"Just us two, sir?" asked Alan.

Rutledge raised his eyebrows.

"You don't want anyone else, do you? I think you have the necessary – er – talent, shall we say? – between you. You'll find the stuff if it's there, Lockyer, I'm sure – and the Corporal can carry on from there. Yes?"

"Oh – yes, sir. I suppose so."

Later, as he lay in his sleeping bag, remembering the conversation, Alan was glad he had not agreed with Jim's appraisal of their commanding officer.

"At least," he thought to himself. "He's not all beef and bull. I wonder if he's really as complicated as he seems? Or maybe it's subtlety?"

He pondered on Rutledge for a moment, and then his thought

16

passed on to the future and the task and responsibility it would bring. The future looked good. Alan was pleased with himself.

So, within the very narrow limits of self-satisfaction which he would allow himself, was Rutledge.

"Poor Corporal Bannerman," he thought with a slight smile. "I must be such a disappointment to him. Pity he trusts Lockyer so much though."

He lit another cigarette, picked up the next report and worked on into the night. At intervals, Sa'ad Ali came to the edge of the shadows and watched him, mutely reproachful.

Chapter 2

"I WONDER how Rutledge sticks it?" thought Alan to himself as he climbed carefully up through the scrub. "His nerves are tight as a banjo-string."

The slope gritted under his boots and a velvet darkness, deep, palpable, silver-studded above, filled the immediate world. Jim was somewhere behind, a solid, slightly-panting reassurance in a void which would have been sinister without his companionship. Wild thyme grew somewhere near, and the dark bulk of the hillside came back under their feet as they climbed over the brow and walked, upright again, across its wide and shallow top. Three miles ahead lay the Martuba Bye-pass which they should reach and cross within half an hour of midnight.

"I wonder *why* he sticks it?"

Here indeed, was food for thought, and as long as he succeeded in keeping one compartment of his mind awake to present actualities, and that other compartment tightly shut, it was a subject of almost infinite speculation. Why did other people undertake this sort of job?

Leaving Rutledge for the moment, Alan considered the subordinate members of the group – O'Reilly, for instance.

Fusilier O'Reilly was a large, fair-haired, raw-boned ex-labourer from Country Cork.

"Well now 'n' why shouldn't I join, will you tell me that?" he asked when Alan idly broached the subject, one night after an extended session of pontoon had died of inanition, despite the efforts of the Irishman to keep it going. "'Tes better than sittin' around all day on your arse in Abbassia Barracks, is it not? Bein' chased from mornin' till night by them Guards Sergeants?"

And Alan agreed, for he too had advanced that reason (but more circumspectly) at the interview with the Intelligence Officer who had selected them.

"Do you think that's a good enough reason to volunteer for work behind enemy lines?" asked the officer.

"Abbassia Barracks, sir," Alan had replied. "Is good enough reason to volunteer for fighter pilot, escort destroyer duty, submarines, paratroops, or just plain death!"

"As apart from fancy?" the officer had asked, amused. "What are the other reasons?"

"Must there be others, sir?" asked Alan, rather too quickly.

The officers stared at him speculatively for a while, then examined his finger-nails. "There usually are . . ." he said vaguely, ". . . but perhaps it doesn't matter – I think you'll do. You and Corporal Bannerman are – uh – together, I believe?"

Alan still half-believed that the officer had taken a firm grasp of the wrong end of the stick, but it was the result that counted, not the cause. He and Jim received their posting from Abbassia within a week – and were respectively delighted and astounded when they discovered that their new abode was a flat in Heliopolis. There they had remained for nearly a month during which they were subjected to a scrutiny of which even Alan was really only half-aware, but which provided material for the pages of a remarkably fat dossier upon each of them, now carefully filed away in subterranean vaults. It was after this pleasant interlude that they were suddenly transported out into the Jebel, but as far as Alan was concerned, the sybaritic note in their emloyment had been well maintained.

"This is the life for me, Jim!" he announced at the end of the first week. "Nothing to do, all day to do it in, and you to help me! I haven't been so happy since the day the Sergeant Major fell down the manhole!"

"It may not always be so cushy!" warned Jim, for his puritanical streak was causing him unease. Although he enjoyed the life, it's lack of hard routine or apparent danger made him feel slightly guilty.

However, satisfaction with the conditions – and all the junior members of the group agreed that – to date – it was far and away their easiest period of service, did not explain their separate and several reasons for originally volunteering – for they were not to know how pleasant they were to find it.

"I suppose McCarran came out because he's too scruffy to hold his commission comfortably anywhere else, and Lewis because he wants a gong."

McCarran and Lewis were the lieutenants, respectively short and dumpy, and tall and stringy. McCarran was much the pleasanter, his fat cushioning his nerves against most of life's trivial annoyances, his only social fault – from the group's point of view – an old-maidish fussiness in routine of duty which accorded oddly with his invariable appearance of having just emerged from a bed in a burning house. Lewis, however, was an entirely different character: a tight-mouthed, beady-eyed menace who, rumour had it, carried about with him a wallet containing a parachute badge, two extra cloth stars, a major's crowns, and the medal ribbons of the Distinguished Service Order and the Military

Cross. Rumour had, in fact, exaggerated: but only exaggerated.

"But as officers, we should have a cave to ourselves for messing in, Major," he had remonstrated upon arrival. "Surely you see that? Can't the men eat outside or in their sleeping quarters – or somewhere?"

"No," replied Rutledge, with unexpected menace. "They can't. But as it happens, I can solve your problem. One of our jobs is to keep watch on the traffic going Northwards from Slonta up to Cyrene. It's too far for the road watch to return here each evening, so we've provisioned a cistern near by. I think that might suit you – you won't have to share anything with anyone out there, and I'll arrange for Sa'ad Ali or his brother to fetch in your reports every other evening. Let me know when you've had enough!"

Much to some people's surprise and everyone's relief, Lewis had remained at his solitary post ever since, presumably, as McCarran was heard to remark, changing into service dress whenever he opened a new tin of bully. Jim alone, had some sympathy for him.

"Poor devil," he commented, when Lewis's name cropped up. "I wonder what it was that turned him so sour?"

But if Lewis was physically isolated in splendour on the Cyrene road, another member of the group, Sergeant Drummond, was isolated mentally and spiritually by a fierce reserve of his own manufacture. A sombre man, gaunt and iron-featured, he was a regular soldier who brought to the group its small proportion of orthodoxy, but he, unlike Jim, who had contempt for no-one, poured righteous scorn on the appearance, the abilities and the military value of the entire organisation.

"In nearly ten years I've never seen anything like it," he would hiss – for he would not honour his contempt with the thunder of his Parade Voice. "Officers – My God! Soldiers! I'd like to have 'em in the Depot for a few days! It's a – it's a" and his eyes would roll in his head in an attempt to find a sufficiently ignominious comparison. "It's a – a heap!" he would finish, beaten by his own indignation.

"Well, why did you join then?" asked Alan, the first time he listened to the denouncement, and was appalled by the effect of his question, for it was as though he had asked Judas the reason for the Betrayal. Drummond's rage left him – and with it, for a split second of bleak misery, went Drummond's manhood and self-respect. His eyes dropped, his jaw went slack, his face hangdog. Then he jerked himself together.

"I've reasons," he said, abruptly, and walked out of the cave. He did not return until early morning, and Alan gathered from the ubiquitous Sa'ad Ali that Drummond had spent most of the time hunched up in the shadow of a rock, muttering to himself. Some nights later, Alan woke to hear the muttering himself – only this time Drummond was asleep. There was something familiar about the rhythm, for the words themselves were indistinguishable – but it was not until Alan was drifting off to sleep again that he realised where their familiarity lay.

'Dum de dedum – Dum dededum – Dum dum –'

The clipped monotone conjoured up a vision of grey parade-ground and barking drill sergeants, and the first phrase came instantly to mind, to flow into the second.

"On the Command – Fix Bayonets – "

Now why should a man dream of bayonets? Even as he asked himself the question, the answer came to Alan's mind, for he had accidentally discovered Drummond's regiment, and by chance possessed the knowledge which enabled him now to make a shrewd guess at his battalion. Theirs was a story which had chilled the hearts of infantry men – Guardsmen, Greenjackets or Ghurkas.

Out of ammunition and cut off from supplies at the end of their first day's fighting in Belgium in 1940, unaware of the chaos and disaster which reigned behind them, the entire battalion (for they had suffered few casualties) bayonet-charged their way through a quarter-circle in an effort to contact their flanking units and re-fill their pouches. Finding no allies, they pivoted and swung on their forward position, clearing all before them with cold steel, and with blood slightly less hot than an hour before. Still no contact – and another swing forward, with their ranks now thinning, their hearts congealing, and still no aid or supplies.

So the shambles continued for a whole day until the survivors, faint and sick at heart, learned something of the conditions behind them, turned, and still without arms less personal and immediate than their bayonets, cut their way back. Three days later, twenty men, sole survivors of a proud thousand, re-established contact with their own troops, but it was over a month before any of them could be induced to give a coherent account of their activities.

"So that's why he joined, is it?" thought Alan. "I don't believe we've got a bayonet between us."

The catalogue of motive was growing. Escape from discipline or routine, desire for fame or glory, avoidance of specific horror: the interaction of personality and circumstance was capable of endless variation.

"And there too, go I!" thought Alan, for with a sudden flash of perception he saw that with all of the group so far, he had common cause. Like the Irishman, he had hated Abbassia, like McCarran he was glad to be quit of blanco and the parade ground, and if he was not specifically after a medal like Lewis, he knew he would be coyly delighted if he got one. Like Drummond, too, there were parts of his military experience to date which he had no desire to repeat.

His mind reviewed Rutledge, who was probably forcing himself to do his duty as he saw it, Jim – who came out of friendship for Alan – and the other private soldier in the group, a man of wide culture, considerable charm and light, sympathetic cynicism, named Whittaker.

"H'm, yes," thought Alan. "Whittaker."

And at the back of his mind came a warning creak, as though the door of the secret compartment was opening. Abruptly, he tried to check his thoughts, but a night march is conducive of reflection and the mind, once set moving along a certain course, attains a momentum not easily curbed.

"Whittaker, too, is running away from something!" Before he could stifle it, the thought was there in his mind – complete, irrevocable impossible to ignore.

"And how do you know that?" asked a smooth, inner voice. "Is it because you recognise a fellow sufferer?"

Wildly, Alan tried to ignore the question, but firmly – and so persuasively, the voice went on.

"You've managed to avoid thinking about this for some time now, haven't you? Why not have a quick peep in the cupboard, and see if the skeleton is still there? After all, it may have gone, or modified, or not really be so terrifying as you imagine."

Tentatively, Alan skirted around the idea. It had its attractions.

Before he could put it to the test, however, practical details interrupted. He found himself standing on the brow of a hill, looking down on the Martuba Bye-pass. It was twelve-fifteen.

"Watch it, Alan," murmured Jim from behind, and they both dropped flat.

Below them, the slope dropped away sharply, and fifty yards of open country separated them from the road. Only the slope and the first few yards of flat were in shadow.

"See anything, Jim?"

"No. Only you, stuck up against the skyline. What happened. Think it was a false crest?"

"M'm," said Alan, unwilling to admit inattention. "I wonder –"

He craned forward, peering down the slope, then stared up and down the length of the road. Shadows patched the ground across the road, which rose far sooner and more steeply than on the near side.

Alan drew back.

"We could risk it," he suggested tentatively.

"What for? asked Jim. "We can cross somewhere else can't we?"

"It'll be a long way round, now – and make us late."

"Look," said Jim, reasonably. "I'd sooner arrive at the cistern tired and late, than not arrive at all. If they've got patrols along the road tonight, and if one spotted us coming over the top, we'll be dead ducks. There are about fifty places down there where they could be lying in wait for us."

"O.K.," said Alan, and slid back behind the crest again.

They made their way along behind the protection of the ridge until the road bent, spent ten minutes watching it from deep shadow, then slipped across it separately each moving under the protection of the other's gun. In the first sizable patch of shadow, they waited again, watching for movement ahead. Then they climbed rapidly up between rock and bush and gained the protection of the first crest. Now the road lay behind them, its crossing uncomplicated, safe, uneventful. Alan had conducted and led it with adequate and commendable precaution.

He took up the cudgels with his inner voice.

"Look here," he addressed himself, firmly. "We'll have a little less of this Grand Inquisitor act, shall we? Not only does it detract from my concentration on the job in hand – thereby increasing the risks, which if small, nevertheless exist – it's also unfair and unnecessary. Why insist that Whittaker is my replica and counterpart? Why not Rutledge? If he has qualifications for his part of the job, so have I for my part! One very good reason I'm doing this job, is that Jim thought I'd be good at it! – and however simple and unsophisticated he may be in some ways," he concluded triumphantly, " – militarily, he's very sound!"

Thus abjured, conscience retired. More, however, to sharpen the hatchet than to bury it.

"And damn it – he's right," continued Alan, following up his advantage. "I *am* good at it – when my attention is not diverted by worries about something I couldn't help anyway."

Conscience struck.

"Whether you could help it or not, the situation exists!" and Alan, caught off mental balance, snapped his brain shut and sought distraction in practicality, glaring nervously and uncertainly into the deep night ahead.

Chapter 3

THE cistern was large – the size of a Bayswater drawing-room internally, hewn from the solid rock, and lined with masonry. The Romans, who built hundreds of these in the Jebel, seem to have handed only their engineering ability and industry on to their descendants, their martial process going illegitimately to the other half of the Axis partnership. Certainly the cistern as a structure, had withstood the test of time, and if only the Arabs had been possessed of the slightest foresight and maintainance ability, it would now have been half full of water. The broken and scattered remains of two dwarf walls, led down at an angle from the hillside above to the entrance of the cistern, designed originally to collect and funnel the water from the torrential winter showers.

Now, the walls were breached, the floor of the cistern cracked, the jointing between the blocks crumbled.

Alan and Jim, arriving just before three o'clock, had stacked their food and spare equipment in one corner, drawn out their sleeping bags, and with nearly three hours of darkness still left to them, bedded down under the bushes out on the hillside, Jim's rifle by his side, Alan's Tommy-gun under the bundle of clothing which served as his pillow.

At dawn they awoke, moved into the cistern and spent the morning dozing and keeping watch from the entrance. After a meal in the early afternoon, they tidied up, hid their rucksacks under bushes away from the cistern, and set out on a careful tour of the area, moving slowly towards the settlement which was their prime objective. Alan was intent, unworried: his mind had now cleared of the introspection of the night's march.

In the late afternoon they reached the crest of the ring of ridges around Guidano Corba, and found good cover midway along its southwest quadrant allowing them to overlook the Derna-Barce road – the Northern one – lying an exact diameter east and west just below. The southern circumference of ridges was wider on plan than the northern, leaving a smaller semi-circle of flat, in-habitable space in the centre.

"Well, it's something, anyway," admitted Alan, staring down at the scene of hive-like activity just below them. "But there must be something else here somewhere. It's too convenient a place for just a repair base."

Opposite them, as they looked due north across the road, lay

24

the repair sheds, the store-huts and living accommodation of an Italian base workshops. Fifteen-hundredweight trucks, three and five-ton lorries, tank-transporters and their cargoes – mostly German Mark 2s – were parked in a neat rectangle bordered on three sides by a double line of huts and on the fourth side by three large repair hangars. A concrete-mixer churned out its grey-green sludge, spilling it out over the black, ash-covered earth in front of one of the hangars, its lurching roar reaching their ears as a low and rhythmic rumble. Through binoculars, Alan could watch the sweating activity of its operators. Overalled mechanics worked industriously among the vehicles.

Bordering the camp along and beyond its eastern edge lay the outlying plantations of the village of Guidano Corba which occupied most of the remaining habitable area of the bowl, a concrete monolith celebrating the rebirth of Italian Glory pencilling upwards above the settlement from the centrepoint of the northern crest. Despite the pretensions which had caused its erection, the monument was impressive.

Alan looked speculatively over the dusty green bowl spread below them.

"Gazala's a hundred miles away," he reasoned, "and although Rommel hopes to go forward, he knows damn well he may have to come back, and if he does, he won't have time to stop for a re-bore here – which from appearances is about all he'd get. Yet he can't afford to ignore a place like this."

He looked down at the camp again.

"I wonder if that's a cover for anything?" he asked Jim. "Would it need all that number of huts for just a repair base?"

Jim raised his eyebrows: there is a limit to subtlety in warfare.

"Depends on the size of the workshops," he said briefly. " – and how long they've been there. Your guess is as good as mine really, but if they can repair tanks, it needs to be pretty large. We can't really tell without going and looking."

Alan glanced at his watch. It was half past six.

"Let's work around to the other side of the settlement first," he said. "It'll be dark in a couple of hours. We might take a look at the road then, and come back through the village about midnight. We'll leave those workshops until we've checked up everywhere else. No point in running after trouble."

Nevertheless, the military camp held a definite attraction for him, and he felt vaguely pleased that the thought of prowling around the Italian base merely revived the lively anticipation which he had felt two nights before. Honesty, however, did make him admit to himself that had Germans been occupying the place, he might have felt far different.

"Still, it's a start," he reflected, as they moved off in a wide circle along the ridge, still south of the road, swinging eastward towards the gap four miles away on the far side of the village, through which the Derna road disappeared.

Guidano Corba consisted at this time of sixty to seventy houses, a few stores and shops, a large concrete hall used now as a cinema and mess for the troops, and those basic necessities of Italian military life, brothel and garage. Commercial establishments had the frontage to the main road, the houses and farms of the hapless colonists stretching back along four sideroads – originally adequate, now badly in need of re-surfacing–which left the mainroad at neat and regular right-angles, two on each side of the road.

They passed along the shoulder of the ridge overlooking the settlement from the south, until they came to a spot immediately above and between the two minor roads which led out towards them. Here Alan stopped and turned his binoculars on the areas bordering and between the roads. The overall effect was not unlike parts of Hayling Island or the beach villas at Dawlish Warren, but except for the fact that a short branch road seemed now to connect the nearer ends of the roads, thus forming a U from the main road, there was little more to be seen than the maps had already told them.

"Wonder what's going to happen to those poor blighters," said Jim. "Can't be much fun bein' an Itie colonist these days. What with the Wogs, and us, and Jerry not being much of a comfort to 'em, they must be wishing they'd stayed at home in Sunny Sicily."

He looked down at the plantations spreading back from the buildings, now uncared for, overgrown, vines broken and trailing, olive patches choked with weeds and thistle. Somewhere in each holding, a wooden shed disintegrated with the sagging blotch of a badly wrapped parcel.

"Seems a shame, doesn't it?" he said. "After all, they must have put quite a lot of work into it at the beginning. Now, I suppose, they can't get the labour, or the tools, or something."

Alan, still busy quartering the area, grunted unsympathetically.

"They're not in much worse state than a hell of a lot of other people," he muttered. "Including the poor devils they pinched it all from. Anyway, take a look at the buildings themselves. There's nothing wrong with them. Even if they can't keep their fields in order, their roofs aren't falling in or anything like that. They seem to have labour and tools to look after their personal comfort."

He put down the binoculars and glanced sourly over the area

again. Uncertainty was rising in his mind: a familiar, corrosive tide.

"Come on," he said to Jim. "There's nothing down there that I can see. Let's get around to the road. We'll have a look at the ground over on the other side tonight, and if we don't find anything there, we'll have a crack at the workshops tomorrow night."

He scrambled to his feet and glared angrily down into the bowl which held the settlement and the camp.

"I know damn well there's something there," he said to himself. "There's got to be!"

They continued along the ridge as it curved north-east now, until it ended in a steep bluff falling down to the road. For the moment it was devoid of traffic, and a few moments later they were moving cautiously westward on the tarmac through the gap in the hills and into the basin, eyes searching for tracks which might lead off towards camouflaged dumps, ears alert for sound of traffic or foot patrols. It was nearly eight-thirty, dark, and the lights of the settlement shone yellow, about a mile in front of them.

"Better move off the road and slow down," suggested Jim. "A bit too early to go in, isn't it?"

Alan nodded and they moved over to the north side of the basin. For the next hour and half they searched deliberately up, down and across the undulating ground which lay in the rough triangle formed by the main road, the first of the northern side roads, and the foot of the curving ridge which formed the north-east sweep of the bowl. There was nothing: no tracks, no buildings, no dumps.

For another hour they lay twenty yards back from the road, watching the occasional traffic, trying to wring vital information from trivial evidence: Jim's sound common sense kept some of Alan's wilder fancies within bounds, but they were both glad when the time came to move off. Just before midnight, they walked down past the outer fringes of the eastern plantations, gained the main road, and turned westwards into the village itself.

As they moved in out of the uninhabited area, an idea flitted across the back of Alan's mind, but before he had time to recapture it, the door of a house just in front of them burst open to emit a blast of tawdry music and half a dozen Italian soldiers, all in a state of maudlin, ineffectual intoxication. Eventually, they wandered away towards the workshops in an amorphous clump, but the incident served to focus Alan's attentions. Vague and unformulated ideas must wait: for the moment, he must keep his wits about him.

27

They walked steadily forward, keeping distance behind the Italians, as much as possible in the shadows, but moving all the time – not lurking, or darting from place to place. Anyone noticing them would have accepted their right to be present, and only they themselves knew of their thumping hearts and sweating hands. After a remarkably short while, however, these discomforts evaporated, and as they turned right, up the first of the Northern side roads, Alan was conscious of a decided elation.

He grinned across towards the dark shadow beside him.

"Piece of cake!" he whispered.

"Could be," admitted Jim. "Anyway, what else did you expect?"

Alan glanced sideways at him, his teeth showing derisively.

"Come off it, cock. Whatever we expected, you had a shake on when we reached the first house."

"Those Wops worried me," muttered Jim. "They ought to have been in barracks by this time."

His voice was almost that of the Outraged Mother.

"They may be over twenty-one," offered Alan, and then, while Jim grappled with the suggestion and sought to apply it, he found a wide path leading off between two houses. At the end was a small garage – empty, and on each side of the path lay the flat, unbroken patches of kitchen gardens. Disappointed, Alan led back to the road and then further up it. Another path, another small shed, more kitchen gardens.

The next time, he left the path, crossed the garden, and penetrated the deeper areas of the plantation. Young olive bushes, stunted, thin, grey-green, oiled the air with their perfume as he brushed through ranks, and barley grew beyond them thick, heavy-headed. In a shed the like of which can be found at the bottom of every allotment plot in the world was a tumbled assortment of garden tools, paraffin cans and seed-boxes: irrigation ditches were wet and muddy. But there was nothing else. No sign of ammunition or fuel dumps, no inconspicuous, anonymous, tarpaulined heaps, no deep tracks of heavy-laden vehicles; just the normal surface disturbance and implements of small-farming.

Grimly, Alan searched all the way up the outer side of the road. and then turned his attention to the area between the two side roads. Once again, there was nothing – nothing, that is, indicative of military activity or interest. About the middle of the patch bounded by the roads an attempt had been made to grow oranges, but the sweet, appetising scent was a fraud, the fruit themselves being small, yellowish and dry. There was no short road connecting these side roads as on the south side, although a footpath had been worn through by use.

"It's nearly two o'clock, Alan," murmured Jim as they stood, tired now, and dispirited, midway along the footpath. The northern foothills rose a hundred yards away and the ground between lay unused, undulating, scrub-covered. Outside the immediate area of the settlement, it seemed strangely deserted.

A recollection came back to Alan. Instead of turning west along to the next, unobserved line of houses and farms running down the far side of the second road, he led across the barren ground towards the hills. Halfway over, he turned west again, and walked along until the northern ridge curved in close, they were clear of the village plantations, and between the spot where they stood and the main road lay the military workshops. They walked down towards them. Cold flashes of violet light warned them that work was still going on in the repair sheds, so they veered East, crossed back into the bottom of the plantations, and went straight on down to the main road. Alan made no attempt now to search for dumps in the areas, for time was passing and they must be well clear of the settlement, and if possible, back at the cistern, by daybreak. They walked rapidly along the side of the cinema – garish posters showing panic-striken British officers fleeing before savage, bayonet-charging Italian infantry – crossed the main road and climbed up to the ridge from which they had first observed the Italian camp.

At the top, they lay down for a rest.

"See any Arabs?" asked Alan, a little too casually, when he had regained some of his breath.

Jim considered the question.

"Should we have?" he enquired cautiously.

"Well, damn it! We're in their country, aren't we?"

When Alan was tired he required brighter co-operation from his cross-talk feed. Jim squinted up towards the stars.

"Not much light," he mumbled wearily. "We might have missed 'em."

"Missed 'em, my foot," said Alan. "There's a black froth of Wog tents around every village and town in North Africa from Cairo to Casablanca."

"You've never been West of Benghasi, chum," accused Jim, a seeker after truth. "Still – I see what you mean. We didn't find any North of the road, and certainly there were none to be seen South of it. Think they've been turned out?"

"I think they'd be there if there wasn't some good reason for 'em not to be!" replied Alan rather pompously, for strain and fatigue had worn through his humanity and the uncertain core was waspish: he would grow old into querulous and insistent self-importance.

"Still," he stated. "I'm sure I'm right now. Unless there was something in that valley to hide, there'd be some – if not a hell of a lot – of Arab tents around the outskirts."

He sat up.

"Come on. Let's get back to the cistern. We'll take another look from up here this evening and we'll go into the camp as soon as it's late enough to try. There's something there, I know. We'll find it!"

They rose to their feet and made their way south, reaching the cistern just before dawn. Weariness drugged the fundamental doubt in Alan's mind and he slept soundly.

Chapter 4

DUSK again, the baking heat of the day was gone – soon it would be cool: beneath Alan's hand, the thin grass was damp. They lay on the crest of the Northern ridge now, just above the place where its curve brought it closest to the camp lying just below – there would be thirty yards of open ground to cross before they reached the outer huts. As far as they could see in the fading light there was no wire, but a prowler guard of three men wandered in a bored and purely routine fashion around the perimeter and up and down between the huts. By midnight, when Alan and Jim proposed to go in, the patrol would be sleepy and even more apathetic: but they would not be cold. Although their thoughts would doubtless be dwelling on fond enchantments in more native climes, they would not be hurrying through their duty – torpid, frozen, intent upon an early return to the guard-room fire, as memory reminded Alan had been his chief concern when similarly employed in England. The patrol constituted a factor of decided weight. It would have to be watched.

The camp consisted of a double line of barrack and stores huts, running around three sides of a hollow square. In each side there were twelve huts – six in each row, and the corners away from the road each held one hut, set diagonally. Thirty-eight huts altogether. Along the fourth side of the square ran the main road, and between the open ends of the U of huts were built the three repair hangars, which backed on to the road.

The rectangle formed by the fronts of these hangars and the fronts of the three inner lines of huts, was the parking ground, almost completely covered by a comprehensive selection of the transport of three armies – German, Italian, and the patched and worn relics of the Eighth Army's soft-skinned vehicles – all presumably in various stages of repair.

Alan rolled over on to his back and looked up into the velvet, silver-sequinned night. Still he was held in precarious doubt, for an afternoon spent scouring the basin through his binoculars had severely limited the area feasible for concealment of a worthwhile volume of supplies. There was no point in bringing raiders in to destroy a thousand gallons of petrol or oil, an ammunition dump containable in the capacity of a Nissen hut. A hundred thousand gallons of fuel or a fair-sized ship-load of explosives would be necessary as a target, to justify the risk, and cause a sufficiently serious loss to Rommel.

Such a target required space – and except within the bounds of the camp, the requisite space appeared either occupied or neglected. Alan had by now marshalled logical reasons to support his belief that there must be something here other than a repair shop. Gazala was a hundred miles away. If Rommel was forced back – then he'd come back in a hurry in exactly the same way as he had rocketed in the opposite direction from Agheila. But we left our transport behind, and Rommel learned from other people's mistakes just as much as from his own. Where then, would he concentrate supplies?

Unless he went back along the Triq el Abd – open, defenceless, with no hope of a stop until Agheila again – then the obvious place was Derna. But that was too obvious and too vulnerable, for the Navy could shell the open port and deny its use – as a re-fuelling stop anyway – to Axis traffic. The next place back was Guidano Corba.

Blast it! The man must have something here!

But where?

South of the road, the ridge ran up, steep and wooded, completely unclimbable by anything but a jeep – except for the areas occupied by the neglected small-holdings which they had examined yesterday from the ridge. To make certain, Alan had again spent some hours in the same spot, but had seen nothing more than he had observed the previous evening. Although the buildings were in good shape, the plantations were neglected and overgrown. Were fuel drums and shells concealed below the matted vegetation? Well, it was possible, but in view of the lack of tracks or even wide paths leading out into it, how could supplies of any sort be loaded in a hurry? – and Alan was certain that anything left there would be disposed for emergency.

"If we find nothing in the camp," he decided, "we'll go across there on our way back to the cistern. But I don't see how they could hide stuff there without leaving signs."

That left the area North of the road, and with the exception of the area contained in the camp, last night's reconnaisance had proved its innocence.

Alan rolled over and looked down at the camp again. Lights had appeared in some of the huts, and the hangars too, were occupied – aprons of light spilling out from the wide doors on to the ground in front of them. The nearer two had concrete-covered entrance bays, the third half-concrete, half-earth. Silent and monstrous, the concrete mixer stood by.

There were two solutions as Alan saw it. Either the litter of transport concealed and broke the lines of stacked drums or supplies – or the fairly innocent-looking huts were packed from floor to roof.

Alan stirred uneasily. Both ideas appeared meretricious, to say the least. Possibly that was where the reason for their adoption lay – it was so hazardous a proposal that no-one would suspect the presence of valuable stores beneath the facade of a repair shop – which may or may not be worth the attention of hard-pressed bombers. To while away the boredom of the road-watch, Alan and Jim had often played the naval game of battleships, and Alan had discovered the occasionally advantageous strategy of placing battleship and cruiser in contiguous squares. On one occasion, Jim had sunk the cruiser early in the game, and then plastered the rest of the chequerboard square in an effort to find the battleship.

"Took a chance, didn't you?" he commented when Alan victoriously showed him his disposition of forces, at the end of the game. "Nine times out of ten, I'd have hit the blighter while I was finishing off the cruiser."

But he hadn't – and Alan's risk had been justified.

Maybe Rommel was gambling in the same way.

One by one, the lights in the huts went out. Occasionally dark diminutive figures appeared in the gaping mouths of the hangars, crossing the aprons into the night and back again: the night shift was on. Alan looked at his watch. It was eleven-thirty.

"Come on," he said. "Let's get down there."

They rose to their feet, brushed the twigs and dirt from their clothes, ran their hands over the reassuring lines of Colt automatic and Tommy-gun (Jim had at last been persuaded to leave his precious rifle behind), and began their scramble down the ridge towards the camp. They both wore khaki drill trousers and shirts, with half-length, wide collared driver's coats and folded, woollen cap-comforter scarves pulled skull-close. Remove cap-comforters and coats, and they could, in the half-light, be mistaken for bona fide members of the camp – a thin disguise, but one which might suffice in the heat and hurry of a chase.

"Hold it, Alan," whispered Jim from behind as they reached the bottom of the slope. "Patrol."

Crouched in shadows, they watched the three men come up from the road, stare incuriously out over their heads from the corner, disappear casually between the rear huts. Alan counted up to a hundred, held his breath, and nodded. Crouching, wide-eyed, they stole across to the corner, and paused in its shadow.

"O.K." breathed Alan, mouth and throat suddenly a parched tunnel.

He tiptoed across to the front of the inner line and heard Jim move off between the two lines of huts.

"Keep level with me, for Christ's sake, Jim," prayed Alan silently, and then relaxed. Jim knew his job, all right. Wherever Alan moved in the parking area, he could be sure that Jim would be on a parallel line, waiting – as usual – with covering fire in case of trouble. He breathed out, slowly, and felt his belly ease gently down into his pelvis. That was better.

He looked across at the conglomeration of transport in front of him. Ten yards of hard-packed earth separated him from the nearest vehicle – a troop carrier whose empty vastness held a faint nightmare threat – the yawning gulf, the toppling cliff: his stomach tightened again. Already, beside him, the dry splintering wood of the hut, acrid and familiar, held him back – almost it had become home, and a strange, hostile jungle lay before him.

He gulped, forced down his stomach, held open the taut hollow of mouth, throat and chest, and impelled himself away from the wooden walls towards the troop carrier. His legs were stiff, his feet were lead, and smashed against the bare earth in galloping thunder. Then he was in protection, the warm shadow of the troop-carrier cloaked him, its steel sides sheltered his fragility. His breathing eased, the lump in his belly dissolved; his heart slowed: soon he was ready to start his search.

He dropped to the ground and peered along under the vehicles. It was too dark to see far, but certainly there was nothing under the troop carrier. On his feet again, peering over the long bonnet, the very familiarity of the scene calmed his nerves and soothed away the remnants of his fear. Cabin box and truck body, half-track and bulging wheels like dusty and gigantic Pontefract cakes, all combined to restore his confidence. Here he was safe: only beyond the circle of his immediate vision was there menace, and relief moistened and smoothed his mouth and throat.

After the tension of the immediate past, over-reaction set in, and he moved down along the edge, peering under the trucks, between the wheels, his heart light and his spirits soaring: what matter if no shells, no drums of fuel, no mines, no chests of bombs or sacks of bullets lay stacked beneath the lorries? The game's the thing! Come the four corners of the world in arms and Alan Lockyer stands with Drake – a pity Il Duce had no beard to singe! However, Alan was at the end of the line and there was the open hangar thirty yards from him.

He sat on the running board of a truck, completely surrounded and invisible, watching the activity in the echoing grey-walled hangar with amusement and rising contempt. Light-headedly, he felt the need of irreproachable Mechlin lace at his wrists. The prowler guard walked along the concrete apron in front of him, and Sir Alan watched them mockingly through gold-framed, quizzical eyeglass. Still, they reminded him of what he was there for, and he'd better get on with it.

Rising, he turned, and with a wave towards the huts, where he guessed Jim was watching for him, walked back along the edge. Some of his elation faded as he left the hangar behind, and he steaded. Then, as he searched among the ranks of squat and slumbrous tanks which formed the majority of the transport along the Northern fringe, his foot caught under a crowbar wedged between track and roller, and he sprawled forward on to a surface composed of loose cinders. The fall barked his shins, took skin from his hands, brought sharp tears to his eyes, and quite possibly saved his life.

As he sat rubbing his leg, cursing under his breath, the remnants of his light-headedness evaporated, and he proceeded more soberly. Soon he became fairly certain that there was nothing concealed in the parking area, and it was what it seemed – a collection of vehicles awaiting repair. At the next corner – North-East – he waited for Jim to show himself, they both waited for the patrol to wander by, then Alan crossed to Jim.

"I don't think there's anything there," he whispered. "What about the huts – Have you been able to see into any of them?"

"I only tried the inner ones," replied Jim. "And they're all barrack huts – beds and blokes asleep on 'em."

Alan thought for a moment.

"Let's go back along the outer line and try some of those," he suggested. "We know the patrol's just gone by so we should be all right for a bit."

The nearest outer hut was locked, but the windows disclosed dark bulk filling the greater portion of the space and they could not see across to the opposite window. Excited, Alan broke the glass – inexpertly, but with surprisingly little noise through the thickness of his coat, put his hand through and released the catch. He clambered through the window. The dark bulk proved to be piled blankets and between diasppointment and fluff, he felt the desire to sneeze.

Seeing no point in unnecessary clambering, he tried the door. There was a key on the inside of the ordinary rimlock, and this puzzled him until he realised that there was a door at each end of the hut – presumably the other door was locked from the outside.

With memories of the simplicity and delapidation of hut doors and locks in the British Army, he removed the key for use in other doors. He was quite right. With some carefully applied force the key opened doors in all except two of the back row of huts, and Alan smashed the windows of these two.

Three of the huts were full of iron bedsteads, one full of assorted clothing and the other of straw-filled palliasses. Grimly, Alan started on the Western outer line – the line through which they had entered the camp. (The eastern double line was still completely unexamined – as was the south-east section of the parking-ground).

The top two huts seemed to hold the answer to Alan's prayer – for through the window they could see drum upon drum stacked, and his hopes rose. Then he went through the window and discovered they were all empty. The chill, familiar breeze of uncertainty blew upon the back of his neck, for the thrill, the excitement, the fear, were all gone now, and disappointment in the first hut had been succeeded by disgust in the second, then growing panic as realisation of the personal importance of success came to his mind; he was too much physically engaged at the moment to feel its horror, but he dreaded a return to the impotence, the failure, the disappointment of life before he discovered and put to use his odd, peculiarly military, talent.

The next hut was empty, and the fourth in the line filled with broken or unserviceable engine parts – blocks, cylinder-heads, axles, spring-leaves, lay strewn about the floor in haphazard profusion. Grey, sullen despair now lapped about the slender sand-castle of Alan's confidence, a menacing and oily incoming tide.

"There's damn-all here," he muttered. "May as well give up, I suppose."

But he knew he couldn't – not until he'd completely exhausted all probabilities. They crossed back into the vehicle-park and dodged between half-tracks and light runabouts which faced the three hangars, making for the eastern row of huts which they had still to search. From the last hangar, a welding plant splashed fitful heliotrope across the scene, lighting it with sardonic clarity.

Uncaring now, and with growing resentment, Alan started across to the double row of unexplored huts. Jim grabbed his arms and yanked him fiercely back, and the prowler guard walked by, down towards the road. Somehow, the men seemed more alert, as though the atmosphere had caught and transmitted the hostile presence in the camp.

Impatiently, Alan watched them go, then started across the road. Halfway across, a wide, shallow pothole had been filled with cinders, and before he could stop himself, he was tramping across it with the ear-filling crunch of a man eating breakfast cereal. The third time his boot went down, the rasp penetrated the fog of annoyance and frustration which wreathed his brain, and he froze – a startled statue in the night.

Behind him he heard Jim drop, and the clink as his Tommy-gun came up. In front, the prowler guard had swung around and were staring at him, open-mouthed. For a moment, the tableau held – and then, with the rapid evanescence of sunlight on a cloudy day, all his anger, bitterness and impatience dissolved, leaving him unguarded and afraid. With what started from his diaphragm as a scream and emerged from his throat as a strangled grunt, he flung himself into the shadows of the huts in front of him. Behind, the Tommy-gun burst into heavy stuttering and the guards pitched to the ground where they lay with the awful pathos of the suddenly and unexpectedly dead.

Then pandemonium broke loose and Jim came across to join Alan in the shadows of the huts.

"This way!"

After the first frantic paralysis, fear played its proper part and lent Alan's brain new keenness, his sinews new strength. With Jim behind him, he fled down towards the road, veered sharply between two huts as men ran out from the hangars, dived over some wire and somersaulted into irrigation ditches at the bottom of one of the Northwest plantations. It was wet, muddy, cold – and for a horrifying second he thought he had lost his gun.

Then he found it lying just in front of him, grabbed it and was just about to fire at a figure climbing the wire when he realised it was Jim. The wire was six feet high – he himself must have taken off like a kangaroo.

"Jim!" he hissed, and slid away down towards the road. Jim caught him up as they reached the high bulk of the cinema, and at the edge of the road, they paused, listening to the uproar and confusion which had broken out in the camp. Jim's teeth showed white.

"Noisy shower, aren't they?" he said, conversationally. It was obvious he held no grudge against Alan for his stupidity, and relieved, Alan grinned back at him, then looked across the road. One of the Italians must have reported the scene of their departure from the camp, for men suddenly debouched into the plantations and began threshing noisily through the crops, towards them.

"Better get across," muttered Alan, and moved out from the shelter of the cinema. Immediately, there was a scream from a building just up the road, a window slammed shut, seconds later a door opened, a stream of shrill and vituperative Italian – undoubtedly feminine – added itself to the night.

"Blasted woman!" snarled Alan as he plunged into the plantations on the Southern side of the road. Automatically, he followed the course he had decided on as part of their search – diagonally across the choked and overgrown holdings – and even as they forced their way through them he derived a slim comfort from the fact that he appeared to be right as far as this part was concerned anyway – there were no drums of oil or stacks of shells beneath this tangled mat of vegetation.

Now closer behind him, he could hear the sounds of immediate pursuit, as the Italian patrols, urged on by the soprano exhortations of the garage-proprietor's wife (the garage-proprietor himself was still in bed with the sheets up over his head), cautiously followed along the trail of beaten down shrubs which marked the fugitives' passage. Unless they could reach clearer ground, they would soon be under fire. Alan turned and made for the nearest point of the sideroad. Ten more yards of shrubbery, onions and lettuce crushing under their feet as they went across a small kitchen-garden, two houses looming on each side, and they ran between walls into the road.

Concrete rang under their feet. They ran down towards the link road and the foothills of the Southern ridge which lay beyond it, but with twenty yards more to go, shouts came from behind them, and bullets whined viciously over their heads. He heard Jim stop and turn, and as the Tommy-gun fired, he turned too. The Colt was heavy in his hand and it bucked powerfully as he fired at the dim shapes far off, giving him a resurgence of courage and strength. He fired again then ran on to the corner, hearing Jim follow after him – but more slowly, stopping to fire twice more.

Alan looked along the length of the short, link road. There were three buildings on the outer side, two-storied, stucco-fronted, flat-roofed, and despite the noise no lights showed in any of them: they were dead, empty of life – and inviting.

"We'll never make the foothills, Jim," he called back. "Hold 'em until I fire twice, then make for the middle building back here. I'll be on the roof."

No sounds whatever came from behind the shutters, a post led up to a veranda, the top of the parapet was within easy reach, and with a quick heave, he was up and over, lying flat on the felt-covered boards. He slid across the roof and peered over back and sides, found nothing and fired the signal. A long burst from the

Tommy-gun followed by a scattered but angry fusillade in reply and Jim came running fast along the road.

"Up, Jim. Give me your gun!"

Alan remained at the front of the roof, Jim watched from the back.

It was nearly five minutes before the first of the Italian patrols came cautiously along the road, keeping to the shadows, occasionally calling to each other. As they were not fired on, they gained confidence, and finally congregated in the middle of the road, looking over towards the foothills. Then an officer came, harangued them, and they filed past the house and out into the flat ground leading to the ridge. They were out there for nearly an hour, and Alan and Jim could hear them moving around and shouting to each other, and then at last they came back and went off down the road towards the camp, abandoning the pursuit and cursing the raiders.

Alan lay in the centre of the roof, listening to the retreating Italian footsteps, his forehead on the cool felt, a contented smile on his face. Jim turned and crawled across to him, eyes shining, teeth white in a wide grin.

"Clever, aren't you?" he whispered, "I suppose you're going to say you knew it was here all the time?"

He inhaled deeply.

"Phew!" he said. "What a stink! Are you sure it's not something they eat? Let's go and have a look."

In the building beneath them, and in the ones on each side of it, and in the first four houses down each side of each side road, they found petrol. Drum upon drum upon stacked drum. Eighty-four of them in the first house, ninety in the second and third, and over a hundred in the bigger buildings along the sideroads. Sixty gallon drums, all of them.

Say a hundred in each house – the average would certainly not be less. A hundred drums, times sixty gallons each, times nineteen houses. Over a hundred and ten thousand gallons of petrol, neatly disposed alongside a well-surfaced road (examination revealed recent maintenance) so arranged as to cause no traffic jam to columns of fast-moving but thirsty traffic.

And over and around it all, hung that faint, elusive sepulchral smell, which betrayed its presence and identified its owner.

It would all go up in a most satisfying blaze.

Alan had cause for satisfaction.

So had Rutledge when, forty-eight hours later, the position was reported to him. The Morse keys tapped, the signals took the air –

and in Cairo, a coloured flag was stuck in a wall-map. Some days later, its importance in relation to other targets was considered and evaluated, and the planning officers of two raiding units were consulted.

"That's going to be a right bastard," said one of them, gloomily slapping horse-tailed fly-swatter against corduroyed leg. "Even supposing these cloak and dagger types lead us in all right, how the hell do we get out?"

Chapter 5

As was only to be expected, Jim Bannerman bore the monotonous but expectant days which followed the pair's return to Rutledge's cave with considerably more equability than did Alan.

"What's the hurry?" he asked in reply to Alan's irritable jibes at an apparently apathetic Headquarters. "If they do want that lot blown up, they'll send chaps in to do it at the best time for the job. No point in doing it if Rommel can just replace it without mucking up his arrangements. Anyway," he added, with unconsciousness tartness, "maybe they've got other things to think about in Cairo."

"You bet they have," said Alan sullenly. "Sherry at Mena House and ice cream at Groppi's – not to speak of the nurses out at Helmieh!"

But these were points upon which Jim would be neither drawn nor prompted, for his was a curiously direct mind which had no comprehension of – or appreciation for – the spites and malices of what passes for sophisticated conversation. He was no fool though, no simpleton in a world of sharp and devious practice, and his directness took him to the heart of several human problems with an apparent cynicism which had, on occasion, left Alan breathless.

"Why should he have stayed with his platoon?" he asked once, referring to a certain young subaltern who had deemed it wiser to allow his men to take up an untenable position under command of their sergeant. "You can't expect a young chap with a nice car and a lot of money to commit suicide – not unless he'd been trained for it," – then added with a certainty which was entirely without smugness, " – like he would have if he'd been a proper officer in our mob!"

For Jim was steadfastly and humbly proud of his position as Corporal on the regular establishment of his county's regiment – a regiment who had worn the rifleman's green ever since the idea of camouflage first played a part in the reckonings of the War Office, and a modicum of subtlety replaced the solid weight of flesh and metal which had ruled on the field of battle up to that date. Jim had joined up in 1935 as a result of a combination of domestic and financial considerations which gave him, in point of fact, little choice but to accept the King's Shilling.

41

His father had been killed in the mud and slime of Passchendaele, and if Bannerman Senior had had any dying thoughts of the child he would never see, they were probably on the lines of heartfelt hopes that the boy would be allowed to fight for his King and Country in less frustrating circumstances than the Western Front must have been for a Light Infantryman. From him, Jim had inherited a sound practicality and a fundamental knowledge of the satisfaction to be derived from right action.

Mrs. Bannerman had married again, in 1923, and from his stepfather Jim had received an impartial and exact justice under which a less sturdy individuality would surely have wilted and either died or rebelled. As it was, Jim grew up with a self-sufficiency which was a satisfaction to all concerned, and when, in 1932, his mother succumbed to the startling thunder of pulmonary thrombosis, Jim was neither deeply stricken by a sense of personal loss, nor severely incommoded by the practical aspect. His stepfather allowed him to remain on in the house, until his apprenticeship was finished, (he had adopted the trade of joiner in the local firm of building contractors), and then, as Jim had fully expected, announced his intention of marrying the woman who had joined the establishment as housekeeper. He also intimated that he considered his duties as far as Jim was concerned, now terminated.

Jim agreed, and as the firm who employed him had been forced by economic competition to underpay the union rate by 3d. an hour, he sold his bicycle, entrusted his kit of tools to his stepfather's care – there was no animosity between them, only unemotional respect – and walked along to the local barracks. Neither Jim, nor Military Authority ever had cause to regret that day.

After the requisite period in the regimental depot, he was posted to the overseas battalion in Palestine where the point of the training received at Aldershot and Shorncliffe was soon apparent. Never, however, despite the most earnest endeavours on his part, was he able to unravel the complex tangle of politics, human need, treachery and nobility, which necessitated his presence in that, in those days, dreary and barren desolation, and with characteristic modesty, he put down this lapse in his comprehension, to his own mental insufficiency. He never dreamed that no-one else understood it either, attributing the same omnipotence to his country's leaders as he did, with reason, to his battalion officers.

But he was content, for there was much in the life of the regular soldier serving abroad between the two wars, which was both satisfying and adventurous. His promotions gave him satisfaction which was deeper in the knowledge that he had earned them, and his troubled apprehension at the outbreak of war, (he had seen enough of bomb and booby-trap in Palestine to realise the extent of the likely carnage) was offset by the likelihood of further and more rapid promotion in the expanding army. He was sent home, attended an instructor's cadre, and was then sent to the Oxfordshire village of Hinton Merrott in company with two other corporals, a sergeant and a captain to await the arrival and commence the training of a hundred recruits.

While awaiting their arrival, and the arrival of the other officers and N.C.O.s detailed for the job, Jim passed the time by falling in love. As with everything else he did, he did it slowly, carefully – but very, very thoroughly.

Chapter 6

"I CAN ONLY PRESUME, ROBERT, that they'll be bringing their own rations. Cairo must know we can't feed twenty extra men, even for three days."

Rutledge and his second-in-command – as far as there was a second-in-command in the loose heirarchy of the group – lay on a hilltop above a narrow wadi. Below them, strung along the floor of the wadi, were three others, each man squatting now alongside a small tin of petrol-soaked sand. Jim was at the farthest end of the line, and Alan was up on the opposite slope at a point level with the nearest member of the line and at right angles to the axis. He also, had his tin. The 'plane was due at midnight.

Robert McCarran grunted sceptically.

"Cairo," he announced lugubriously, "know damn-all. It'd be just like them to send half a battalion out here with instructions to live by local purchase."

Rutledge sighed. "I should like to hope that you were wrong, Robert, if only to temper the edge of your satisfaction when you prove, as usual, to be right."

He glanced at his watch.

"Quarter of an hour to go," he muttered, "I wonder how late they'll be?"

By his side, McCarran fidgetted, small, pudgy hands smoothing the black cylinders of torch and Tommy-gun barrel, wide, flexible mouth twitching. He wore no hat, and untidy hair swept back in waves from a high forehead. The chin was dimpled and round.

"Shall I go around again and make sure they're all clued up on what to do?"

"They're hardly likely to have forgotten in the last hour, Robert," said the older man gently. "Do you think we might risk a cigarette?"

McCarran looked at him in alarm.

"Perhaps you're right," said Rutledge, catching the expression on his face. "Although with all this moonlight around I shouldn't have thought it would have made much difference."

"Wait till they've dropped. Then it won't matter."

Despite McCarran's steadfast belief that everything would always go wrong, he invariably obeyed to the letter the detailed minutiae of the instruction booklets.

"Suppose the L.R.D.G. can't get to the pick-up rendezvous in time," he asked, harking back to the original subject of discussion. "What do the parashots live on then?"

"They'll live on what they've brought with them or what they can find, Robert," answered the older man. "Now stop fussing like a bloody old Grandmother. If these chaps weren't prepared to look after themselves, they wouldn't have volunteered. Anyway, from what I can gather, there will be so many of these parties scattered between Gazala and Benghasi, that the L.R.D.G., will be running a sort of bus service. If our lot miss one bus, they'll catch the next."

McCarran digested this information and ruminated – bleak, sceptical, then suddenly apprehensive.

"There wouldn't be some vague but over-riding suggestion on the part of Cairo, that the pick-up on the edge of the desert won't be necessary anyway, is there?" he asked. "Due, of course, to the swift and relentless advance of our gallant troops coming up from Gazala?"

"You worry too much, Robert," replied Rutledge. He tore a leaf from a nearby bush and nibbled at it, glancing ironically under his brows at his subordinate. "Also your cynicism is too well grounded. There is, I admit, a suggestion – not in words so much as in phrasing – that the end of all our troubles is in sight and we need no longer exercise such rigid economy with our stores and ammunition."

"I see."

Gloomy relish interspiced the foreboding in his voice. "And where do we hide while the battle rages past us? Always supposing it gets this far?" He broke off speech for a moment to follow another line of prognostication. Suddenly he started to laugh, silently, but with a genuine hilarity which shook his dumpy body and brought tears to his eyes. Rutledge watched, gravely but with perception.

"Yes," he said at last, "it's quite a prospect, isn't it? Twenty parashots and eight of us – always supposing we all survive the raid – plus any leftovers from other raids – plus any survivors from the L.R.D.G. after they've been dive-bombed off the road. That's what you have in mind, isn't it? With the Eighth Army in full retreat to Alexandria and most of the Navy sunk, I suppose?" He sighed again. "Why have you never learned to keep your imagination under stricter control, Robert?"

McCarran wiped his eyes and looked down at his chief.

"Why should I," he asked, derisively. "I like a good laugh now and then. That's what keeps me fat!"

There was no reply from Rutledge, who had suddenly raised his head, staring into the darkness. "Listen! I believe I hear the 'plane."

Above the sounds of the cooling earth, the insects, the soft sighs of their own breathing, came a sporadic but familiar hum, its continuity broken as the angle of the ground beneath the plane formed sounding–board or block. Suddenly it was close around them, the note a growling, querulous thunder as the plane circled like a bee searching for pollen.

Both men stood up, staring towards the noise, waiting for the first sight. Like a black bird of doom, she came low-flying over the crest of a hill, heading to pass them too far north. McCarran flicked the signal torch, swearing softly and unconsciously to himself as he spelled out the code letter. There was a tiny speck of yellow from the black beak of the bird and she altered course and began circling. McCarran turned and flashed the torch down into the wadi. In response, four reddy-yellow dots appeared, flickering intermittantly at first and then steadying.

The 'plane disappeared behind a low hill towards the coast and spent endless minutes buzzing and whining away to herself out of sight.

"Where the hell have they got to now?" muttered McCarran. "Those blasted fires'll die any minute. Do they think we're swimming in petrol?"

Beside him, Rutledge stood rigid, nerves holding his fear-tired body in a paralysis of anticipation – only in the deepest recesses of his brain was there any relaxation, where a cool intellectual detachment viewed his physical paralysis with a mixture of sympathy and contempt. Suddenly, much higher and apparently faster, the 'plane came back, flying true now, along the line of the wadi and the yellow dots. Moonlight softly greyed the near side of her fuselage and then, surprisingly, in silent and effortless parturition, she left a bundle behind her in the sky. Then another, and another, and another. For the time of a heartbeat, or a sudden breath, or almost eternity, they lay, unmoving in the blue clarity of the night.

Then they kicked and fell, and above them canopies burst open in black, hard-edged relief. The bundles swung, jerked, swayed and took shape, three the conventional silhouettes of airborne soldiers, the fourth retaining lifeless rectangularity. Silent and controlled, they swiftly dropped into the blackness of the wadi. Beyond the hills once more, the 'plane was circling for her second run.

"They'll take all bloody night if they don't drop more than that each time!"

"Here they come again."

Two men, two containers. The next run, four containers. Below them, in the wadi, men cursed and stumbled, fought their way out of their harness, and greeted one another with the bright exuberance of slight intoxication.

"If I haven't got concussion it's only because I must have a rubber neck! God! I came in like a bomb!"

"You wouldn't 'ave concussion, man, if the chapel fell on you! Bit rough isn't it? Not like what we've bin used to! Where's the Corporal?"

" 'Ere! 'Oo chose this coppin' place for a D.Z.? Some perishin' penguin, I'll bet a dollar – talk abaht landin' rolls, I came dahn smack between a ten-foot thorn bush an' a bloody great boulder! 'Ullo, sir. Ring the bell ternight?"

"Not tonight, Corporal – *and* I kept my feet together!"

"That's the ticket, sir. Carry on like that an' we'll let you try it with a parachute next time. 'Ere they come again – 'oo is it this time? 'Ere, anyone seen these blokes 'oo are supposed to meet us?"

"Oh – they're around somewhere. Christ! What the hell's going on up there?"

Above the thunder of the returning 'plane had come a higher and a thinner whine. A wasp-like viciousness pierced the growing tumult over their heads and the familiar roar choked, burst forth afresh and climbed higher above them. Yellow-white balls suddenly cross-crossed the sky, and then far up in the heavens, the watchers saw a red, glowing finger of fire point out from the wing of their aircraft. Appalled, they waited.

Clumsy now, and heavy, the aircraft cartwheeled across the night, and as her assassin whined away far off into the dark reaches beyond her, she seemed to level off, and start sliding back in towards the wadi.

"Jump you clots! Jump out of the thing!" one of them whispered, and as if his frantic plea had been heard, a dark shadow fell from the belly of the 'plane, thin rigging lines just visible, reaching back towards the umbilical safety point. Then came a tearing whistle from behind and under her, a racketting clatter of anger and spite, and the fighter screamed by again, pumping white globules up into the stricken 'plane. She shuddered, up-ended, soared and fell, lumpish and dead until the wings turned lazily to take the weight, fluttering and ungainly afterwards. No parachutes opened.

The crest of a hill shut her from sight, they heard a thump, a pause, and then the close horizon was outlined with a rosy, yellow-shot glow which flared briefly and died. There was no explosion.

"This is the way the world will end – not with a bang but a whimper." Unconsciously, McCarran said the words aloud, his brain stunned by the sudden violence of the catastrophe, only the trivial edges of his mind still percipient. Then he started running down into the wadi, in automatic obedience to studied and remembered instructions.

"Clear the wadi first!" he shouted. "Look at the wreck after! Find the containers!"

Already the parashots were scrambling up the other side, their thoughts, their hopes centred on the broken and littered chaos out in the hills beyond. Alan's voice joined McCarran's, and being already on the farther slope, he ran along to intercept them. As McCarran crossed the floor of the wadi and started up through the thin scrub, he heard the urgent and rising anger in the voices.

"Come on, sir! Some might still be alive!"

"No – wait a minute all of you."

McCarran panted up the slope, sweat dripping down his face, soaking his shirt to black sogginess. In the centre of the group stood Alan and a slight, white-faced youth with etched features and two cloth stars sewn on each of his smock epaulettes. Thanking God that he hadn't a senior officer to deal with, McCarran reached the edge of the group.

"Look chaps, this is bloody grim!" he panted. "But for Heaven's sake, think! None of 'em can be alive – you heard her hit, and there were no parachutes opened. We've got to get this stuff cleared out of the wadi and back to the cave before the Jerries come looking over the ground. They'll be over at first light. We can't do it if you all waste time examining the wreck."

He looked around the group. It had a corporate appearance of angry and lowering heavy strength, and yet its focal point was in the slim tautness of the officer.

"I'm McCarran. Second-in-Command out here. Major Rutledge is back on the hill-crest, watching the approaches from the road. We must get moving."

"Yes". The voice was light – almost unemotional. The young officer looked up at the hillcrest towards which they had clambered in their rush of anger and mercy. Then he turned back.

"Yes," he said again, and then, coolly, "One of us must go to the 'plane, though. Now! – with one of yours to guide him."

He looked questioningly at Alan.

"We can't spare them, old chap, honestly!"

"One of us goes – or all of us, McCarran. My name's Perowne."

The voice was cold, the tone flat. There was cool ruthlessness in it, and McCarran nodded – recognising a superior power of will.

"You can find your way back to the cave, Lockyer?"

Perowne spoke quietly to a grim, hard-faced giant with hooked nose and black, flaring moustache who replied with a terse "Aye, sir. I'll do that!" and climbed rapidly to the crest, not pausing to wait for Alan. As Alan clambered up after him, McCarran took the parashots down into the wadi and with Jim, Sjt. Drummond and Whittaker, they searched for and found the containers and chutes, re-packed them and carried the lot back to the cave.

The work was done in a dead oppressive silence, without hostility, but with no sign of sympathy expected or extended. Time is tragedy's only balm.

Alan found the crumpled remnants of the 'plane lying against a low stone wall running down a shallow hillside to the mouth of a cistern. Opposite it, the second wall forming the water funnel had been torn apart and on the other side of the gap lay the charred and still smouldering pieces of the port wing; farther away still, smoking chunks of metal completed the story. She had come in with the blazing port wing down, and this had hit first. Wing, fuel tanks and engine had been ripped clean away from the main fuselage, which had then plunged on to bring up against the solid stone ahead, outside the ring of fire, and protected from it by the first wall. The reek of petrol from the starboard fuel tanks choked them at first, but inside the fuselage, the scene of compact and quintessential horror stunned the mind and reft away the senses.

There were no survivors – that was obvious, unless the one who had jumped before the second attack by the fighter was alive somewhere out in the hills. Although Alan was appalled by the physical prospect, his human sympathy was deep enough to offer to search the bodies and remove the identification tags.

"They're my lads," replied Serjeant Orr grimly. "I'll do what's necessary. You busy yourself wi' the other containers. We'll likely have need o' what's in 'em."

It took over an hour – an hour of nightmarish sweat and piteous agony of the mind. Then it was done and Alan and Serjeant Orr stood beyond the broken wall looking at the grey hulk of the fuselage and starboard wing. At their feet lay four containers, and in their pockets were the fuses of the grenades, the bolts of the Stens and the pistons of the two Brens which were inside them: the containers would be collected later. A package of mail which Alan had found in one of the containers was also in the patch pocket of his trousers, forming a heavy pad against his thigh, and an oppressive, sinister menace in that part of his mind which had not been numbed by the immediate tragedy.

In his hand, Serjeant Orr held a grenade.

"God rest your souls, lads," he said, and flung it over into the fuselage. Alan and he ducked below the top of the wall. A silence, a roar, a pause – and then with a swift crackle which rose to a deep gusty howl, the petrol caught. Ammunition still in the plane cracked and spat; all around, fantastic shadows danced and writhed over the flame-lit earth. Alan gripped the serjeant's arm and together, numbed and exhausted in spirit, they fled from the flaming sepulchre.

Away from the place and the sight, soothed by the physical effort of movement and the mental distraction of finding the way, Alan recovered fairly soon, and with recovery came the urgent need for personal and private re-assurance.

"Hang on a minute," he said to Orr, and took the package of mail from his pocket. Halfway through the bundle, his heart turned to ice and lurched drunkenly down through his guts. The envelope was white and cheap and square, the writing spidery, ill-formed, familiar. It was addressed to him.

There was nothing else in the bundle for him, and nothing at all for his friend who had waited patiently, week in, week out, for news from home, of his wife who he loved so much and so simply, and his child, whom he had never seen, but of whom he was so proud.

Bitterly, Alan slit the envelope, took out the letter and read it by the light of the moon. As he picked out the words, cold sweat glassed his forehead, his throat contracted and his mouth dried. When the full import of the letter had sunk in, and he had re-read it enough times to know that there was no loophole in his predicament, no other interpretation to put on the shabby, mis-spelt, accursed message, he folded it with shaking hands, replaced it in the envelope, and stuffed it into the inside pocket of his smock.

Then he rose to his feet and stumbled off again, instinctively leading back towards the cave, followed by Serjeant Orr. Both men moved with the automatism of those who are for the moment deep in their memories. Serjeant Orr's thoughts were in the recent past with his training stick – of which he was now the sole survivor.

Alan, however, was back two-and-a-half years – in England.

PART TWO

Chapter 7

IN THE YEAR; before Chamberlain's Day of Disappointment, Alan had been a bank clerk, hurried straight from school into the revolving cage of business by a fashionable philosophy which held that Security was the only God, and 'Pension Rights' his creed. He had sought escape from suburban monotony in the amateur theatre.

He undoubtedly had a flair for the stage, but his immediate meteoric rise to local fame was due far more to the intelligence and ability of the leader of the local dramatic society, a man who by application and observance had turned himself into that rarity, an amateur theatrical producer who knew what he was up to. Under his tutelage and direction, Alan gave two performances in succeeding productions which would have been a credit to a repertory theatre.

The public being what it is, Alan received the acclaim which should have gone to his mentor, his head reached the clouds, where the rarefied atmosphere expanded it, and its subsequent shrinkage was painful in the extreme. Scorning the excellent advice which was offered, he attempted to form his own society, and the dismal production which resulted was laughed ironically off the stage. The fact that he had done much to deserve his fate, did little to alleviate the pain and resultant sensitivity which followed.

When therefore, he eventually received his call-up papers in the Autumn of 1939, they appeared at first as a welcome means of escape from an environment which still fascinated, but now frightened him.

It was not long, however, before the harsh realities of army training quenched his ever volatile enthusiasm. He had expected companionship – there was only propinquity: he had expected gallantry – there was only dullness and fatigues: he had expected at least a modicum of intelligent and intelligible conversation (preferably, of course, with himself as scintillating hub) – and there was only the dull profanity which had become the lingua franca of the services. Worst of all, he had secretly hoped that his swift elevation to the heights of the local theatrical coterie would be repeated by rapid promotion in the army, and he would be able to return to the scene of his humiliation sheathed in the armour of an officer's uniform. With influence and luck, of course, he might have done this, but having neither, he was forced through the mill of recruit training. He was not a promising young soldier.

Compared with the manual dexterity of the garage mechanic, his efforts to strip and re-assemble the Bren were clumsy. Beside the brawny weight of the navvy, his attempt to dig a slit-trench was futile, and the weight of his pack almost too much for him to lift. Beside the faultless turn-out of an ex-chauffeur to landed gentry, his battle-dress was shapeless and his boots dull.

Not all of army training or efficiency, despite the pseudo-cynicism of malcontents, depends upon such matters as those catalogued above, but during the first three months of recruit training, they do loom large, and this was quite long enough to extinguish the unsteady light of Alan's military enthusiasm. Hardly out of an adolescence, extended and exacerbated by the febrile juvenility of the amateur theatre, he reverted even further, and sulked. Petulant, querulous, sneering, he took shelter behind a pose of aloof superiority and his wounded egotism supplied ex-culpation and creed in one: what he could not do well and easily was not worth doing anyway, and those who could master the basic simplicities of military life were obviously moronic.

It was in this frame of mind that he attended the first Company Dance, lounging self-consciously against the proscenium of the village hall, watching with bored expression but yearning eyes, the hot milling throng of Cockney conscripts with their brightly-garbed rustic girl friends.

"Who's the tall chap by the stage, Jim?" asked the village siren, eye roving for more ambitious conquests.

"Who?" asked Jim, hot, moist. and already devoted. "Oh him! Chap named Lockyer. La-di-da, but he'll be all right. Look Cora – what about a shandy? I'm sweating like a pig!"

"There's no need to be vulgar," stated Cora Simmonds, suddenly refined. "I think he looks rather nice. Take me over and introduce me!"

And Jim, made suddenly and sadly aware of his chivalric deficiencies, obeyed. It was a fateful moment, tawdrily enacted.

"Pleased to meet you, I'm sure," announced Cora. "Are you one of the boys Jim has in charge? Fancy that!"

There was a slight pause while Alan choked back his first eager re-action to attention at last.

"Fancy that indeed," he managed, endeavouring to hide his relief and appreciation – for despite her conversational disadvantages, Cora combined copper hair with a pantherine grace which would have repaid lacquering and a Wardour Street setting.

"I'll have a gin and lime, Jim please," said Cora, determined to impress.

"Gin and – ?" asked Jim, thunderstruck and unfortunately showing it. "Are you sure?"

"Allow me," cut in smooth Sir Lancelot, and while Guinevere dimpled and King Arthur stood by shaken but unsuspecting, the prologue commenced.

Cora and Alan danced together, ("Don't be silly, Jim. You know you can't tango. Come on, Alan. I'm sure you do it lovely!") and in the first heady intoxication of flattery by innuendo, Alan's motives were natural and patent. Physically, she was far and away the most attractive girl present and after two months of a masculine disregard amounting almost to contempt, he found in her attentions an irresistible delight.

"See Lockyer's pinching the Corporal's girl friend," commented one Smalley, a Stepney ironfighter. "Bastard!"

"Oh, I dunno," replied another, a brawny bricklayer from the dusty greys of Finsbury who rejoiced in the name of Bert 'Slasher' Craggs. " 'E's a bastard all right, but I don't reckon it's all 'is fault this time. Corp' 'd be well rid o' that bit o' frippet – tho' 'e don't know it yet."

He ran his eye coolly over the curves and contours under discussion – sleekly enhanced by tight blouse and even tighter skirt. "Wouldn't mind a go meself, come to that. On a cash an' carry basis, 'o course – nothin' permanent."

Jim, as was by now his established right, escorted the girl home, and any suspicions which might have arisen in his mind (but hadn't) as a result of her unprecedented request to be taken home early would have been dispelled by the graciousness of her goodnight kisses. Hitherto, she had alternated between a casualness which hurt and a fierce exhorbitance which rather shocked him. Such passion, he felt on these latter occasions, should await the marital blessing.

But tonight, she was fond, and sweet, and restrained. Jim went back to his billet a happy and contented man.

Meanwhile, in the village hall, Alan found himself next to the sardonic Craggs in the press around the bar.

"Enjoyin' y'self, Bucko?" enquired that worthy. "Pity she had to go 'ome, wasn't it?"

Alan smiled in secret satisfaction.

"Tho' o' course," continued Craggs, deliberately, " 'eadaches 'ave been known to disappear in the cool night air,"

The smile wilted under the shrewd, hard eyes.

"Ah, well," said Craggs, philosophically. "Someone 'as to be Joe Runt!"

Some hours later, as Alan strolled carefully and watchfully back to his billet, he remembered the bricklayer's cryptic valediction, and some of its double edge was evident. The cool night air had not only cured Cora's headache, it had accompanied Alan's un-buttoning fingers through her blouse, and when eventually his cupping hand had been withdrawn, cooled overwarm and swelling flesh which Alan had been intrigued to find firm enough to need no support of brassiere or corset.

Alan had been pleased, surprised and then – as other, more physiological adjustments had in due course taken place – restored to much of his battered self-confidence. With this return came a modicum of mental balance – sufficient anyway, for him to realise that Cora had been more disappointed at his acceptance of her final, belated resistance, than he had been at its encounter; but that his acceptance had in fact, been wise. She was no longer misted in the heady attraction induced by alcohol, excitement and bright lights, and her statement – twice repeated in the shadows of the village church – that she had known at once that Alan was 'her type', had sounded a strong note of warning to a not inex-perienced ear.

"In fact," said Alan to himself. "Except for undeniable physi-cal attractions, she is a possessive bitch – with the temper of the hounds of hell into the bargain, from the colour of her hair. Corporal Bannerman is welcome to her."

But Fate had other ideas.

The following morning was one set aside for inspection of kit, personal turn-out and drill, to be followed by an afternoon on the ranges with Bren and rifle.

In the course of the morning, several lists of names were com-piled. The first list was made out by the quartermaster-clerk at the direction of his principal, consisting of those men checked for deficiency of kit. The second was at the instance of the Company Commander, and the third and most ominous, taken by the Regimental Sergeant Major.

Owing to lack of (a) spare bootlaces, (b) attention of the bar-ber's scissors, and (c) ability at split second's notice to distinguish between right and left, Alan's name figured on all of them, and by an unfortunate co-incidence, at the end in every case.

The afternoon provided that concentrated misery for all con-cerned, which is the speciality of rifle ranges. The weather was dull December, squalls brushing the sodden and despondent men at the firing point with fingers of wet ice. Alan fired in the last detail, the desire of those in charge for once co-inciding with his own. He shut his eyes against the bitter wind and fired through the sleet with the simple desire to have done with the miserable business as soon as possible. So did everyone else in that detail, but only Alan failed to hit his target at all.

Wet and cold, the Company marched back to the village where they halted for dismissal outside the Orderly Room. From this comparative haven of warmth came the neat, efficient form of the Corporal of the Day, that epitome of military life – who had incidentally, been spared the ordeal on the ranges – Corporal Bannerman. In his hand he carried the lists.

"The following will report to the Quartermaster's Stores, draw items of equipment as detailed and remain on duty until dismissed." Then followed a list of names, ending " – Jarrold, MacKenzie, Lockyer."

Jim started on the next list. These offenders were due to rectify matters of dress and appearance and work out their salvation in the cookhouse. The list of names went on until finally, " – Bryant, Fleming – " a slight pause, " – Lockyer."

The Regimental Sergeant Major wished to interview those catalogued next with a view to organising extra drills for them, and this time the pause was pronounced. " – Erskine, Barrett." Blank, blank. " – Lockyer."

There was a sycophantic snigger from the back row. Jim glowered in the offender's direction, but neither the culprit nor the subject, hidden from Jim by front files, saw the annoyance in Jim's eyes, or realised his innocence of deliberate irony. He flourished another list.

"Here are the results of the firing on the range this afternoon. Rifle – "

He read out the scores in descending order, and as he made his way down the list, the spirits of the assembled Cockneys rose in anticipatory derision, while Alan's heart congealed with humiliation.

"——, ——, Butterworth, seven, Haskins, five, Lockyer – " Here, to make matters worse, Jim's eyes boggled, "nought!"

From the ranks came a loud, highly artificial, cough. Alan flushed. Jim glared.

"Bren Gun!"

Once more the dismal descent was made, and Jim, incapable of deliberate cruelty – was utterly unaware of the incredulity which entered his voice as name after name was reeled off and the attributive scores sank lower and lower – many among the hearers connecting his tones with the events of the previous evening. If there was going to be strong difference of opinion between Corporal Bannerman and Rifleman Lockyer, Jim had the popular support.

" —— Cowall, eight, Winchester, six. Lockyer – nought!"

The disbelief in Jim's voice was drowned by the howl of laughter. When order was restored, the Company listened to a brief homily on behaviour in front of the Company offices and then dismissed. During the respite, however, Alan's humiliation had thawed out in the heat of rising anger, and when Jim, unconscious of the possible connections between personal and official relationship, spoke to him, it was all Alan could do to stop himself striking his unconscious tormentor.

"You don't appear to have done very well, today, do you, Lockyer?" said Jim, severely, as he walked past into the Orderly Room.

"I'll do a bloody sight better than you do tonight, though!" thought Alan savagely to himself as he turned and walked away.

At the corner, out of sight of the office, Alan doubled back and ran along to the general store where Cora served behind the counter.

"Hullo Cora! What about tonight?" he demanded with a direct abruptness which brought a sparkle to Cora's sea-green eyes.

"Jim's coming round," she said, automatically employing delaying tactics, for she had considered herself somewhat slighted by the fact that Alan had not solicited further meetings immediately before their fond farewell. "I don't . . ."

"Look! Get rid of him by nine thirty and meet me afterwards!"

"Well, I don't know that I can!" She bridled slightly, torn between unprecedented desire and a habit of mind which expected obedience, not direction. "Anyway, why should I?"

For a fleeting second she saw the calculation in Alan's eyes but any caution she might have felt as a result was swept away as his gaze left her face and dropped. She was not to know that the fire which now seemed to burn away the cotton of her dress, was compounded just as much of rage against Jim as it was of desire for her: all she knew was that suddenly, in the shop in daylight, she was experiencing similar emotions to those belonging to moonlight shadows and that for a second she seemed actually to feel again Alan's cool, exploring hand amid her unbuttoned and disarrayed silk and Celanese.

"Come on Cora. You can get rid of him easy enough. I'll be at the cross-roads beyond the school at quarter to ten!"

"Wait over by the gate then," a hard practicality made her warn him, despite her tumult. " . . . or that cat Shiela Groves'll see you!"

As Alan turned to go however, she recaptured some of her presence of mind and put back into play technique absorbed from cinema and novelette.

"I'm not saying I will, mind, but I'll think about it!"

This she did – with a growing excitement which rendered her dismissal of Jim unduly brusque and brought her to the rendez-vous only ten minutes late.

"Well," she said breathlessly. "I've come, but I'm not sure you deserve . . ."

We rarely get what we deserve, but psychological balance was such at that moment that Alan could have just what he was ruth-less enough to take – and by the time caution or scruples might have intervened, promptings of the blood were far too urgent in both of them: whatever effect Cora felt from the removal of much of her clothing, the disarray of most of the remainder and the ruin of the flimsiest, it was not the cold which caused her to tremble.

Afterwards, as they lay together on Alan's greatcoat under frost-tipped hedges and Alan's nerves and muscles were slack with release of tension and his mind was ten million miles away, she asked the inevitable question.

"Well, why did you do it then?" she asked, when Alan eventu-ally indicated a firm negative. For a moment he was tempted to tell her – and there had been many times since when he had bitter-ly regretted not doing so – but at that moment under the Autumn clouds, it seemed best to temporize. With the same deliberacy which he had employed in the shop, his eyes travelled from her well-shaped ankles up the entrancing length of her silk-stockings, across the gleaming strip to the rumpled swathe of her skirt, then on across the opened blouse until they met her own.

"If you could see what I can, you wouldn't ask!" had been the smooth reassurance which Alan had intended to offer, but almost as a reflex, his hand had followed his eyes on the last part of their journey, and as it slid between silk and warm invitation until once again it could gather no more into its hungry fingers, Cora's arms drew his head down and her mouth blossomed under his. He felt her thighs move under him again, the questing hands, the vacancy, the sucking breath: then the world began once more to tip away.

"I wouldn't have believed it possible," he murmured to himself, ten minutes later.

Beside him now, Cora breathed slowly in deep content – almost he could hear her purr.

During the weeks that followed, of course, the driving animus behind Alan's seduction of Cora – if such it could be called –

slackened with achievement and lack of further stimulus in the cause of revenge. Alan's intelligence began to make up for his deficiencies in the routine and purely physical side of the training, and when such subjects as map-reading, navigation and simple tactics replaced the eternal weapon stripping and drill, he began to achieve some of the pre-eminence which at first he had desired.

But the return of his self-confidence, and his continued liaison with Cora, gave him little chance to appreciate his future comrade's qualities. His attitude to Jim at this time was one of amused superiority, tinged with slight guilt when some action of Jim's revealed the latter's generosity or steady capability.

It was this occasional twinge which made him persuade Cora not to break with Jim (not that she needed much persuasion, for she had a solid, rustic belief in the safety of numbers), and to co-operate in keeping their affair on a clandestine basis. Craggs, of course, divined all about it, but kept his own counsel, and the majority of the Company were aware of the probabilities inherent in the situation, but Alan was intelligent and in a number of ways lucky, and although speculation was rife for a while, interest flagged through lack of evidence, and the small, deliberately spiteful element found that in any case, Jim's honest trust was proof against their casual insinuations.

Christmas and the New Year passed – Alan spending his week's leave at his parent's home in Ruislip, while Jim's devotions to Regiment and Cora kept him in the village. January froze and sparkled. February drowned and congealed, and in March, by which time Alan was no longer interested in Cora, and she was reacting fretful and shrewish, the Company started training manoeuvres. Alan's abilities over ground and cover were noted by the watchful Corporal Bannerman, and the intuitive sense of opposing tactics came to light.

"You ever live in this part of the world, Lockyer?"

"No, Corporal. London or Hampshire, that's me!"

"London's not so far away, didn't you ever spend your holidays out here?"

"Never. Why the interest in my home life, anyway? Taking up slumming?"

"You got in first on the exercise last night. I thought you might have known the way. What happened – did you get a lift?"

"Of course I didn't!" Alan was mildy offended. "It was dead easy. You gave me a map didn't you – and a compass?"

"Other chaps had maps, too. Haskins came in next after you – just before two o'clock!"

Alan had been in before midnight.

"Look, Corporal, be reasonable! You gave me a trip of eight miles. I did it in two hours – that's not so wonderful is it? What everybody else got up to, I wouldn't know. Maybe they found some gypsies in the wood!"

It was Alan's lack of realisation of what he'd done that really raised Jim's suspicions, for eight miles in two hours on a metalled road in broad daylight is commendable – over unknown and broken country on a pitch-black night, it's phenomenal. Jim set out to prove his suspicion, and the opportunity arose a week later, when another night exercise was held.

"You are now," he announced to the squad, at the beginning of the exercise, "at Map Reference 585988. Got it?"

Ten men, bulky, inept but not uneager, clustered around the tailboard of the three-ton lorry, cavernous and huge by the side of the road. There was a mumble of voices, and a rustle and flapping of stiff paper.

"Wot did 'e say? 585 – ?"

"988. 'Ere it is. Blimey! Clarissant Court, formerly a nunnery, it says. 'Ullo, 'ullo, 'ullo! Corp'ral – where 'ave you brought us? Nuns, eh?"

"That'll do!" Jim's voice held faint distaste. "Anyway, you're too far South. Try up a bit."

"Richmond 'ill?"

The voice was shrill, incredulous, offended. An indignant chorus drowned it.

" 'Ere? Blimey – they got a nerve!"

"You got it wrong Buster. You must 'ave!"

"Wot abaht a pint at 'The Lass', eh?"

"Shut up, the lot of you! You're supposed to be a patrol just approaching the enemy positions. The row you're kicking up, you'd have half Hitler's artillery on you by now! Soldiers – my oath, give me the Girl Guides any day. They've more chance of living through the first day's action than you lot!"

What Jim lacked in poetic imagery, he made up for in righteous indignation. The babble died.

"Lockyer. Have you got it?"

"I think so, Corporal – yes. Just below the 'a' of Brampton, isn't it? Unless my eyes deceive me more than usual."

Despite the change of milieu, he still affected a theatrical drawl when, for a moment, he was what he still thought of as Stage Centre. The bright, wily eyes of the products of Whitechapel and neighbouring districts met in cynical and slightly contemptuous amusement.

"Right!" said Jim curtly. "That's the start point. Look down to that little place, Oakenden, past Milton St. Johns. That road leading through Oakenden is the enemy front line. Your job's to reach it without being seen, and report to Sergeant Grayson who'll be in Oakenden Village. Pushed out from the enemy front line will be his forward positions – that'll be me, Captain Brant, and at least four other chaps, so use your imagination, work out where we'll be, and keep clear of us. Any questions?"

"Do we 'ave to keep together Corp'ral, or can we go through on our Tod?"

"You're supposed to be a patrol so you want to keep more or less together. Split up if necessary when you reach the danger area. Until then – let's see. Lockyer! Suppose you take charge?"

"Good heavens above, Corporal! Me? But what an honour! Fame at last!"

Alan glanced around at the circle of shrewd, sardonic faces. Apprehension goaded him.

"Do you think the men will follow me, Corporal? I should hate to be shot in the back!"

There was a moment's silence.

"You'll be all right t'night, chum," remarked one of them, drily. "We only got blanks!"

Unable to think of a sufficiently crushing retort, Alan flushed and turned away.

"Come on then." he muttered. "Let's get it over with." And led off through the thin trees, followed tardily by the rest of the squad.

"Silly ass!" muttered Jim as he climbed back into the truck, but in view of his suspicions, he drove straight down towards Oakenden, turning off along the narrow track which was to constitute the mythical forward positions. He patrolled this path, on foot, for nearly three hours, and during the last hour he was joined by Captain Brant and four other experienced and long-service N.C.O.s. Yet despite their vigilance, the entire squad infiltrated past them, and when Sergeant Grayson, giving himself as he thought, plenty of time, arrived at Oakenden Village, they materialised from the shadows to greet him with triumphant, but slightly awed, hilarity.

"I don't," said Bert Craggs to Jim the following day, "know 'ow the perisher does it – and it don't make me like 'im any the more for it, 'cos 'e's a la-di-da bastard 'oo can do with a good kick up the backside. But you got to 'and it to 'im – 'e can find 'is way abaht at night like a ruddy cat. 'E never 'esitated once – just bashed straight on till we came to that farm'ouse place. Then we waited while 'e went on by 'imself."

Craggs scratched his chin, reminiscently.

"That's funny, too, now I come to think of it. There weren't no arguments. We just did as 'e told us to – 'e seemed so certain of 'imself. Different to what 'e is usually."

"Go on," said Jim, hopes crystallizing.

"Eh? Oh, yes. Where was I? At the farm'ouse! Well, 'e came back after a while and whispered, 'It's as I thought. Captain Brant is just along the road by that clump of trees, and Coporal Bannerman's up in the shadow of the barn. I reckon there are two more chaps up past the barn, Brant'll have one the other side of him, and the fourth I should say will be sculling around at the back. We'll have to watch out for him the other side of the road.' "

He looked questioningly at Jim, who nodded. Alan might have been present at the N.C.O.s' briefing.

"Well," said Craggs, continuing. " 'e told us 'e'd sorted out a place for us to cross the road, but we'd 'ave to keep dead quiet. So off we went, 'im leading, straight down towards the clump of trees where the Captain was. After a bit, we all 'ad to lie dahn be'ind some bushes, and we could see the Captain leaning against one of the trees. 'We'll wait 'ere,' says Lockyer, 'until 'e shoves off. 'E's going to want a fag pretty soon!' – and blow me, we 'adn't bin there more'n abaht five minutes, when the Captain starts patting 'is mac pockets, brings out 'is fag case, and shoves off into the middle of the clump for a spit and a draw. I could 'a done with one meself by then, too, but old Lockyer, 'e 'ad us divin' across the road, with 'im watchin' the clump and also keepin' an eye open for you, and before the Captain could 'ave got properly lit up. I reckon we was all across and on our way to Oakenden. 'E didn't seem to worry abaht the other bloke further back – but we didn't see any sign of 'im."

He looked across at Jim.

"I suppose 'e's the bright sort of bastard 'oo's goin' to make an orficer some day?"

"From what you say we could do worse, couldn't we?"

Craggs stroked his chin and lower lip with the blunt top of his forefinger. Then he shook his head, decisively.

"Don't fancy it meself. I grant yo 'e could take a section or a platoon where they were supposed to go, and 'e'd probably keep 'em aht o' trouble. But that's just it – yer can't keep aht o' trouble all the time in this lark, and when it does catch 'im up, well – " he sucked expressively at the corner of his mouth, " – I can't see young Pansy-face givin' much thought to anything but 'is own skin."

But Jim, who tended to judge people by his own standards, thought otherwise, led further astray by memories of one of the

61

Regular Battalion officers, who also possessed uncanny ability over country, and intuitive foreknowledge of the opponent's intensions. If Alan shared this gift with Lieutenant Greville, then surely he also had the brilliant officer's courage and devotion to his men.

"You could be wrong," he said to Craggs.

"Oh, yes," replied that worthy. "I could. But I don't think I am."

But Jim's pilgrim spirit had found it's cause. Here was material to be nursed and shaped into the finest type of Light Infantry officer – a conscript recruit who would one day stand beside the Grevilles, the Wemyss's, the Fanshawes who had officered the regular battalions since the formation of the regiment.

But of course, when it came to it, Alan refused to be nursed or shaped. He was quite prepared to lead the way in night patrols or suggest means of outwitting or bypassing the "Red" or "Blue" forces pitted against them in mock battles – in fact, he preferred to, for if he led, then time was not wasted by the mistakes which everyone else seemed to make, and could retire to his blankets that much earlier.

But as for improving his shooting, or smartening up his dress, or even remembering to read Daily Routine Orders, they were matters with which Rifleman Lockyer just could not be bothered. After all, everyone knew that the Maginot Line was impregnable, so was the Siegfried, and Hitler was a gentleman. Both armies would sit tight and the politicians would solve the matter in good time. Meanwhile, the phony war was a joke – in not very good taste, mark you – and the best thing to do was to get through the dreariness with as little effort as possible.

At first, Jim's lack of comprehension of Alan's outlook was only equalled by the patience with which he sought to alter it, but as the nature and extent of Alan's intransigeance became evident, Jim, that slow, stolid, kindly lad, gradually became angry. Angry with the burning anger of the social reformer who sees waste and want side by side, coupled with the frustrated violence of a proud craftsman defeated by a piece of superb but somehow obdurate material.

And with anger, Jim discovered a use for irony. From the memories of his apprenticeship days, he recalled the tones and expressions of the master joiners who had taught him. Great gobbets of sarcasm were unearthed almost from his subconscious – the relics of his raw days at the Regimental Depot – and his recollections of the Drill Serjeant at the Barracks at Tel el Kebir, a man with a tongue like the bite of a centipede, supplied him with many a titbit of descriptive allegory. All this, he unleashed on Alan.

"Straighten yourself up, man," he snapped at him. "Your chest's like the back of a spoon and your shoulders are like beer-bottles. Pull your belly in! You look like a pregnant duck!"

"What the hell have you been using to clean this with?" he asked, peering down Alan's rifle barrel. "The flue-brush dipped in treacle? It's damn near as black as your neck!"

And on the parade ground, when Alan had the misfortune to be halted on a patch of ice, with the result that his feet shot from under him and he slid forward flat on his back, Jim was there, looking sardonically down at him, when finally he came to rest.

"Feeling sleepy?" asked Jim. "Sonny?"

All this benefited the principals not at all, but it provided the rest of the Company with some amusement at Alan's expense – for his new-found abilities had in no way decreased his unpopularity, and, such is the waywardness of destiny that Cora also reaped solace. Stung by Jim's taunts back into the vengeful fury which had driven him during the early days of his punitive liaison, Alan renewed his interest in, and attacks upon, what a considerable number of people regarded as Jim's property. Cora was delighted.

Delighted, that is, until the Battalion was formed up and ordered to France to join the B.E.F.

"You ought to marry me, before you go, Alan, really you did."

"Marry you?" asked the startled Alan, and then diplomatically stifling the incredulity in his voice. "What about Jim?"

"Oh – him! I'll tell him about us before you go!"

"Christ! Don't do that! Do you think I want to be shot in the back first time we go into action?"

Ever practical, but of course, entranced at the possibility of men fighting over her, Cora agreed, and when they landed in Cherbourg, both Jim and Alan were at peace with their own private worlds, Alan relieved of what had once more become a stale and unrewarding affair, Jim steadfast and confident in his love.

Chapter 8

SOLDIERING ABROAD – even in a foreign land so nearly contiguous as France – was completely, astonishingly, and in late April 1940, delightfully, different from training in England. First of all, for Alan as much as any other of the Battalion – for he had been too poor to travel – there was the excitement of new surroundings. They were stationed at first in a grey and cream village in the Sarth district, a place of wide, dust-blue roads, sleepy farms, short, dumpy girls, gauche and giggling. For Alan the place was epitomised in the soft, bland, unexciting Muscat which he drank in some of its ubiquitous and ever-open cafes.

With the change in surroundings, there came also a change in Alan's relations with the rest of the Company. Now, instead of being one man, isolated among many because of differences of class and sympathies, he was one of a group of men, isolated – or at any rate different – among a countryside of strangers. On his part he unconsciously shed some of his protective affections – on their part, they no longer looked on him as self-consciously 'officer class' and therefore as a potential enemy. They included him into their companionship.

"He ain't such a stuck-up sod as you'd first think. 'E might even be 'uman!"

The words were spoken by Craggs, but the feeling was general – in fact the only dissentient voice was Jim's, still nursing his frustration at his own inability to transform Alan into the pride of the regiment. This continued hostility was once more construed as jealousy by the other men, but with the shift in relationships, Jim began to occupy the ignominious position of cuckold, while Alan had acquired some of the tawdry glamour of the successful rake.

Then the battalion moved up to the Belgian frontier.

On the evening of the ninth of May, Alan was sitting in the corner of one of the larger estaminets in Baillieul, unexceptionally stating his views upon the probable employment of the Battalion, and more especially the Company, during the immediate future.

"Bert," he said, "Be your age!" For Craggs had suggested that the sudden move up towards the frontier had been made for genuine – as opposed to 'administrative' – military expediency, and that they might soon be firing their rifles at living targets. "I can tell you exactly why we've been sent up here. France, with one or two exceptions, is a beautiful country. Summer is coming. You

64

don't think G.H.Q. are going to let infantry – the likes of you and me – get a look at the best parts, do you? The scenery anywhere else in this land is much too good for peasants like us – we might start enjoying ourselves! No, chum! The reason why we've been sent up here is because it's the dullest, the flattest, the dirtiest and the smelliest part of the country. The fact that it's nearest to Jerry is just co-incidence!"

"Beer's lousy, too," agreed Craggs, lugubriously regarding the thin, pale liquid in the glasses, " – which strengthens your argument. I see all that, Bucko, and I admit you've got a point. But I still reckon old 'Itler's going to move. I can feel it in me water."

"What if he does?" asked Nick Barrett aggressively. "If he shoves his snitch ahtside 'is own country, 'e'll get done!"

"Ah – maybe!" said Craggs. "But p'raps 'e don't know that, see? P'raps 'e don't know that facin' 'is tanks is a fine body o' British infantry, fully armed with rifles and bayonets – steel ones at that – some of 'om 'ave even fired their bond'ooks, and as a result know which end the bullet comes aht of! See what I mean? 'E may not know that!"

He examined the bottom of his glass somewhat grimly.

"Then again," he added, " – 'e might know all abaht it and just not care. We all know 'ow silly some geezers can be!"

There was an uncomfortable pause.

"You gettin' cold feet, Bert?" asked Smalley, eventually.

"I dunno!" admitted Craggs, "I reckon I'm as game to 'ave a bash as anyone else – but whatever they say in the papers I don't see it bein' a picnic, once it does start!"

" 'Oo said it was goin' to start anyway?" asked someone uncomfortably.

At that moment there was diversion, for Alan felt a hand on his shoulder.

"I'd like a word with you, Lockyer. Can you spare a minute?"

Jim, paler than usual and tense, stood behind him.

" 'Ullo, Jim," said Craggs, quickly. "Thought you were on duty. What's yours? I don't exactly recommend the beer but it's better than a slap in the kisser with a wet 'addock."

"No thanks, Bert – I am on duty really, but I just nipped out for a word with Lockyer, here. I've got to get back to the Orderly Room. Will you walk back with me Lockyer? What I've got to say won't take long, and you can come back again afterwards."

Alan felt his spine grow cool, and hoped that he hadn't turned pale as well. Then he flushed – and felt that, too. Shrewd eyes watched his face and divined his feelings. He swallowed the remainder of his drink and rose to his feet.

"Sure," he said. "What's on your mind, Corporal?" He followed Jim out, leaving a speculative and slightly hilarious group behind him.

"Aye – aye!" sang one of them, and . . .

"Trouble in the old 'ome tonight, eh? Reckon Corp's forcing a show down, Bert?" asked another.

But Craggs was not amused. Puzzled, yes, but not amused.

Outside on the pavement, Jim and Alan walked along until they were clear of the main street and the sauntering crowds. Alan using the time to prepare his defences. At last they walked together along a fairly deserted road leading out of the town towards the Company billet.

"Now, look here, Lockyer," began Jim. "I want you to listen to what I have to say, because I'm dead serious, and if what I hear is correct, we may all need every bit of common sense and intelligence we've got during the next few weeks."

This was so different to any approach that Alan had envisaged that it bereft him of speech. In desperation he essayed a grunt, choked, and started a fit of coughing. Jim watched him with surprise.

"What's the matter? Swallow a fly or something?"

Red-faced, wheezing slightly, Alan shook his head.

"Something went the wrong way," he gasped, and then, as he quickly regained his breath – "what was that you were saying?"

"I reckon we're in for trouble, Lockyer. I heard tonight that Jerry's massing troops on the Dutch and Belgian frontier, and that the moment he crosses one or the other, we're to go forward and meet him."

Like a chess-player surveying the board in relation to his opponent's latest move, Alan wondered whether he should shift his mental basis of defence.

"Surely he's not going to do a ' – if I die, I know that you will take good care of Cora – ' act, is he?" he thought. Jim was speaking again.

"I suppose you think I've been picking on you lately, just because I don't like your face or something. Don't you?"

For a moment Alan considered a bland denial that he had even been aware that Jim had 'been picking in him' at all, but abandoned it as futile.

"I expect I'm pretty awful at times," he said vaguely, not wishing to lead anywhere specific.

"You are!" said Jim, succinctly. "Bloody awful when you know how good you could be if you tried!"

"What the hell are you talking about?" asked Alan, surprised out of his amorphous smoke-screen.

"I'm talking about you," replied Jim earnestly. " – and believe me, it's for your own good. Look, Lockyer, whether you like it or not, there's a war on. I've been trying to din that in to your thick head for months, and get you to take it seriously. Well, now I can tell you that it's nearly on us – I reckon we'll be in action within a week!"

"What?"

Surprise mingled with a quite understandable panic for a second, but then Alan, rapidly readjusting his thoughts, steadied his voice. It must be remembered that he had never as yet, heard a shot fired in anger.

"So what, rather! We're ready for 'em."

He looked across at Jim.

"Aren't we?"

"I'm not saying we aren't ready," said Jim, doggedly. "But what I am saying is that you at any rate, could be a damn sight readier. Look, Lockyer, I'm serious and I know what I'm talking about. You've got the makings of a first-class officer!"

This somewhat apocalyptic announcement took Alan back to his fond dreams upon call-up, long since put out of mind. That Jim, of all people should suggest their re-emergence was a twist which was lending an already baffling conversation some of the febrile inexplicity of delirium. With vague memories of astronomical casualty figures among junior officers in 1914, Alan wondered for a moment whether this was all part of some murky plot to get rid of him.

He peered suspiciously at Jim.

"What's all this leading up to?" he asked.

"It's not leading up to anything," answered Jim, pursuing his course, " – except a last attempt to make you see reason. I'm not doing it for my own good, Lockyer. It's for all of us – for the battalion! Unless we all pull our weight when we meet up with Jerry, well–" his imagination rejected the suggestion of defeat, or even worse – retreat, (how Jim's mind survived the events of the next three weeks, is proof of the indestructibility of the psyche) and he finished with a halting " – it's going to be pretty tough for the rest of us."

Abruptly, Alan stopped, and when Jim swung around to see why, the taller man was staring down at him with the beginnings of troubled comprehension in his face.

"Do you expect me to believe that you've been roasting the pants off me for my own good?"

"Of course I do! What other reason is there for me to have chased you?"

Bewilderment stared down at honest ingenuousness.

"Do you think I'm jealous of you or something?"

Ah! – That's more like it! Triumphantly, suspicion returned and showed itself in facial expression.

"Oh, don't be so bloody silly, Lockyer. I know I'll never be offered a commission – not in my own mob anyway, and I'd never leave them for some other lot, commission or not! Come on, I can't stand around – I've got to get back to the Orderly Room."

Jim turned and started off again. Alan stared at his back for a second and then hurried after him.

"Of course I'd like to have your brains – but I haven't and that's all there is to it. What I've got's enough to do my job." went on Jim when Alan caught him up. "But what makes me so fed up, is to see a chap like you, with your brains and education, who can find his way over country like you do, and who can work out what the other bloke is up to – but who won't take the trouble to use 'em. Didn't matter so much when we were just training, but – " Here Jim hesitated, then stopped and looked up at Alan. " – I'm not supposed to tell anyone this, Lockyer – I'm not even supposed to know it myself! G.H.Q. thinks the balloon is about to go up, and when it does, we shall be outnumbered and outgunned, and the chances are that the R.A.F.'ll be shot out of the sky so we'll have no air cover."

Stupified by the incredible revelations which were beginning to pile up, one on the other, Alan looked blankly at the worried, dogged, and so patently honest young face before him. Somewhere in the pit of his stomach (for the heart, despite the lady novelist, is purely functional) he felt the rather abrupt awakening of a conscience, and the beginning of shame. Some of this caused an alteration of expression, for Jim grinned – almost paternally.

"Don't worry chum – we'll get through somehow. That is – we'll get through if everyone pulls his weight! So now do you see why I've been chasing you? Now do you see why I came and fetched you tonight?"

It was Alan who moved on this time. He was seeing a lot of things – including Jim in a new light. The political and military situation could wait – there was something else he wanted to know. But how to get the conversatoin around to it?

"Going to be a lot of casualties," he ventured at last, clumsily working around towards the subject. Jim was unimpressed, but sympathetic.

"Of course there'll be casualties," he said. "But don't let it worry you!"

"I wasn't thinking of us so much," replied Alan, carefully, " – as the people at home." He hesitated, drew breath, and plunged. "Your girl friend, for instance, Cora. She'll take a poor view of things if you buy it, won't she?"

Now here Alan made a mistake. It was one caused by lack of intelligence (in the military sense) as well as lack of appreciation of character, for even had other matters been serene and straight-forward between Jim and Cora, Jim's native shyness would never have allowed him to give a natural answer on such a subject to one whom he considered worldly and sophisticated. There was also the fact that, despite the regular despatch of a dutiful letter to Cora every day since they had arrived in France, he had never received one in return, and even Jim was beginning to suspect that this was not entirely due to postal inefficiency.

"I doubt it," he said briefly. "Cora's all right for a bit of fun, but I reckon that's about all!"

If Alan had pursued the matter, he might have got at the truth, as far as Jim's feelings were concerned, but he was so relieved at the apparent lack of ardour in Jim's reply, that he took it at it's face value.

"Good time girl, eh?" he commented, native caution forbidding the full concordance which he could have expressed.

"Could be," grunted Jim, embarrassed anyway, and unhappy in the subject. "Here's the Orderly Room."

He stopped at the doorway and turned to Alan.

"Well – there you are, Lockyer. I've got it off my chest now, and I can't do any more. It's up to you! As I've told you, you've got the talent to make as fine an officer as we've got in this battalion – with the exception of the Colonel of course," he added loyally, for the C.O. was a regular. "Think it over."

"Oh, I will," replied Alan. For the moment he considered offering to join Jim on duty, thus relieving one of the runners, but he decided instead that he'd better devote a little solitary thought both to his own position in the light of Jim's prognosis of his military worth, and his own future actions concerning Jim himself. He was beginning to feel very guilty – not so much for his dalliance with Cora – for that, to judge by Jim's recent reaction, was of no account – as for the derision and dislike with which he had regarded Jim hitherto.

"Goodnight, old chap," he said. " – and, er, thanks very much."

Slowly – and suddenly rather humble – he turned and walked off into the night.

Four hours later, Luftwaffe Bombers crossed the dividing frontiers and bombed the Arras G.H.Q., and the grey waves rolled forward into Belgium and Holland. Within twenty-four hours, Alan, Jim, Bert Craggs, and all the rest of the Battalion were moving forward to meet them.

Among Alan's platoon, only Craggs and Jim had the remotest conception of what they might be up against. Perhaps it was as well.

Chapter 9

ALWAYS THE STUKA! Incessantly, ceaslessly the Stuka! Be it day or night, or dawn or dusk, or even time for tea – the Stuka! A bowel-curdling horror at first, by reaction a thing of derision second, thirdly a vicious nuisance which presaged the shock of prowling tanks, and from then on, as body tired and nerves stretched, a howling and ever-present menace.

"Where's the bloody R.A.F.?" asked the dog-weary troops, and perhaps, out of all the thousands of Allied troops in Belgium, Alan alone cried "No!" in his heart.

"Not more noise, for pity's sake!"

Shaken by the hordes of refugees, his nerves keyed up to shrieking pitch by the long, wearisome approach marches to the various lines of defence which were abandoned before they were attacked, his over-riding objection to war when it finally caught up with him seemed to be to its noisiness.

Now he lay on the floor of an open barn, Craggs on one side of him, Smalley, Calderhouse, Barrett and other members of the platoon lying in the straw behind them. The platoon officer had gone off to try to find Company or Battalion Headquarters, and with the incredible inconsequence which reigned in those days, taken Jim with him. As their platoon sergeant had disappeared two days previously (disappeared: just like that! Eighteen months later Jim met him as a Captain of Artillery – what he'd been doing in the meantime, he and God alone knew;) Jim had received temporary acting promotion and was the only other authority in the platoon. With both officer and Jim absent, the platoon was leaderless. Leaderless, that is, with the exception of such natural leaders as time and necessity might produce.

"What we going to do when this perishin' swarm buzzes off back to its nest, Bucko?"

"Thank God for the quiet and go to sleep, I should think," mumbled Alan. "Why? Do you think there's any hope of 'em going?"

"They'll go all right, Bucko," answered Craggs grimly. "And then, if I've got the idea right, in comes 'is tanks."

"We're all right, Bert. We're Reserve platoon aren't we? One and three platoons are up front.

"Where," asked Craggs, pointedly, " – is up front?"

Alan rubbed his eyes wearily. What with the noise, the lack of sleep, and the dust in the barn, his head ached abominably. Almost unaware of what he was doing, he rose to his feet.

"I'll go and fine out shall I?" he asked, and walked out of the barn and halfway across the rich, malodorous yard. It was almost as though the Stukas were as surprised as the other members of the platoon, for there was a silence. In it, Alan turned and shouted.

"I'll go up as far as the cross-roads."

He paused.

"Back in ten minutes," he added, only slightly aware of the incongruity of the statement, and then walked on across the yard, turned the corner by the main farmhouse, and started along its length.

Behind him, the section looked at each other incredulously.

"Where's 'e orf to, Bert?"

" 'E's gone to 'ave a look rahnd!" said Craggs in tones of wonderment.

"Wot 'im? Blimey! Take back all I ever said abaht' im. 'Oo'd a thought 'e 'ad the guts!"

From the other side of the farmhouse came a short, sharp burst of fire.

"Come on!" yelled Craggs, and to a man, the platoon leapt to their feet, grabbed their weapons and raced after Alan.

As the first of them turned the corner around which he had disappeared, they saw him run forward, apparently pursuing three grey-green figures, then fling himself sideways into a ditch as another burst of machine-gun fire pitted the road alongside him.

"After 'em!" roared Craggs again – a mighty man now action was joined, but as the platoon swept forward, Alan's hand appeared above the ditch. Obedient to the somewhat imperious gesture, they too, flung themselves sideways – across to the opposite side of the road. Cannon shell and Spandau bullet ricochetted off the farmhouse walls and scored the surface of the tarmac.

In the ditch they lay, eyes on the road ahead, waiting for Alan's next command, spoken or signalled. In their hearts they marvelled at the innaccuracy of their previous judgment of him, and were grateful now for his presence and leadership. They remembered his uncanny abilities over country.

" 'Oo'd a thought it, eh?" they repeated to themselves as they watched the road.

All in all, it was an extremely good thing for their peace of mind, as well as for Alan's sudden glory, that they could not actually see into the short trench into which he had flung himself.

"Christ!" he thought as he lay quaking with fear. "What's

72

happening? What did I come out here for? Why didn't someone tell me the Germans were around?"

For the simple facts of the matter were that Alan, his thought processes numbed by weariness and noise, had been completely unaware of any possibility of danger when he walked across the yard. He had simply been going to find a place free from Stukas, and his bewildered comprehension had registered the fact that beyond the farmhouse, the sky was clear: his spoken intentions had been more in the nature of an excuse than a proposal, and nothing was further from his mind than contact with the enemy. Then suddenly, when he was halfway along the length of the farm-house, his heart rising in the post-Stuka calm, bullets sang about him, and looking up, he saw three slightly blurred but undoubt-edly hostile figures advancing down the road.

He saw something else, too, a small ditch about ten yards in front of him – and an incredibly acute sense of self-preservation told him to go forward to it, and not to attempt the long and assuredly fatal retreat back down the length of the building. As he advanced, the Germans – who were aware of the tanks and machine-guns coming up behind them and who were in any case, only a reconnaisance unit, probing forward to find Allied oppo-sition – quite naturally retreated.

This was the situation upon which the rest of the platoon burst, and in the frantic paralysis which gripped Alan's mind, Cragg's defiant roar of attack sounded like the crack of doom – just, in fact, like more of the enemy closing in on him from the rear. Almost instinctively, he put his hand up in an effort to propitiate the angry warriors behind him, and as he brought his hand down, tank and machine gun opened up in response to information re-tailed by the three reconnaisance men now safely back under their protection.

Cannon and machine gun ceased fire. Silence. The world waited, and the painful thudding of Alan's heart eased slightly, for realisa-tion had suddenly struck him that the enemy in the rear had not arrived. Had they been shot down by their own bullets? In such a disordered world as this had become, anything was possible. He stuck his neck up out of the ditch, and there being a Fortune which protects the drunk, the very young and the incredibly fool-ish, was not shot for his pains.

Instead, almost opposite him, he saw the head of Bert Craggs also tentatively emerging from cover. Immediately it was trans-formed by a broad grin, and to Alan's complete astonishment, he was given an enthusiastic thumbs up sign. "Bloody good work, Bucko!"

Excitement had reduced Craggs' language to that of his officers. "Can you see the bastards?" asked Craggs, recovering.

Alan turned his head and peered forward, his brain slowly disentangling the situation. Ten yards ahead of him he saw, slowly rising above level of the road, the top of a coal-scuttle helmet. He had the immense advantage of time – about three-quarters of a second. As the brim of the helmet cleared the road level, Alan's rifle was coming forward from under his stomach. As the eyes came up high enough to see over the road, the rifle butt came into Alan's shoulder, and automatically his hands gripped stock and barrel. He fired.

Where the bullet went, no-one knew, but the report was enough to send the German back into his ditch.

At this indication of the enemy in front, however, Cockney pugnacity burst its cautionary bounds, and Craggs, followed by the rest of the platoon, leapt from the ditch and charged up past Alan. What they all expected to see, no-one knew: what they saw, was Alan's startled German re-emerging from his ditch, with three more behind him. The action which followed was brief, chaotic, bloody. During it, one of the platoon dropped a grenade.

Alan, crawling out of his ditch and running belatedly up behind the others – more for company than any desire to close with the enemy, be it said – picked up the bomb.

The action finished, the surprised Germans were despatched, and the platoon stood back, puzzled, uncertain what they should do next. A grey-blue half-track hurtled around a near-by corner, and screamed to a halt. Alan pulled the pin of the grenade and flung the pineapple over the heads of the platoon to land with inspired accuracy in the half-track.

"Come on!" yelled Alan, his brain suddenly shocked back into activity by the resultant explosion. "Get to hell out of here!"

As he turned and fled back up the road, machine guns and rifles opened up on the spot where they had all been standing, and the rest of the platoon – chasing after him – marvelled again at his prescience. They swept past the barn in which they had been resting, and only stopped half a mile back when they met their platoon officer – one Lieutenant Rose – to whom between excitement and a faint feeling of guilt at not stopping at the barn and fighting a 'last round, last man' action, the Cockneys gave a highly coloured account of the events of the preceding quarter of an hour in which Alan's named figured conspicuously.

If there was gratuitous praise for him, there was also – but not in Bert Cragg's heart – a shrewd tactical manoeuvre which would provide a scapegoat if, by some incalculable interpretation of events on the part of Authority, they had done wrong.

As it happened, all was well.

"First class, Lockyer!" said Lieutenant Rose, "and as it happens, on Sergeant Bannerman's recommendation, I was considering promoting you to Corporal anyway. You can take it that that will go through."

Thus Alan achieved his first – and only – promotion.

It was, of course, Temporary, Acting.

The platoon saw no more of the enemy for three days.

They heard him though. At any and all hours of the day and the night, sudden action would flare up in diverse and completely inexplicable directions. The enemy were everywhere; they were nowhere. The line was in front and then along the left flank and there it was certain, and stabilised. Then tanks roared upon them from behind, and the rear echelons dragged their rifles out from the welter of cooking pots, ambulances, and filing cabinets, fixed their bayonets and gallantly charged a heavily armoured column – which promptly withdrew.

Between seven and eight o'clock one morning, D Company on Alan's left flank was completely decimated, yet all Alan heard was a scattered rattle of shots and the revving up of heavy engines. They were less than half a mile away, but when the few survivors came in and attached themselves to their company, they had a look of blank, uncomprehending horror in their eyes. Jim was attached to Headquarters Company and Lieutenant Rose told Alan he would have to act as Platoon Sergeant and Bert Craggs was given a stripe.

All the time they were moving, but no-one could say whether it was an advance or a retreat, and as they marched, counter-marched em- and de- bussed, the air of complete unreality deepened, and what with men getting lost, and sharp, sudden actions whittling away the lengths of the nominal rolls, the battalion strength sank lower and lower, until it was little more than that of a company.

On the evening of the third day, the platoon was ordered to dig in along a line of hedges. On their left flank was a wood, held, so they were told, by crack troops of the French Army – Chasseurs Alpins was the name most suggested – their right flank was held by other platoons of their own company, while the remains of C Company was beyond them, and Headquarters and the D Company survivors were behind.

"Don't believe it," announced Bert Craggs. "That's a 'ighly

intelligent arrangement, that is, and what – " he enquired bitterly, " – is a 'ighly intelligent arrangement doing arahnd 'ere in this war?"

"We've got along well enough without one so far, I must admit," agreed Alan softly.

Somehow, what with this further responsibility, coupled with the passage of sufficient time to allow him to start believing the current report of his behaviour three days previously, he had gained confidence. Action, fear, excitement too, had stripped him of his last remaining affections, and this evening, he was a confident, fairly relaxed, popular young man, among friends who admired and trusted him.

Twilight deepened – oh, those mauve, almost purple twilights, fantastically lit with golden flash and platinum-white flare!

"What the hell's that Belisha Beacon doing, stuck up there?" asked Alan, looking towards a huge orange sphere suspended in the air about half a mile away, apparently a hundred or so feet above ground level.

"Search me," muttered Nick Barrett, beside him. "What the hell's anything in this war?" He examined the sphere, still suspended, still stationary. "Maybe it *is* a Belisha Beacon and there's a pedestrian crossing underneath it! Wouldn't surprise me!"

They waited, and the darkness thickened.

By midnight they were cold with inactivity, and in their inexperience, bored. Came footsteps, buckets clinked behind them, and who should it be but the cooks, bringing up cocoa? The platoon looked at each other suspiciously.

"I give up!" announced Craggs, wonderingly. "Rifle platoons in front, Headquarters be'ind – *and* cocoa! Someone," he continued bleakly, " – 'as been organising! I suppose 'Itler knows it's Naafi break, does 'e! We don't want 'im bargin' in 'ere with the goo only 'arf drunk, do we?"

Finishing his drink quickly, Alan felt his bowels move, and as a general air of break-time invested the whole proceedings, decided to take his ease in the fringe of the woods behind and to their left.

"Back in a minute, Bert," he announced. "Keep an eye on my bondhook."

Others had been in the woods before him with the same intent. Now, others were there again – presumably similarly engaged, thought Alan – as he made himself ready to return to the platoon. There was a movement, just to his left. Being by nature, reticent – as far as the body's needs were concerned – Alan waited, unwilling to embarrass or to be embarrassed.

Two forms stepped from the edge of the wood and peered after the returning cooks, now clinking their buckets away in the direction of Headquarters Company. Alan froze with suspicion. The forms moved further out from the wood, followed immediately by two more. Clear of the shadowing copse, they were silhouetted as bulky, jack-booted, coalscuttle-helmetted. One of the leading pair lifted his arm, pointing towards the platoon positions. Silently, the four moved down towards the unsuspecting Cockneys, each drawing a stick-bomb from his belt.

Behind them, fear paralysed Alan's throat and he clutched at a tree-trunk. If he shouted – they would turn and kill him – this he knew. He closed his eyes to blot out the position, and then, realising he could not, screwed up his courage to sacrifice himself. As he opened his eyes and his mouth to shout, two more heavy figures stepped out from the darkness of the trees, and their sudden appearance unnerved him again and he remained silent.

Slow, deathless time ticked by.

Then a violent explosion split the air apart, followed immediately by three more as red and yellow flame erupted from the platoon positions. From well away on the right, where the other platoon lay, came shouts and the sporadic crack of rifles, and then suddenly, in front of him, were the four first Germans, come back to join the last two. A murmur of voices, a chuckle, they all moved back into the woods, passing within six feet of Alan.

Occasionally, Fate is kind. Alan fainted.

Chapter 10

LOSS OF MEMORY, so the psychiatrists tell us, is not always caused by physical damage to the brain or nerve structures. It can be caused also by the sub-conscious mind blanking off memories too painful to be borne or loads of guilt too great to be carried, by a conscious mind already over stressed with the day to day problems of life.

Alan's case had vague, but not sub-conscious, similarities.

Not so much by a deliberate effort to forget, as by a deliberate effort to make himself believe that he *did not know* what had happened that night, did he eventually manage to persuade both himself, and the official and unofficial enquirers as to events, that he could have had no responsibility in the death of all the other members of his platoon.

At a later stage in the war, he might not have got away with it, but now he was considerably assisted by events. The cooks, who could have told of his leaving the platoon – without his rifle – were not present when the first enquiries were made by Company and Battalion Commanders, and when, only a matter of hours later, the main weight of the German Forces in the area were turned on the battalion, all concerned were too busy fighting for their own lives to worry overmuch about the manner in which other people had lost theirs.

What had in fact happened, was that Alan eventually came completely to his senses about half an hour after he lost them. He had partially recovered twice before, coming up from the depths like a submariner escaping, but as soon as conscious thought began – however fumblingly – the flood of memory combined with harsh actuality to frighten him back again into insensibility. In the end, however, no matter how hard he might try to avoid it, he had to return to danger and discomfort.

The first thing to do was to get away from the wood – having emitted six Germans, it might well start producing more. With no wish to start giving explanations, he must avoid Headquarters – which meant that he must either return to the position of his own platoon, or bye-pass it and go on to the flanking platoons. Wild horses could not have dragged him back to see the shambles which he might have prevented, so he started off for the trenches which had neighboured his own.

Halfway across to them – almost instinctively, so little thought or consideration did the precaution take – he altered his route to join the direct line between his objective and his platoon position. Once on the line, he removed his tin hat, flung it back towards his own trench, and then crawled on. Even as his hands and knees scraped along the earth, he was preparing himself for the part he was to play. Five yards short of the nearest platoon position, he managed a sobbing moan. Ahead, something rustled in the grasses.

"Help! Help!" he cried in a strangled whisper.

More rustles, metal clicked and chinked.

"Don't fire!" he called, momentary panic restoring strength to his voice. "It's Lockyer!"

There was a short silence and then a voice answered him.

"Where are you, chum? Can you come in?"

"I think so!"

In view of the fainting weakness in his tones, however, the platoon sergeant and one of the riflemen came out, looming suddenly in the darkness, picked him up by the arms and half-carried, half-dragged him into their own trenches.

"What happened, Corporal?" asked the young Lieutenant in charge. "We went over to have a look, but there didn't seem to be anyone left alive. Where were you?"

"I went after 'em sir!"

The outlines of the story were already in his mind. Faintly, and oh, so hesitantly, the rest came out.

"I was – at the end of the – the trench, sir. I heard something – behind us, and tur- turned, and saw the bombs coming!"

Here he paused – with effect. He passed his hand wearily across his forehead.

"Here, chum. 'Ave a pull o' this!"

Rum coursed hotly down his throat. Carried away by his own art, he choked and coughed (in the dark, with a most sympathetic audience, he was giving the performance of his life).

"I chucked myself sideways out of the trench, rolled over and went after them. Then the bombs went off behind me, and – and – "

He faltered.

"You don't remember any more I suppose?" said the Lieutenant sympathetically.

He shook his head, wretchedly. Only the sergeant was not impressed.

"Where's your rifle, Corporal?"

Alan looked up, bewildered, hurt.

"It was quite possibly blown out of his hands, Sergeant" said the Lieutenant in terms of mild rebuke. "Get Corporal Lockyer evacuated as soon as possible. He needs rest after what he's been through."

But the sergeant, who had considerably more experience of both the effects of bombing and of human nature than the Lieutenant, was by no means satisfied. He had not been particularly willing to accept the popular version of the previous encounter between Alan and the enemy, and as a result, his mind was not so conditioned to overlook discrepancies in Alan's story as other were.

"I see you lost your helmet, too, Corporal. That get blown off your head?"

"I suppose so, Sergeant. I – I'm afraid I don't know."

"Pity! If you'd brought that back, we might have been able to see what had knocked you out. Ah, well. You'd better get back I suppose. Can you find your way alone?"

"Send a man with him, Sergeant," said the Lieutenant firmly, much to Alan's relief. The Sergeant regarded both officer and Alan with basilisk stare.

"Very good sir. Kellatt!"

With a brief jerk of his head to Rifleman Kellatt he both detailed Alan's escort and signified his dissent. It was not the hero's triumphal discharge which Alan would have liked – and at one time looked like getting – but by this time he was glad to escape without threat of immediate court martial.

Together he and Rifleman Kellett stumbled away through the dark, occasionally dropping flat as white or coloured fire curved lazily up into the night.

"Have any trouble getting him back?" asked the Sergeant when Kellatt returned to the platoon.

"No, Sergeant," replied Kellatt. "We made it all right."

"H'm. Yes, I thought perhaps you would."

Meanwhile, back at Headquarters, Alan was repeating his tale to a variety of people, from the Battalion Commander who listened grimly, his mind occupied with the inexorable laws of logistics and man-power, to Jim and the office clerks who saw the events in more human terms and were more impressionable as a result.

Alan's reputation grew, but with the memory of the platoon sergeant always at the back of his mind, he played it down as much as possible, genuinely desirous of avoiding too much totally undeserved credit.

Shortly after three o'clock in the morning, fighting broke out on the extreme flank of the battalion position and in the space of twenty minutes, six subalterns were killed, with four of their platoon N.C.O.s. At four o'clock, the Colonel returned and sent for Jim.

"Corporal Bannerman," he said, "take any men who you consider capable of bearing arms down to the small farm beyond the road. You'll find the remains of Lieutenant Cator's platoon and Liuetenant Mackeson's. Hold the farmhouse until ten o'clock this morning. After that you can retire."

He looked up at the erect and unperturbed figure in front of him.

"Good Luck, Corporal," he said. "Perhaps we shall meet again in England!"

Jim saluted, turned about and marched out of the room to carry out his orders. Behind him, the Colonel tidied up a few outstanding matters, put on his helmet and walked outside to have a final word with the Chaplain and the Medical Officer, and to cheer up those casualties who were conscious. He picked up a rifle from under one of the stretchers.

"This shouldn't be here," he said brightly, and took it out with him.

He still had it with him the following morning when he was killed at the head of yet another scratch platoon, holding a line of ditches on the outskirts of Oudenaarde. Oddly enough, one of his ancestors had been killed there, over two hundred years before, serving with the same regiment under Marlborough, and the two lie buried now less than a quarter of a mile apart, although over three hundred from the house in which they were both born, and which they had both inherited upon reaching man's estate.

The attacks on the small farm began at six o'clock.

"Thank Gawd for you and Sarn't Bannerman," said one little Cockney clerk to Alan. "Makes all the difference to us to feel we got proper fightin' soljers wiv us!"

Alan glanced at him suspiciously, then stared.

"My God," thought Alan. "I believe he means it!" and a look around at the other pathetic, frightened but somehow pugnacious faces, confirmed the fact. The assorted clerks, runners, sanitary orderlies and stretcher bearers were genuinely heartened by the presence of Alan and Jim among them.

Alan swallowed, and suddenly the vision of Bert Craggs was conjured in his mind.

"I'll do my best Bert – honestly I will!" he said.

And when the attacks came, he did.

The first wave of storming infantry was shot down by Bren and rifle – Alan had the Bren – and there was not even a graze among them. The platoon were delighted.

"What'll they do next, Alan?" asked Jim.

"Try to creep around the flanks," he answered, surprised at the question.

Disposition of firing points was altered. Half an hour later, Jim broke up a patrol with bombs, twenty yards away from the farm, and another patrol walked down on to Alan's Bren almost the same distance the other side.

"Let 'em take the farm this time, Jim," counselled Alan. "We can't stop 'em with what we've got, but we can clear 'em out again afterwards!"

Jim looked doubtful.

"Colonel said we must hold it until ten," he said.

"Well, we won't if we try to hold it now, Jim – they'll wipe us out. Let 'em have it for ten minutes – we'll get 'em out again!"

The Stukas came over at eight o'clock, set a small outhouse on fire and put one bomb through the roof. The noise, as usual, was far in excess of the damage and Alan surprised himself with a genuinely derisive grin as they flew away. From a small hillock a hundred yards away, they watched the German infantry creep into the farm.

They left the Bren with the little Cockney clerk, and strict and precise instructions as to when and along what lines he was to open fire. Grim and determined, like a pugnacious sparrow, he lay behind the gun, tears in his eyes and exultation in his heart.

"Coo!" he said to himself, over and over again, " 'Oo'd 'a' thought it, eh? eh? 'Oo'd 'a' thought it?"

Jim took one side with four men, Alan the other with three. In ninety seconds of incredible and brilliantly deliniated confusion, the farm was cleared, and Alan came of age: he had seen the face of fear and its owner wore grey uniform and jackboots, weighed two stones more than Alan and whimpered for his mother as he went down before the charge. One of the platoon was killed and another shot through the upper arm – painful but not serious – not even to the recipient.

"It's me left arm an' I can still shoot!" he said. " – an' that's all that matters!"

And indeed, in the heat and excitement, it was. The Bren was brought in.

"Did I do all right, for you, Sarge? Did I do all right?" asked the sparrow, and glowed with pride when assured that he had.

"What now, Alan?" asked Jim.

"Back to our first positions – and quick! They'll be coming to find out what's happened."

Moving figures behind the thinning hedges were watched until they stepped out, lulled into false security by the silence from the farm. Two officers fell, and the rest retreated under the fire, but Jim was becoming worried by the ammunition problem.

"We've an hour to go, Alan. How soon before they come again?"

"They won't come without Stukas, Jim. We could send out and search for ammo. if you like. Tell the blokes to come back as soon as the 'planes come over."

They sent the sparrow and one other. They both returned within half an hour, bringing a boxful of .303, and, best of all, another Bren. The Stukas had not returned, and although there were sounds of severe fighting on both sides, the enemy had apparently decided to leave the farm alone for the time being.

"It's a quarter to ten, Jim. Let's beat it back to the hill again. We can set up both Brens, and if Jerry walks in before ten o'clock we can pour in cross-fire. That ought to make 'em keep their heads down."

"What do you mean by cross-fire?" asked Jim. "That hill's a hundred yards away, and the farm's only twenty feet wide. They might fire down parallel lines."

"Oh."

Alan came down a little closer to earth.

"Well, what do you think?"

Jim considered, eyes flicking over ground in front and behind the farm.

"How many grenades have we left?"

A tally revealed eight.

"O.K., Alan. Take the Brens back and site them to fire into the yard and through the windows. Don't let the outhouse mask you."

Alan was back on the hill and the Brens in position before he fully realised that Jim was not with him. It was five to ten. Sparrow and the wounded man had one Bren, Alan and an orderly-room runner, the second. The back door of the farm opened and four men came out and ran back to the hill. That left Jim in there, by himself.

"That'll fix the bastards," said one of the new arrivals. "We wired grenades to the front door and windows, and Sarge is fixin' one to the back door. That'll sort 'em out all right!"

At ten o'clock – and not a second before, Jim climbed out through one of the back windows and ran across to join them. He'd hardly reached the hill, when the Stukas came back.

"Come on," he said. "Let's get out of here."

"Aren't we going to wait and shoot up the Jerries when they come in?" asked Alan.

Jim shook his head.

"We've done the job we were asked to do," he replied. "Now we've got to keep alive. You'd better lead the way Alan. Take one chap with you and keep your eyes open. We'll follow twenty yards behind."

He looked back at the Stukas, weaving and diving in the air above the farm, and then at a much larger swarm almost directly in front of them, about two miles ahead along their presumable line of retreat.

"I suppose that's Oudenaarde," he said. "It looks as though we'd better give it a miss. However, you're the best judge of that. You lead. We'll follow."

And with that working arrangement, they joined the great retreat.

The first day, Alan led them in a huge arc, across the Scheldte (they swam it – closing their eyes and mouths against the horrific evidences of war which swelled its muddy water) and then down on to the railway line running back towards Courtrai. The others wanted to go on further South and reach the main road which they could see was packed with slow-moving khaki traffic, spilling off the roads to each side as Stukas flew their harassing patrols.

"Not likely! Look at the way they're crawling. We'll make much better time by ourselves – and we'll have more room if a Stuka sees us."

"But there might be some of our blokes there!" objected one of the group.

"And there might not!" said Alan. "And even if there are – what of it?"

Jim backed Alan up, and so did the sparrow, who, what with his lone responsibility on the hill and his office as Number one on the second Bren, had developed a marked personality – one, moreover, completely devoted to Alan and Jim.

In Courtrai, they were directed back along the main road by a weary and disgruntled Military Policeman who had been in the Metropolitan Force four months before.

"Joined up in order to get away from this sort of thing," he stated. "Worse than Hammersmith Broadway on a Saturday lunch-time this is – all you get there's load o' flies off the river." He glared morosely up at the Stukas. "Perishin' nuisances!" he added. "Yes," he said, recalling himself to the matter on hand. "Carry on down the road. They're forming a line somewhere around Menin, I think. Who are you? Oh, yes, some of your blokes went through about an hour ago. Had a bit of a bashing, haven't you?" he asked, sympathetically.

It was getting dark by now and they were tired, but urgency kept them going, and a desire to know what was happening. They reached the Menin-Tourcoing Road and were directed South along it.

"Two Brens, eh? Jolly good show!" said a tired voice about a quarter of a mile further on. "Would you chaps care to join us? We've got a bit of a brew going."

Ten minutes later they were fast asleep beside their arms, part of a mixed force which, it was piously hoped, would hold the Northern approaches to Roubaix and Lille for two days.

It didn't.

The following morning revealed the owner of the tired drawl as a blond-moustached Major of the type which was later to become the glass of fashion in the desert. The force under his command was rather less than forty, gaunt, red-eyed, unshaven scarecrows and looking around at them, Alan felt compassion and pity, until some minutes later when he realised that in all probability, he looked exactly the same. Then, the first shock of dismay over, he discovered that his basic emotion was one of quiet satisfaction.

Then the attacks came. The pattern was obviously only too familiar to all present, and the first wave of German infantry was beaten off with cool, unexciting efficiency.

"Ten minutes' break, now chaps," remarked the major. "Time for a brew!" – and the incongruity of the announcement, though apparent to all, was taken for granted.

"Stukas!" came the cry, ten minutes later from down the line, and every one flattened for the dive-bombing.

"Don't waste ammunition on 'em, chaps," – it was a suggestion more than an order. "We'll probably need all we've got fairly soon."

The grey infantry came forward again, a probe at first, which developed into a vicious and sustained drive against the line about a hundred yards along from where Alan and Jim lay. The major came back towards them.

"I'll give you the line of fire. Would you open up with the Brens, now? I think it might relieve the pressure a bit."

He stood upright behind them, directing their arc of fire.

"Just a little to the right, now, please. Jolly good! Lift it a bit, can you? That's the stuff! I think we must be doing all right, now." He listened to the slackening fire further up. "Yes, I think so – hold it a bit. I'll go and look."

Five minutes later, the firing died completely, and shortly afterwards, the major came back. From somewhere in front of them, the sounds of heavy engines tightened their throats.

"I think it's time you blokes went," the major suggested. "I've sent the other chaps off already – what was left of them. I don't think there's much point in your hanging around now."

He paused, embarrassed.

"There is one thing, though. I wonder if you could possibly leave me one of your Brens and a few rounds? Just to put up some sort of show, you know!"

Silently, the sparrow got up from his gun, and the major lay down behind it.

"Thanks awfully," he said. "If I was you I'd make for Cassel and then up to the coast. I think they may try to arrange something there."

He was very vague, and apologetic.

"Won't you come with us, sir?" asked Alan.

There was a pause.

"Um – no. I think I'd better stay, if you don't mind. Thanks very much for the offer, though, jolly decent of you! But I think perhaps I'd better stay."

They picked up their arms, tightened their straps, climbed out of their trenches.

"Cheerio then sir," said one of them, inadequately, and turning, they moved slowly and awkwardly away. Ten minutes later, Alan broke the uncomfortable silence.

"You know," he said softly to Jim. "When I get back to England, I don't think I shall be able to believe that this really happened."

"Why not?" asked Jim. "He's a proper, regular officer. That's all there is to it."

But when, shortly afterwards, they heard the Bren suddenly start its chatter, then falter, the re-start, then finish in the crack and roar of a stick-grenade, Jim paled, and stared bleakly before him.

"I should have stopped with him," he said whitely. "I'm a regular, too."

It was the only time Alan ever saw Jim deviate from simple but inexorable practicality.

At Steenworde, just North of Armentieres, they were drawn off the road to hold a piece of yet another thin line of defence, but the order "every man for himself!" was given almost before the enemy were engaged, and although Alan and the sparrow stayed back with the Bren (and Jim, needless to say), to give covering fire if necessary, they started the next stage of the retreat without exchanging a shot.

In Cassel, they took the remaining Bren up on to the roof of one of the outlying buildings and joined in the attempts to shoot down the Stukas when they came, but they had no success whatever for physical and nervous strain was beginning to tell, and repetition had robbed action of its first exhilaration.

So on to Dunkirk, and there the party merged with the thousands, got separated and, with the exception of Alan, Jim and the sparrow, completely lost sight of each other. Reaction set in. With the disappearance of responsibility, his individuality submerged and no outlet for his developing talents. Alan's nerves went to pieces and his courage evaporated: it was as though his whole personality deliquesced, and in the dull, disheartening monotony of waiting, it seemed to him that he sank to become a shaking, amorphous, jelly-like lump of fear.

On the second day, after two nights spent lying on the sands between Jim and the sparrow, quivering with apprehension, he waded in his turn out to sea, and was picked up by a thirty-foot cabin cruiser which turned to take its load straight back to Ramsgate without bothering to offload on to one of the larger ships standing out to sea.

Three miles from the shore, two Luftwaffe fighters roared out of the sun at them, and with a frantic yell – uncontrollable as a reflex – Alan flung himself over the side. Convinced he had been hit, Jim and the sparrow went after him.

The fighters circled and came back. A rising crescendo of engines, a heavy stammering, white beads dropping towards them from the leading edges, waterspouts – and the sparrow flung up his hands and disappeared, Jim straightened up out of the water, rigid with pain and shock. As he fell, Alan re-discovered his manhood and went to him, finding him just below the surface. He turned him on his back and towed him towards the circling cabin cruiser, now slowing to pick them up. The fighters had gone.

" 'Ere, can yer tike the rope, chum?"

"Chuck him a lifebelt, someone."

"Shall I come in and give you a hand?"

"Orlright, orlright! I got 'im. Easy chum – where's 'e 't, d'yu know?"

Willing hands lifted them out of the water, Jim carefully, Alan, once they were sure that he was unhurt, more quickly.

"Bleedin' good, chum, that was! Went arter 'is mate, sir, 'e did – like a flash! Pore little bugger was 'it the first time they came over, I think, sir, an' this chap an' the other went arter 'im. Copulatin' 'eroes, both of 'em! 'Ow's the other one?"

Jim was not too bad, the bullet having passed clean through his shoulder, chipping blade and collar-bone, grazing the top of his lung.

"Good show my lad," said the owner of the boat, a tall, athletic aristocrat who was, in due course, to command his own destroyer. "I think I've got a few cigarettes left. Like one?"

Under the beaming approval of all on board, Alan lit up. What with the fact that he rarely smoked anyway, coupled with rising shame, he didn't enjoy it very much.

Chapter 11

To Alan, England after the mental dislocations of Dunkirk, was a foreign country in which what familiarity he found served merely to underline its strangeness. He was drowned in tea thick with sugar – and he preferred his unsweetened; cigarettes were practically forced into his mouth, and greying, sweet-faced women gave him plates of thick, brown stew, and were naturally but gently reproachful when his fumbling hands spilt it down his battle-blouse, and he swore, unconsciously, automatically, with the fluid repetition which all had used in France.

"There's no need to use language like that now, is there?" they asked.

Unfortunately, the incident was witnessed by an immaculate, red-tabbed officer, hot from Whitehall, who had never crossed the Channel in uniform and was, in the circumstances, sensitive about it.

"Enough of that!" he snapped. "Where the devil do you think you are?" – and as Alan moved guiltily off – "Don't you salute officers in your regiment?"

Worst of all was lack of friends, for having spent most of his life without any but casual acquaintances, he believed – in retrospect – that Belgium had taught him the deep truth of brotherhood, only to deprive him of its security. Jim was in hospital – the rest had disappeared or were know dead, and his mind rocketed away from any thought of the sparrow.

The first night in England he spent in a railway carriage packed full of tired, filthy men, who although apparently in the same straits as himself, revealed no similarity of experience, or having that similarity, spoke of it in a different language. They were Northerners, and as such imbued with contempt for the countryside, the customs and above all the manner of speech of the South.

The following afternoon, Alan arrived at his home to be embarrased and further upset by the reactions of his parents, whose overwhelming relief and gratitude for his deliverance turned their unambitious, lower middle-class respectability towards churchgoing and a burst of evangelism. Alan sought immediate shelter in sleep, but it was long in coming, though once it did come, kept him senseless for fourteen hours.

The following morning, he went out for a walk about ten

o'clock, and having borrowed some money from his mother, called into a public house for a drink about eleven-thirty. As alcohol released the tension in him, and the bar filled, he was drawn into conversation by some of the regular customers who guessed from the state of his uniform where he had been. At two-thirty, he arrived home stupid with drink, to find a tearful mother, frightened and now outraged father – about to inform the police that their returned hero had been abducted.

"Thank heavens it was a week-day!" said Mr. Lockyer to his wife when they had at least got Alan up to bed. "At least not many of the neighbours could have seen him, although what the vicar will think when he hears of it," for experience had taught Mr. Lockyer that the vicar would, " – I dare not think!"

Then he went back to the office, puzzled, disturbed, rather frightened.

For three days Alan tried his best to re-settle himself into the smooth contours of suburban life, but the events in Belgium seemed to have cut him off from his former life, and estranged him from everyone who had not shared his experiences. A stranger in his home, an object of wonder and curiosity in the immediate vicinity – for he was the only local son to have returned – the only place where he could break down the barriers was in the pub, and his own desire not to wound his parents again, kept him out of there.

On the morning of the fourth day, he put on his uniform, and with a tale of hearing that all troops were to report back to their units, took the train to Hinton Merrott. The first person he saw was the Platoon Sergeant who had shown such reluctance to accept his version of the death of Bert Craggs and the rest of his platoon.

"Well, well," he said, "I was wondering when you'd turn up. The conquering hero himself!" He looked narrowly at Alan, sighed, and then seemed to relax. "At any rate you were there, which is more than anyone else in this dump was! Let's go and have a drink, somewhere, for God's sake!"

Over a pint, Alan learned from Sergeant Blackman what the known position was – as far as anyone knew anything.

"We've got a new Colonel – used to be major in the second battalion, and we're being re-formed as soon as possible – that's what I've been told. The rear party we left behind when we went to France are still here – never budged apparently – and practically every day, a few names come in of chaps who've managed to get back."

He took a pull at his beer.

"Not likely to be any more now, though – if the evacuation has definitely been called off. Jim Bannerman's in hospital in Oxford, by the way. I went along to see him and he told me you'd got back and what happened down at that farm place."

Blackman stared hard at his beer.

"Beats me," he said, shaking his head. "I've known Jim now for some years, and although he's not an Einstein or any other sort of genius, he's not a fool – no more of a fool than anyone who's absolutely dead straight, anyway. Yet he thinks the world of you, Lockyer. Thinks you're a bloody wonder. Thoroughly believes all that stuff about you chasing single-handed after the Huns, and all that!"

He put his empty glass down and looked steadily at Alan.

"If you let him down, my lad, you'll have me to deal with. Jim's the kind who made this country, and he's the kind who'll pull her out of this mess, too. You aren't. Nor, for that matter, am I – perhaps that's why I understand you so well. We'll have another beer, now, and then you'd better get along to the Orderly Room and find out what's happening to you. Oh, by the way, you can forget about being a Corporal. Even if the promotion went into Orders – which I doubt – it wouldn't hold now. Cheers – and remember what I said!"

At the Orderly Room, Alan was interviewed by a strange officer, and then told to go back to his old billet. He would be re-kitted the following day, and appointed to duties. The rest of the day was his own, but when he asked if he might go to Oxford and visit Corporal Bannerman in hospital, he was suddenly and incomprehensively forbidden to leave the village. Why, he never knew. Nor, actually, did anyone else, but the military doctrine of obstruction had not yet been swept away by High Authority, and in the aftermath of Dunkirk, it behoved regular officers of a certain stamp, to walk warily. This officer was of that stamp.

He was also of the stamp which insists upon the luxuries and appurtenances of rank. At three o'clock, Alan was fetched from the billet and interviewed by the officer again.

"Can you drive a car, Lockyer?"

"What type, sir?"

"My Humber Staff car."

"I've never driven a Humber, sir, but I expect I could manage it."

Major Smith-Hennessey looked him up and down.

"I need a batman-driver. Let's see how you handle her."

So Alan spent the afternoon first cleaning the Humber, then driving the Major around the countryside.

"All right then, you'll do. Put the car away and be at my billet at seven o'clock tomorrow morning."

Deliberately, Alan made no answer, merely saluting and sliding back behind the wheel of the car. There was no compulsion to undertake the duties of batman, and he could refuse it if he wished, but at the moment he wanted time to think the matter over. The job could be cushy – there was no denying that – and if he could stomach the servitude and put up with the Major, it might be worth his while.

He decided to wait and see.

In the meantime, it had been a hot afternoon and the strain of driving the Humber for the first time, especially under the eye of a new officer on the lookout for faults, was conducive of thirst. The Rose and Crown being open, he called in, and was fairly soon giving an account of the fighting in Belgium to the landlord, and answering enquiries after several of the men who had patronised the place and made friends with the landlord's family.

By eight o'clock, he was the centre of a crowd of local inhabitants – a fringe of disgruntled khaki on the edges, now displaced from favour by someone who had 'been there', – the air was blue with tobacco smoke, and Alan's voice a shade louder, a tone higher than usual – but he was not boasting. He was enjoying himself, he was drinking a lot of beer paid for by other people and he was trying to answer their questions honestly. Somehow – almost for the first time in his life, he felt no compulsion to embroider his own adventures, indeed he avoided discussing them – and although this was wise with regard to some, not all of his actions had been discreditable.

At nine-thirty, Cora came in. She brushed off two members of the quartermaster's staff who had been paying her attentions during Jim's absence, and made straight for Alan. He turned in order to speak to someone else, saw her, and speech and movement were halted abruptly – cut off in astonishment at her tawny, feline beauty. Away from her, his memory had retained only the cheapness and voracity of her nature; he had forgotten her body.

On her part, she stopped too – for the first time in her life overcome by a feeling not engendered by greed or spite. She had entered with anger in her heart and its force gave her carriage an added sweep, her colouring even more fire and sparkle. When the crowd parted to reveal each to the other, her anger left her, but the emotion which replaced it retained the same symptoms – the flashing eye, the blush, the pride. As far as it was possible for her to be, Cora was in love.

"You might have come to see me, Alan," she said, but the

92

words lacked the venom with which she had intended to invest them.

Alan put his glass carefully down on the nearest table. His intentions also, were undergoing revision. The heat, the alcohol, the shock of Cora's presence, all combined to dissipate the faint shame he had felt whenever he thought of their joint deception of Jim.

"Hullo, Cora," he said. "I was coming along but – well, I wasn't sure where you'd be." His smile robbed the remark of offence, but she bit her lip to keep back the protest. "What are you drinking? Have you seen Jim yet – or is that all over?"

The hubbub in the bar re-started, the glasses clinked, the rounds were bought and the bigger group which had centred around Alan, broke into the smaller, habitual clumps of drinkers. Only the jealous and the gossip-mongers paid further attention to Cora and Alan, but there was no intense focus on them for Jim had been absent for some time and the villagers had presumed the 'understanding' between he and Cora dead. Gradually, as the crowd about them thickened and pushed them closer, as the temperature rose and the alcohol quickened them, silk-covered thigh pressed urgently against khaki and every movement which feminine guile could cause to do so, would reveal the shadowed valley below the misty, Marks and Spencers, pearls.

There was no unusual notice taken when, ten minutes before closing time, Alan and Cora slipped out together into the sweet, summer night.

"Where?" asked Alan urgently.

"This way," she whispered, and led out of the village, through four-barred gates and along hedges until they came to a barn. The moonlight slanted down from a skylight, and in its rays – having first barred the door from the inside – Cora removed her clothing with the lingering technique of a strip-tease artist, posed for a second on tip-toe like a Tanagra statuette with necklace, then flung herself across the barn at Alan, lying Pasha-like among the sacks: for the rest of his life, the smell of dry earth and hessian would always link in Alan's mind with exhorbitance, and bursting anguish. and Californian Poppy.

"I wonder if I *have* done Jim out of something worth while?" he asked himself as he eventually made his way through the early dawn back to his billet. "No!" he concluded. "She wouldn't have treated Jim like that. She'd have led him a hell of a life!"

The next day, Alan fulfilled his duties as batman-driver, and found they were in no way arduous. When things went well, Major Smith-Hennessey could be affability itself, and there were not enough men actually under his command or in his charge as yet to form too burdensome a duty. That evening Alan went to Oxford to see Jim.

"What's the news of the other chaps?" was Jim's first question, and: "Has the new Colonel arrived yet?" the second.

He was quite cheerful, the damage to his shoulder in no way likely to affect his ability, the grazed lung mending nicely.

"It'll take a bit of time though, so the M.O. says," reported Jim. "I hope they don't post me to another battalion. I wonder who the R.S.M. will be?"

Alan was to find out the next day, and decided to hang on to his job as batman. R.S.M. Wiles was a warrant officer of the old school, and when he spoke, the world was hushed.

Four days later, the troops started arriving – new intake, the men who got back from Dunkirk, N.C.O.s and officers posted in from other battalions, reservists. The tempo rose, the Colonel arrived and took command, Major Smith-Hennessey became much busier and his temper shortened. However, he was a lesser terror than Sergeant-Major Wiles, and watching the endless drilling, the inspections, the wearying night marches – never in groups of less than twenty – Alan was glad of his servile but unexacting duties.

The summer days passed.

Alan again visited Jim whenever he was in Oxford, but somehow the frequency with which he could do this seemed to drop with the passing of time. The situation between Alan and Cora was not dissimilar: there is a limit to erotic variation beyond which lies a dark labyrinth outside Cora's imagination or Alan's interest, and when this limit was reached, Cora's failings became blatant and Alan tired of her purely physical attractions – and showed it. She accused him of callousness, and with memories of the way they had both treated Jim Alan laughed in her face, to be almost stunned by the force of the slap which his own then received. When she repeated her pre-Dunkirk assertion that he ought to marry her, he told her flatly that he wouldn't, and they parted in violent anger – but with relief on Alan's side. Cora found several men only too willing to act as escort, and these she flaunted in front of Alan and was bitterly chagrined when he was obviously unaffected.

By the end of July, Jim was convalescing still and it was fairly evident that the battalion were about to be embroiled in a large-scale movement. As driver to the battalion's second-in-command, Alan picked up news not available to others, and when Major Smith-Hennessey realised that he was not a gossip and could be trusted not to repeat everything he heard, less pains were taken to keep facts from him.

Thus he learned that they were going abroad. He visited the convalescent camp and told Jim.

"Look Alan, the Colonel knows me," pleaded Jim. "I'm practically better. Be a pal and ask your officer to put in a word for me. I'm sure the Colonel could get me out if he tried – I'll be sick as mud if the battalion go without me!"

"I'll see," said Alan, "but I don't hold out any hope with my bloke. He's not too hot on doing anything for anyone else even when he's got all the time in the world, and now he's chasing around all day like a blue-arsed fly!"

"Do your best though, Alan, won't you?"

The opportunity came much sooner than Alan could possibly have foreseen, for the next morning his name was down for interview with the Colonel. Heart beating, belt blancoed, conscience carefully scrutinised and found exceptionally clear, Alan stood erect before the Power of Life and Death.

"There's a need for officers, Lockyer. Going through the nominal rolls, I came across your name. Would you like me to put your name forward for an officer's course?"

Alan stared at him in surprise in which there was an appreciable percentage of dismay.

"But we're just going abroad, sir," he burst out.

The Colonel coughed.

"You're not supposed to know that, young fellow. Well, what about it?"

"I wouldn't be allowed to stay in the battalion as an officer, would I sir?" asked Alan.

"No. You'd be commissioned in another regiment."

Alan considered. He had hardly given a thought to becoming an officer since Jim had talked to him about it on the night before the advance into Belgium. Now it came at the wrong time. He was keyed up and excited at the idea of going abroad again, especially as all indications were that it would be to Egypt: Alan had always felt an attraction for the countries of the Middle East.

"Well?"

"I'd sooner stay with the battalion, sir!"

The Colonel was surprised – and pleased, though he had formed no particular high opinion of Alan. 'Perhaps,' he thought, 'I was wrong in my estimation'. He smiled.

"Very well, Lockyer. We shall, of course, be pleased to keep you!"

"Thank you sir! There is one matter though – "

The guarded look, the down-turned mouth, the thought – 'I was right! He's after something!"

"Well?"

"It's about Corporal Bannerman, sir!"

"Bannerman? Bannerman? Who's he?"

"He says he served under you in Palestine, sir!"

"Good God, yes – I remember. First class chap! Well, what about him?"

"He's in Number four Convalescent Camp, sir. He was wounded in France, but he's practically better, now – almost due for discharge. He wondered whether you could get him to the battalion before we go sir."

"Oh! Well, I wonder – . You're sure of this are you?"

"I was with him last night sir. It will break his heart if the battalion sail without him, sir."

The Colonel was much gratified. He was well aware that his adjutant dealt almost daily with men requesting compassionate posting which would keep them in England, and he also knew that at least ten men would go absent without leave when the move started. It always had happened and it always would – here were two men who were anxious to reverse the process.

"I'll have to see what can be done!" he said.

"Left turn. Quick march. Left, right, left, right, left, right, Halt!" shouted Orderly Sergeant Blackman. "Maybe you're not such a bad bastard after all – though I wouldn't bet on it!" he added in minor key.

The turmoil rose to a crescendo, Alan drove Major Smith-Hennessey from one end of the country to the other, at the wheel from morning till night. He was thoroughly enjoying himself. Then they were all given embarkation leave.

As they waited on the station for the leave train, Cora walked on to the platform. Alan was loading his own and Major Smith-Hennessey's kit into the train.

"I've got to talk to you Alan. I've got to."

"Well, talk away! No-one's stopping you."

She waited until he turned back to pick up the next piece of luggage. They were a fair distance from the nearest group, although many eyes were watching them curiously.

"You'll have to marry me now, Alan. I'm going to have a baby!"

Alan put down the suitcase he had just picked up, and stared at her.

"You don't expect me to believe that, do you?"

"It's true! It's a wonder it didn't happen before!"

"You're right there – by any one of half a dozen chaps, I should think!"

"No, Alan, you're wrong! It was you! You're the only one it could have been!"

"Now, Cora, my dear. I should have thought we knew each other a little better than that. Run away and don't try those tricks with me – I told you once, and I'm telling you again – not under any circumstances whatever, will I marry you! And there's no need to get upset – you knew that from the beginning. Look out – here comes the boss!"

The major boarded the train with a brief, important look at Cora, and as the station-master was waving his flag and the men all scrambling aboard, Alan took advantage of the situation to shut the door of the carriage with himself inside, making good his escape through the train corridors. The train moved, leaving Cora, torn between anger and dismay on the platform.

Alan was not, however, quite as heartless as the last episode may have indicated. During the leave, he thought quite a lot about Cora, and what he should do if, by any chance, she had been telling the truth. It was damned awkward – but really, he could not think it any concern of his. He had not been the first or the last, he told himself uncertainly – and incorrectly as it happened, although he had no means of knowing this. "If she *is* in trouble, that's no reason why I should tie her like a millstone around my neck.

"However, we'll see when I get back. I'll have a talk with her," he promised himself – and settled down to enjoy his leave. Almost he succeeded, but there was a tiny, nagging worry at the back of his mind, practically all the time.

Leave ended and he went back.

Almost the first person he saw, was Jim.

"Come and have a drink Alan. I owe you one – the Colonel told me how you'd seen him about me, and I got out the day you went on leave – just missed you! Two pints, please, Mr. Brooks. Got some more news too, Alan. Wanted to wait until you got back, but she wouldn't hear of it! Dead keen she was – shook me! Well, drink up Alan, and wish us luck. Cora and me got married the day before yesterday!"

PART THREE

Chapter 12

JIM was worried. He lay on the top of a shallow hill, halfway through his stag, watching the shimmering heat haze above the approaches to the cistern. Guidano Corba was four miles North, and when dusk fell, he and the three others in the cistern would start out for the dump. If they all carried out their particular tasks with speed and precision, the petrol would go up about four o'clock the next morning, by which time they should all be nearly ten miles away.

If! – for there was no margin for accident or error. The shooting down of the transport 'plane had so reduced the available man-power that only firmness on the part of Rutledge had averted the complete cancellation of the operation as far as Guidano Corba had been concerned.

"The destruction of the petrol dump is only secondary from our point of view!" Lieutenant Perowne had said. "Our main target is the German post at El Machli. That's the rendezvous for all our parties in the area, and the place where the L.R.D.G. are coming to pick us up! That's why they dropped so many of us – ten would be ample for the petrol dump. Come to that, you could have done it yourselves. But El Machli's essential. None of us'll get out alive if we don't take that place in time."

Signals had flashed back and forth, but neither additional men nor transport to drop them had been available, and Headquarters had confirmed the priority of El Machli as a target. As Perowne had said, the taking and holding for twenty-four hours of this traffic junction was essential for the success of the overall strategy of raiding operations in the area. Not only was the dump at Guidano Corba to be destroyed that night, but also similar fuel dumps near Slonta and Maraua to the West, and an ammunition dump South of Martuba to the East. The men taking part in these raids would then make their way as best they could to El Machli, which was a central position for all of them, but thirty miles South, on the edge of the desert.

There, if the attack on the post had been successful, would be waiting food, water, medical aid for those needing it, and transport to evacuate them to the main L.R.D.G. base at Kuffra. Siwa Oasis, which was an L.R.D.G. *rear* base, would in actual fact be nearer, but as it was the intention of G.H.Q. that a full scale battle should be raging across the country in between, it was obviously safer to travel the greater distance.

There would be another mass evacuation of raiding parties going on further West at the same time, for a similar pattern of sabotage was planned for the Western half of the Jebel, and parties raiding bases near Benghasi, Barce and Regima would concentrate West of Msus for evacuation by a second L.R.D.G. patrol. It was expected that the two groups would meet up on their six-hundred mile return journey, near the oasis of Jalo, a hundred and fifty miles South of the Jebel foothills.

All very pretty on paper – but Jim, who was no dog in a manger, sincerely hoped that all other operations had got off to a much better start than theirs had. Not only were they short of men in quantity, but even to Jim's uncritical mind, they could have been luckier in the two who had been detailed to accompany him and Alan.

One of them was Lieutenant Lewis, ordered in from his lone position on the Cyrene Road, to meet the party at the cistern here, and take command – an instruction he interpreted by listening superciliously to all suggestions about how the job was to be done, and then curtly ordering an entirely different system and timetable. The other member of the party was Whittaker.

Whittaker!

At even the thought of the man, Jim's lips tightened in disapproval, and his heart sank in despair.

How could the man be such a bloody fool?

For Whittaker's secret was out – had come out during the twenty-four hours following the dropping of the parashots and the supplies. When the heavily-laden men had arrived back at the cave, one of the new arrivals had produced from his pocket a flask of brandy and offered it around. It had not gone far, of course – a gulp each, but all the parashots had their flasks, and by the time Alan and Sergeant Orr arrived with the report on the crash, they were all empty – with little effect on anyone, it might be said, for a pint of brandy shared among ten exhausted men does not constitute an orgy.

After listening to the grim news brought by Alan and the Sergeant, however, one of the parashots remarked that he wished he'd saved his drink, for he could do with one now.

"There's some rum amongst the supplies that were dropped," said Perowne. "I reckon we could do with another one each, if we've brought in the right containers."

It was remembered by everyone during the days which followed, that Whittaker refused any more, saying he'd had enough, and making his way to the end of the cave where his sleeping bag was already laid out. In the morning, however, Jim noticed that he seemed far more blear-eyed than anyone else, and also, to Jim's non-smoker's nose, his breath reeked more of rum than of brandy.

However, he thought nothing more of it until he heard a brisk ejaculation from one of the parashots.

"Christ!" said the man. "We properly caned the rum last night, didn't we? Two bottles gone!"

"Two?" asked Perowne. "I only opened one!"

But there were the two empty bottles, and although Perowne was obviously suspicious, no-one else was either sceptical or concerned. The stuff had gone – and there was no-one there who had not experienced similar dismal and surprising accountancy after a private or mess party.

"A bottle's like a pound note," said one. "Once you crack it – it's gone, and no-one knows where!"

And that summed up the general attitude.

But in the afternoon, it was discovered that two more bottles had disappeared, and later, that Whittaker was missing. Unfortunately, it was dark when this absence was noted, and only a cursory search of the immediate neighbourhood could be made.

Some time after midnight, Jim was awakened by a faint clink of bottles, sat up abruptly and challenged. There was a louder clink, a scuffle, and as others in the cave woke and enquired diversely what was happening, a heavy figure, recognisably Whittaker's tore aside the camouflage netting and staggered out. Hindered by their sleeping bags, the man in the cave were a long way after him, but he was seen and chased by O'Reilly who was on duty as sentry and whom Whittaker had with drunken cunning, eluded on his way in.

The chase was brief and inglorious. Before O'Reilly could get to him, Whittaker lurched off the path and fell nearly ten feet down a steep bank, doing, of course, no harm to himself, but breaking the two remaining bottles of rum. When O'Reilly dropped beside him, Whittaker's face was buried in the soil, and he was trying to suck the sticky spirit back from the grit into which it was fast soaking.

" 'Twas a terrible waste, I agree," said the Irishman when relating the story afterwards. "But he'd a' done far better to lick around the inside of the broken pieces o' the bottles. Like I did!"

Until the effects of the alcohol were out of his system, Whittaker was truculent – almost triumphant – but when he finally sobered up, his dejection was pitiful. Unfortunately too, there was something humiliating and obsequious about his attempts to regain the respect, or at any rate the affection, of his former friends, which not only embarrassed them, but increased the natural hostility which the parashots had for him.

"We don't want Whittaker on our party to El Machli," stated Perowne. "I don't care what you do with him – he's not coming with us."

As the entire group was being evacuated, even Rutledge going back as far as Kuffra, there was no alternative but for him to accompany Alan and Jim.

"Must we have him, sir?" Jim had enquired of Rutledge.

"I have it on good authority," replied the older man, sadly, "that if Whittaker comes with us to El Machli, he'll never reach the place alive. The parashots are convinced that he is a menace and a liability, and as such, would most likely get them all killed. They live by a ruthless code."

"He'll probably get us killed too," said Jim dismally to Alan, and felt the last straw across his back when he heard Alan's answer.

"That's about the best bloody thing that could happen!"

For it was the change in Alan which really constituted Jim's deepest worry.

What on earth had happened to him? Overnight, he had plunged from light-hearted satisfaction and contentment, to a despondency which Jim sometimes suspected – and felt guilty for the suspicion – bordered on suicidal. Alan had been miserable and short-tempered before during their friendship – notably in the transit camp and at Abbassia before they volunteered for the Jebel – in fact it was Alan's despondency which had led Jim to suggest the move for he would never have left the battalion himself, being not only quite happy in regimental life, but also, of course, far better placed.

"What do you want to volunteer for that sort of job for, Corporal?" asked the R.S.M. when Jim put his name down. "Take my advice and stay with the Battalion, lad. I can't say any more at the moment, but both the Colonel and me are regulars, and so are you! 'Nuff said!"

But Jim insisted, for he knew that Alan was attracted by the idea, and he guessed that there would be far more opportunity for the development of Alan's gifts in irregular military activities, than with the battalion. The relationship between them had by now undergone a complete change, for they were no longer instructor and recruit. They were friends, comrades in battle, muckers – to use the current phrase, and in Jim's code, this relationship ranked above all others. It was not only a code either, for there had been no outlet for the affection in Jim's nature until he and Alan had solidified the friendship begun under fire in Belgium.

Jim's wooing and sudden winning of Cora, had of course, engaged his affections, but somehow – and Jim, being Jim, blamed himself and events – it had not been so satisfactory a fulfillment as he would have wished. After the war, when they settled down in a little place of their own, everything would be all right – especially now, with the nipper growing up. But it hadn't been all that he had hoped so far and that was a fact, for in addition to the separation, Cora just didn't seem able to write letters at all, and when she did make the effort, the results were unsatisfactory – hastily scribbled, short, rather grumbling missives which dealt mostly with the unpleasantness of life in Hinton Merrott and how much better a time she could have elsewhere. She very rarely answered any of the questions he was continually asking in his regular despatches to her – in fact, one might suspect she never even bothered to read them. But still, she must be awfully busy looking after the nipper, and he'd make it up to her for the worry and anxiety she must be undergoing when he got home. Then everything would be all right.

Reluctantly, Jim tore his mind away from the picture of domestic bliss which he envisaged for the future, and returned to present actuality and Alan's dejection, for Alan had never been as bad as this before. It was as though he'd lost all interest in everything: no ambition, no humour, no liveliness – just dull acceptance of everything that happened, coupled with an inertia that usually managed to make things worse.

Perhaps he'd buck up tonight when the raid started. Jim profoundly hoped so, for it would need every particle of keen awareness they could muster between them if they were to achieve their object – let alone make good their escape.

He looked at his watch. Ten more minutes to go – then Alan would come out to relieve him. He might with a bit of luck come out a few minutes before so that they could have a bit of a natter together, and Jim might be able to cheer him up – certainly something ought to be done. In the meantime, Jim sent his thoughts once more back to Hinton Merrott and thought fondly on his beautiful wife, and proudly of his son and the future, in which – who knows, with the world so topsy-turvy? – his son might be a serving officer in the first battalion.

Jim, of course, would have to leave the regiment and probably give up the army altogether, so as not to embarrass the boy – but he could always go back to carpentering.

"If what this Wog says is true," said Lewis contemptuously, " – and there *are* sentries around the place, then I will have to rely on you, Corporal, to see that the charges are properly placed and that my orders are carried out. The sentries are probably only these brats from the Fascist Youth anyway, but they could make nuisances of themselves, so I will keep watch outside each of the houses."

"Very good, sir," said Jim, resignedly – and as his brain catalogued the faults in the speech, he wondered how it was possible for a presumably responsible officer to give tongue to so many, so briefly.

Understandably, the Senussi tribesman who had – gratuitously as far as Jim could make out – arrived with up-to-date information regarding Guidano Corba, having caught the sneer in Lewis's voice, was now wrapping his jerd about him in proud withdrawal: with a little tact he might easily have been persuaded to co-operate further, possibly as look-out, possibly even helping with the demolition charges, certainly as guide.

And if Lewis thought that Facist Youth on guard would only make nuisances of themselves, he could obviously have no idea of the menace that a bunch of frightened, trigger-happy children could be.

Jim sighed: Lewis, overbearing and obviously keyed up towards breaking point, Whittaker completely unreliable, Alan in the depths of despondency – and now, fresh sentries posted between the houses.

It was not a prospect to arouse enthusiasm.

Chapter 13

WARM smell of the night, thick dust, Tommy-gun heavy in his hands, band on the inside of his beret rather tight around his forehead: Lewis was creeping along in front, Alan and Whittaker were behind carrying between them the rucksack which held the majority of the charges, the time-pencils, the cordtex. Grenades weighted the pockets of Jim's smock, two primed charges were hard and oblong against his chest in the slack above his belt, safety-fuse and detonators were stuck in the top pockets. Just in case.

The back of the house farthest down the inside of the Western side road, was ten yards distant. Lewis, tight as a banjo string with nerves, tiptoed past the nearer corner of the house and went on along the wide path which separated it from its neighbour as far as the road in front. Jim started to count. When he reached a hundred, he rose to his feet, crossed to the house in a silent, crouching run, heard Alan and Whittaker move up behind him. Once again, that unmistakeable smell assailed his nostrils, and he blew down them, un uncontrollable reflex.

Along the passage, he could make out the dim silhouette of Lewis, flat against the wall. The officer raised his arm in signal, Jim gestured to the dark shapes behind him, and waited, listening to Alan and Whittaker force the window. The night was black, the plantation a jungle behind them, the Southern ridge circling all around, palpable, unseen. Somewhere on the top of it was cached the rest of their gear.

Alan was inside now, Whittaker clambering after him: Jim left the corner and moved along to the window. Inside he could make out the shapes of the piled drums and the smell of warm metal and oil was everywhere. Whittaker came back to the window and handed out to him a coil of white cordtex, nodding. Jim noticed the sweat pouring down the dust-caked, wide-boned face, and heard a faint click from inside the house which he took to be Alan loosening off some of the stoppers on the drums, so that the place should be full of vapour when the explosion occurred.

He took the cordtex, and uncoiling it, walked backwards to the corner of the house, crossed the passage to the next house along, and found the appropriate window. The cordtex snaked across the ground, surprisingly invisible. One up for Lewis – for this was done on his insistence, Alan and Jim wishing to rely solely on the time pencils.

"But the cordtex may be seen and give us away," protested Alan.

"We're doing it this way!" snapped Lewis. "If we run into trouble while we're there and are only relying on time-pencils, then the enemy (he always referred to them as 'the enemy') will find the charges and remove them before the time-pencils go off. Understand this, all of you! That petrol's going up! If we do run into trouble, I shall set off one charge and as they're all connected, the lot will blow. Any houses we've not visited by then will have grenades flung into them!"

His words would have been more impressive had they not been delivered in such a shrill monotone.

Jim found the window, put the cordtex and his gun carefully on the ground, drew his knife and forced the blade between the ill-fitting sash and frame. Heat had dried and warped the wood, and the flimsy catches burst easily away. Alan was behind him, Whittaker bringing along the heavy rucksack. With a grin at Alan, slightly mischievous, for Lewis had said that Jim must remain outside the houses, he climbed in through the window, gesturing to Alan to follow, and Whittaker to remain on guard with Jim's Tommy-gun.

The drums were huge in the darkness, and cold. Those at the back were on their sides and Alan gestured forward. About the middle of the house, he found drums piled upright, Alan handed him the steel bar, and while he wedged it in the slot of the stopper and began to turn it, Alan pushed a charge between two of the drums, primed it, and fixed both the cordtex and the time-pencil. The second of the stoppers moved with a sudden squawk – ear-splitting in the silence. As they paused, listening, they heard, coming down the road from the Southern link, the slow stamp of sentry's boots – a German sentry, and not – praise be – one of those infernal children. Alan gestured towards the window, Jim quickly unscrewed the stopper, and they tiptoed back. Alan handed out the cordtex to Whittaker, who then disappeared, un-coiling it as Jim had done.

Alan went out first, and Jim waited, still inside, as the sentry was now passing their house. In the darkness, one each side of the sill, they looked at each other and Jim could see that Alan had lost some of his despondency in the excitement, and his eyes were alight and gleaming. Relieved, Jim put his hand over the sill and punched Alan's arm. Some of the light died, some of the despondency came back.

Then the sentry went past, Alan turned and Jim climbed out and went after him. Whittaker was already inside the next house, and Jim took his Tommy-gun back and re-assumed his detailed duty. He peered around the corner and saw once more the faint bulk of the officer against the wall. He wondered whether Lewis was moving up in front of the houses, or coming around the back. Back would be safer, but that would mean losing sight of the sentries. Jim was glad he was not faced with making the choice – either for himself or anyone else.

Whittaker handed out the cordtex, and Jim went on to the fourth house – the inside corner one where the link road joined the Western side road. Sentries patrolled in the road and along the backs of the outer houses, but not, apparently, along the backs of the inner ones. Jim forced the window, but stepped back and let the other two go in – having been in once and discovered that it was no worse a duty than the one allotted to him, he saw no reason to strain further his natural sense of obedience.

He heard the sentry return, heels ringing in leisurely time on the tarmac, turn along the link road, meet and pass his opposite number with a soft, derisive remark, heard the other approach, turn and pass. Then the coil came out of the window, he took it, moved to the edge and hissed softly. Lewis materialised from the shadows. Jim nodded, Lewis led away down through the kitchen garden at the back of the house, into the garden which backed on to that one, through and up to the top, inner house of the Eastern sideroad. Alan and Whittaker followed, carrying the rucksack while Jim uncoiling the cordtex through the tangled undergrowth.

The next four houses were dealt with in exactly the same way as the first four, except that Jim remained outside all the time, always uncoiling the cordtex, always forcing the windows. Alan and Whittaker were both sweating furiously now, smocks patched and wet, their bodies emitting a hot, sickly, humid odour. Whittaker's hand was bleeding where he had torn it on a nail.

They all waited in the shadows of the bottom house, furthest from the link road, for an opportunity to cross and start on the first of the outside houses. Now the greatest danger would start, for the cordtex would lie across the road in full view of the sentries if they came down as far as this, and there was the additional danger of sentries patrolling through the thick, shadowed areas at the back. They would be the greatest menace of all.

The sentry in the link came around the corner, strolled down to just abreast of their house, turned and strolled back. As he turned the corner, they could hear, faintly in the distance, the footsteps of the other coming along the link from the other end. Lewis turned, nodded, and sped off across the road, moving like a dancer, a tense spring. Jim waited to hear if he ran into trouble, then, waving the other two to cross in Lewis's path, he himself circled down and across the road, looping the cordtex in a wide curve which he hoped would lie beyond the vision of the sentry when he turned on his beat.

For these outside houses, it had been decided to use the windows in the side walls, taking the cordtex through one window, connecting the charge in the middle of the drums, then taking the cordtex out through the opposite window, across the passage and into the next house. This meant that Alan and Whittaker would be in the houses practically all the time, and Lewis and Jim would move parallel with them respectively front and back.

Jim watched Alan climb through the first window, then moved to the corner of the house and looked out over the shrubbery at the back, straining his ears for sound of movement out there. He could neither see nor hear anything which might be construed as dangerous, but the ground at the immediate rear of the building was clear, and anybody posted in the jungle would see him if he crossed the width of the house. He circled out until he reached the edge of the vegetation, remained watching for a while, then moved across through its shadow until he was level with the next passage. He was just in time to see Alan climb out of the window, cross the passage and climb into the next house, followed by Whittaker.

It was while he was watching the back of the third house along, that he saw the sentry. The man was in the garden of the top house, in the shadow of a dilapidated shed, carefully watching the ground which led over towards the foothills of the ridge, occasionally turning to look at the backs of the houses in which Alan and Whittaker were working. It was obvious that he was alert, and probable that he sensed trouble.

Jim lay down below a clump of bushes, his fingers busy checking the reliability and readiness of his arms (he had a Colt as well as a Tommy-gun, but prayed he would have to use neither that night) his eyes searching everywhere for other sentries, keeping the one he had seen under observation. He was sweating himself now, his hands greasy on the wooden stock, his throat dry. He swallowed to stop a cough.

From the house in which the two were working came the sudden squawk of another tight stopper. The sentry's head came around with a jerk, staring in the direction of the sound, Jim's hands tightened on the gun and his heart thudded. Instinctively, he too, glanced in the direction of the house. When he looked back, the man was gone.

For a second Jim came near to panic then he controlled himself, staring wide-eyed into the space which he knew the man must cross to reach the backs of the houses. Unconsciously, he held his breath in suspense, until the pain in his chest became unbearable and he let go with a rush: still there was no sign of the man! Had he gone some other way round? Jim's eyes flickered right and left, then back into the space. Had the man crossed then, when Jim looked away? Sweat trickled down into his eyes, he blinked, his eyes glazed and he blinked again. Then the thought struck him that the man had gone to fetch others. Grimly, Jim rose to his feet and watched the house which held his friends, Tommy-gun ready, bombs to hand in unbuttoned pockets.

Then Alan climbed out of the window of the third house, took the rucksacks and cordtex from Whittaker, moved in incredibly slow motion across the path followed by an equally lethargic Whittaker. To Jim's agonised mind it seemed hours before they forced open the window of the top house, and days before they disappeared inside – his sobbing exhalation of breath when the casement was pulled to after them would have been audible five yards away had there been anyone to hear it.

Then he saw the sentry, walking slowly but carefully down past the back of the house into which Alan and Whittaker had just disappeared.

Relief claimed him for a second, washing down through his body like a cool and cleansing wave; then he raised the Tommy-gun, pulled the stock into his shoulder and centred the man in his sights: perhaps just one single shot would not be noticed. Then the man suddenly quickened his pace, turning the corner into the passage which Alan and Whittaker had just crossed and disappearing into the shadows before Jim had time to decide to shoot. Frantic with regret and appalled that he might have let danger in on the others, Jim raced across to the back of the house in a silent, crouching run which justified years of training. He paused at the corner and listened.

The sentry had reached the front end of the passage and paused – irresolute. Then Jim heard him turn and start quickly back. Nearer, nearer, a check, the man stopped. Leather creaked as though he stooped, there came a sudden guttural exclamation, and Jim sprang round the corner at him.

Surprise, anger, realisation all played across the man's face as he straightened up, his eyes wide, his mouth opening to shout. Then Jim glimpsed a darting shadow beyond the sentry and an arm whipped over the man's shoulder and under his chin, snapping his head back, strangling his cry. Jim caught his rifle as it fell, whipped off the bayonet and struck upward under the man's ribs, catching the body under the arms as it slumped forward out of Lewis's grasp.

The window beside them opened, and Alan looked out. At a sign from Lewis, they half lifted, half pushed the limp form through the window, Alan helping, and they heard the thump as it fell to the floor. Lewis passed the rifle through, returned his knife to his belt, sweat pouring in floods down his face – which had suddenly lost its rigid mask. For a split second he looked as though he were about to burst into tears, then incredibly, he put out his hands, gripped Jim above the elbows and shook him, his teeth a white line in the darkness.

"We're winning, boy! We're winning!"

Then he was gone.

Trembling appreciably, Jim returned to the back of the house, picked up his Tommy-gun (he had no memory whatsoever of putting it down before he sprang), and moving in shadow, crossed to the far side of the house.

There were still seven more houses to be visited – three along the link road (including the middle one where Jim and Alan had hidden on their retreat from the search of the base workshops), and the four outer ones along the Western sideroad.

Carefully, keeping level with Lewis who crept along the outer edge of the link towards the front of the first house, Jim crawled through the straggling vines towards the back, cursing the limited vision, but blessing its protection. Alan and Whittaker were still in the top house of the Eastern side road, watching for the all clear before bringing across the charges and uncoiling the cordtex. So much was now in position that the remainder was light enough for just the two of them to handle.

The heat, the dust, the strain were beginning to tell, and feeling faintly guilty about it, Jim decided he must take a benzedrine tablet during his next wait.

Behind the first house, Jim crouched in the shadows, watching across the back areas. Where the blazes was the sentry for this lot – surely they must have one somewhere? He could hear the clear footsteps of the two men patrolling the road and envied Lewis the simplicity of his duty. That was unfair: Lewis was in far more danger.

He moved across the clear space immediately behind the house – queer how they all seemed to conform to the same pattern – and reached the shadows of the first bushes – olives this time.

Lying flat, he stared at the backs of the other two houses along the link. Relief surged up in him as he saw a shadow move in the veranda of the middle house. The sentry! Lazy one, too, sitting on the window sill, lounging back against the sash. Deal with him later.

Jim shivered, faintly sick at the memory of the other sentry, hoping this man's conscience would make him move from his comfortable position, hoping his life need not be taken, hoping, if it must, that someone else would do the deed, then angry and disgusted at himself that he would wish unpleasantness and danger on his friends rather than face it himself.

He went back to the corner of the house, and along the side wall facing the one in which Alan and Whittaker waited. There was a dark movement in front of him.

"O.K.?" whispered Lewis.

"O.K., sir."

They waited until the sentry came up along the Eastern road, turned and went past them along the link. The cordtex across the road had not been noticed yet and Jim blessed his luck, but thought poorly of the sentry. As the man went by, Lewis lifted his torch and with Jim's hands cupped around the glass, flashed it twice. The time which elapsed before the other two could leave their hiding place seemed endless, owing to the dawdling of the second road sentry walking down towards them.

"Could we hurry this up, do you think, Corporal?" whispered Lewis, and Jim suddenly realised how surprised he would have been at the question at any time before the episode of the sentry, yet now it seemed natural, unforced. He thought for a while.

"I know where one sentry is at the back here, sir," he whispered back. "If he doesn't move, I reckon I could get through the side window of the middle house while the other two are in this one, deal with the sentry, then place the charge myself and connect it. That'll save them one lot."

They could just make out the shadows of Alan and Whittaker leaving the bulk of the last house.

Beside him, Lewis nodded.

"We must do something like that. How can I help?"

"When these two are inside, sir, come around the back with me, and I'll show you were the chap is. When you're sure that your sentries in the front are all right, come back between the houses and keep an eye on mine."

"O.K. Let's get this window open for them."

It creaked slightly but it was open by the time Alan and Whittaker arrived – hot, begrimed, gaunt but not tired, for both had taken benzedrine before leaving the cistern.

"What I could do with a pint!" muttered Alan as he went through the window. Jim whispered the new proposal to him, he nodded, closed the window, disappeared. Lewis came back along the wall.

"Took a quick shufti to see my chaps are not making a nuisance of themselves. Let's have a look at yours."

As they watched from the shadows of the bushes, the sentry straightened up from the window sill, stretched himself, yawned, slung his rifle and moved to the corner of the veranda, looking out across the plantations.

"Could we rush him!"

"Risky, sir, with the others on the roadway. I don't know if there are any more around the back here. Pity that Arab didn't give us more information about them."

"M'm. But we've got to get rid of him somehow."

Lewis lay still for an instant, watching. Then the sweat started out on his forehead.

"All right," he said tightly. "I'll go around the front, come back along the passage. You attract his attention somehow and I'll jump him from the back."

The shrill, snappy note was back to his voice, and as he went away down the side of the house, his silhouette was taut again, vaguely unpleasant. Jim crouched, ready to make some sort of movement when Lewis arrived behind the sentry, who still lounged against the corner post of the veranda.

The seconds ticked by.

Then, from the roadway came a sudden shout and then the sound of running footsteps. One sentry was coming in fast from the Eastern sideroad, there was an answering shout from the West end of the link and the man on the veranda spun around and jumped down off the step. Then Lewis's Tommy-gun hammered out in front. As Jim's sentry turned to run down the passage towards the noise, Jim pressed the trigger, felt the spastic surge of the gun, saw the man thrown violently sideways against the wall of the passage, and then he heard Lewis's voice.

"Get out and bomb the rest! I'll blow this lot!"

The high, almost hysterical shout was drowned in another burst of fire, and Alan suddenly appeared above the still-twitching body of the sentry. As Jim ran forward, Whittaker piled out through the window.

"Get out into the road with Lewis!" yelled Jim. ' He's in trouble. I'll deal with this."

He whipped the spare charges from his smock, tore the rest of the coil of cordtex from Whittaker's hand, and as the other two ran away down the passage, wrapped it around both charges. Then he smashed the side window in the middle house. pulled a grenade from his pocket and followed to the front end of the passage. In the darkness he could see the shape of one man lying in the road, Alan and Whittaker were running away from him along towards the last house in the link, and shouts and many running footsteps came nearer along both side roads as men poured out from billets further down towards the main road.

Then Lewis materialised suddenly, coming across the road in a fast, swerving run. Jim tore detonators and safety fuse from his pocket.

"I've wrapped a charge in the cordtex, sir. Shove these in and they'll go. Leave the middle house to me."

Lewis went past and crouched above the charge in the middle of the passage, Alan was smashing in the windows of the last house along the link road, men were running down towards them along both legs of the U, and they were all trapped in the middle of the horizontal. Lewis rose and came back, leaving a hissing snake lying in the passage. Jim pulled the pin from his grenade, let the clip go, flung the bomb through the window he had smashed – and he and Lewis raced along the road after Alan and Whittaker, still intent on bombing the remaining four outer houses of the Western sideroad.

Automatically, Jim was counting. He reached six and flung himself across the road, diving for the only cover he could see.

"Drop!" he yelled at the top of his voice.

As he hit the ground, he heard the grenades go in both houses. There was a rumble of toppling drums, a red glow on the dust under his eyes, and then the charge at the end of the cordtex blew.

Cordtex ignites at the rate of six thousand feet a second. There was less than this stretched between the first charge placed in the bottom house of the Western sideroad, and the last charge, placed in the first house along the link. These two charges – together with the eleven connected between them – went up to all intents and purposes instantaneously.

In two of the houses, so placed to catch all the sun, the temperature had been such that the vapour emanating from the opened drums had practically filled the free space, and when the cordtex flashed and the charges blew, the vapour caught. Both houses exploded like vast bombs in themselves.

In the remainder, the charges burst the drums, petrol spilt everywhere and if it was not ignited by the flash of the charge, fell on metal hot from the explosion, vapourised, built up the explosive content in the free space and either reached its own flashpoint, or was caught by sparks or burning debris from one of the neighbouring houses.

As Jim got to his feet, two houses were already nothing but spreading lakes of burning petrol with a few still unburnt drums marooned in the centre, flames shot from the roofs of four more houses, and crackled angrily inside the wooden casings of the rest. The heat was well-nigh unbearable. He tore the remaining detonator and safety-fuse from his pocket, flung it away, and with his right arm raised to guard his face from the worst of the heat, ran down the road towards the spot where he had last seen Alan. As he ran, he became conscious of Lewis slightly behind him and to his left. Lewis was shouting something, but in the howling din of flames springing up all around, the words were lost.

The Jim saw Alan. Crouched in the outer corner of the road, his face a flame-lit mask, he was firing long bursts down the side road, the gun at his shoulder steady as a rock. In contrast, Whittaker sat just behind him, legs out in front, automatic in hand, staring open-mouthed at the scene around him like a child at a firework party.

"Get moving, you idiot!" Jim shouted as he ran – and unpierced drums in the house on the inside corner – now a flaming shell – burst violently in the rising heat. High above the clangour came Whittaker's scream of terror: then he scrambled to his feet and fled out into the darkness behind him.

Now Lewis and Jim reached Alan – a new magazine in, picking his targets now with single shots.

"Beat it!" yelled Lewis and there was triumph in his voice. "The others will go without our help!"

They dragged Alan to his feet and turned and fled after Whittaker, racing to get away beyond the light of the flames before they were fired on. Sweat poured down Jim's face as he ran, Lewis well ahead shouting after Whittaker, Alan running fast just in front of him. Jim's back felt naked and he tore over the ground with little sense of effort.

Then he reached the shadows of the bottom of the plantation and the thick undergrowth absorbed his momentum, slowing him up. Soon his clothes were soaked, his trousers clinging to him like jam, his socks a slimy mess, his feet on fire, and in the gasping tumult of his chest, his heart thudded as though trying to break his ribs apart. Explosions behind told of still-bursting drums, and at intervals, one would be blown into the air, dripping curtains of fire below it to end like a vast rocket in the sky above.

They could hear no sounds of pursuit, but once – when Lewis halted and they caught him up to stand together for a brief pause, chests heaving like accordions – they heard the sounds of single, lurching movement somewhere ahead of them. Their eyes met, mouths twisting wryly, and it was Lewis who voiced their common thought.

"Poor bastard," he wheezed.

Then on they went again, climbing now and more slowly, the holocaust behind still painting the ground a dull red, a magenta carpet across which danced elephantine shadows.

Rocks tore Jim's hands as he pulled himself up, stones slipped away under his feet, the bushes caught his trousers, ripping the drill and scratching the flesh beneath, his belt was a chafing weight about his waist. The Colt banged his hip-bone, and the strap of the Tommy-gun cut into his shoulder.

Lewis paused again in the shadows of a bush, and as Jim came up and sank to the ground beside Alan he pointed down behind them.

"See!" he panted. "The others have gone up, too. We did it! We did it!"

Beside him, Jim felt Alan jerk his head up and stare at the officer, arrested by the new note in his voice. Lewis was smiling, eyes no longer beady, tight mouth relaxed. He turned from the fire and looked at them, rather tentatively putting out his hand.

"Well done, boys!" he said as they shook it in turn. "Bloody well done!"

It was ten minutes later, as they climbed up the last slope leading to the ridge top, that they heard the shot. It came from further along the crest, from the position in which they had left their food, their sleeping bags, their spare ammunition.

When they arrived at the spot, they found Whittaker, Colt in his hand, blood trickling from a small wound above his right ear. As they turned him over, they saw that whatever failures had attended him in life, whatever forces had overborne his courage and driven him into the treacherous haven of alcohol, in death he had found peace.

His eyes were open and steady, not yet glazed: his mouth smiled contentedly.

Chapter 14

IT is so easy to see the waste, the inefficiency and the duplication of effort which an open system of free enterprise allows – and in somes cases brings about. It is also easy to see how centralisation, in one brisk, pragmatic movement, should reduce the waste, cure the inefficiency and totally abolish the duplication: what is almost never foreseen, however, is the tragedy which then ensues. The Epitaph of many a time-study and efficiency expert is a hor-rified "Oh – I never thought of that!"

From the moment in June, 1940, when Wavell had first demon-strated that any force moving against Egypt possessed two long and immensely vulnerable flanks, private armies – and navies – had mushroomed into growth in order to attack those flanks. By the end of 1941, there were at least two so-called 'demolition squad-rons' loose in the desert, two separate and distinct organisations landing saboteurs from the sea, the Special Air Service still experi-menting with paratroop parties and the L.R.D.G. running their highly-efficient taxi-runs to almost anywhere in North Africa. In addition, there were groups like Rutledge's spread from Tripoli to Bomba.

Eventually the inevitable occurred and one group attacked a post already in the hands of another: casualties fortunately were light and none fatal, but in Cairo, heads were both shaken and nodded portentously and the need proclaimed for a central, guiding authority. This authority was set up in early 1942 and the paper strategists looked on delightedly as operation was smoothly dovetailed into operation, logistic tables assumed a pleasing symmetry and faint lines on the map divided it into zones of activity.

The central authority, they said would streamline effort. It would also cause a great saving in valuable war materials, in the demands on even more valuable man-power, and moreover – and this was proclaimed with especial emphasis and satisfaction – it would impose an overall *pattern* on para-military activity, and this, as all will agree, is always a good thing.

A pattern, however, is something generally visible to anyone – and everyone – who has eyes to look for it.

("Oh – I never thought . . .").

By ten o'clock in the morning of May 26th, Oberst Graf von Schwebel decided that there were no more reports to come in, marked up his map, read through the list of reports again, picked them all up and walked out of his tent and across the sand towards the huge captured British command trucks which constituted Rommel's Field Headquarters. Beneath a tarpaulin rigged out from the side of one of them sat a young Oberleutnant, working on papers spread over a collapsible table.

"Is he free yet, Schmidt?" asked the Oberst softly.

The Oberleutnant glanced up, then sprang to his feet.

"Jahwohl, Herr Oberst. General von Ravenstein left a few minutes ago. I'll just go and make sure . . ."

The Oberst hesitated fractionally, then asked, "How's he taking it?"

Schmidt grinned. "Nothing to worry about, Herr Oberst. I think he might even be pleased!"

"Pleased?" asked von Schwebel, both relieved and incredulous. "Then it won't make any difference?"

Schmidt shook his head.

"We attack tonight!" he said. "He says that if the British were expecting us to do so, all this . . ." and he indicated the papers in von Schwebel's hand . . . would have occurred four nights ago. As it is, these raids confirm that the British intend to attack next Saturday – which we knew anyway."

Two minutes later, von Schwebel entered the 'Mammoth' and the presence of his commanding General.

"Ah, von Schwebel," said the great man, coolly. "And what is the extent of the damage? Are all the reports in?"

"I think so, Herr General," answered the Oberst. "I certainly hope so!"

He placed the map on the desk, and as Rommel's eyes went from coloured cross to coloured cross, he read out the details. Near Jedabya an Italian convoy had been ambushed, north of Antela an airfield attacked and fourteen Savoias left burning: the road between Soluch and Benghasi had been temporarily blocked and everything which approached the block had been shot up.

"At El Abiar . . ." continued von Schwebel, ". . . the Italian police garrison . . ."

"Nothing at Benghasi?" interrupted Rommel quietly.

"Benghasi?" For the moment the Oberst was flustered, missing his stroke. "Nein, Herr General – no report from Benghasi."

The cool, granite eyes of the Desert Fox glanced once up at von Schwebel, then back to the map.

"Continue!"

"At El Abiar, the Italian police garrison was attacked and blown up, and the airfield at Barce was also attacked, Herr

General. Some Stukas were lost, but of course most of them were up here."

Rommel nodded, a faint smile touching the firm mouth.

"From Slonta, General Piatti reports that he is dealing firmly with an uprising among the local Arabs, some of whom entered Slonta last night and threw bombs into a vehicle-park."

"General Piatti," said Rommel succinctly. "Is a fool."

"Jahwohl, Herr General" dutifully answered von Schwebel, and then remained silent, awaiting further comment. Rommel's eyes however, had carried further eastward along the road from Slonta until they reached the cross north-east of it. There then followed a silence which extended too long: when the General eventually looked up, there was a cold glitter in his eyes.

"The petrol at Guidano Corba!" he said. "Under our own guard – did they get that, too?"

"Every drop, Herr General!" replied von Schwebel sadly – and thanked God that is was Rommel he was giving the news to, not a dozen other Wehrmacht Field Commanders, any one of whom would have wrought havoc in his immediate neighbourhood until rage was spent. As it was, even with Rommel an entirely different atmosphere now reigned inside the command truck.

"What happened at Derna and Martuba?" snapped Rommel.

"At Martuba a convoy was redirected and the two leading trucks pitched down the escarpment and an attack was made on an ammunition dump. At Derna – nothing."

"Pah!" spat Rommel in exasperation. "Of course something happened at Derna last night – and at Benghasi, Herr Oberst – whether the reports have come in yet or not! Look at the map! Do you think the British would leave gaps like that? Their minds are just as symmetrical as ours once they rise above the rank of Colonel – or once they start planning! Get through to Gerhardt at Derna and that fat fool Mersagli at Benghasi and find out what happened there."

His eyes went momentarily back to the map.

"And at Marawa as well something was at least attempted – find out what. And also send for whoever was in command of the guard at Guidano Corba!"

As the Oberst hurried from the command truck, he heard Rommel's voice calling for his Chief of Staff and his aide-de-camp.

"Someone's going to pay for the night's work," he thought as he entered the signal office. "Will it be us – or the British?"

Half an hour later when he re-entered the General's 'Mammoth,' he saw that plans were being laid to ensure that the British should pay the price of their own misdoings: the map was now covered in wriggling, coloured lines, all leading away from the points of sabotage towards the open desert. They represented the possible escape routes.

"Well?" asked Rommel curtly.

"At Benghasi, an attempt was made to blow up ships in the harbour, Herr General, at Marawa a petrol convoy was shot off the road and at Derna, the Ftaiah airfield was attacked."

"Ah!" snapped Rommel triumphantly – and rapidly sketched in a few more lines. Then he stepped back from the map and looked at it: the effect of his work was obvious, for like two almost solid triangles, the escape lines funnelled down east and west,

Eastwards, they met near Msus, westwards at El Machli.

"Send instructions to Mersagli to stop staring out to sea for the Royal Navy, and to Piatti to release the Arabs he has wasted his time collecting as hostages," snapped Rommel. "Tell them to rush every man who can bear arms southwards to the Trig el Abd and to patrol northwards from it as far as Msus and at least twenty miles each side. As for El Machli," he turned to a young Staff Officer standing behind him. "Did you get through?"

"Jahwohl, Herr General." The Staff Officer shook his head. "Nothing as yet. No sign of trouble at all!"

"Good – I was afraid we might be too late."

The granite eyes dropped to the map and flicked quickly over its salient points, ensuring that he had overlooked nothing, that no other interpretation could be placed upon the unmistakeable patterns which the map revealed. He glanced up again at the Staff Officer.

"We must ensure the British a proper welcome when they do arrive. What is the strength of the force now concentrated at Location 5X?"

When the required information had been both obtained and verified, Rommel gave his orders rapidly and decisively, and soon signal-sets were burping out their messages and telephone lines humming: a Panzeroffizier received an explicit briefing. Back in the Mammoth, the Desert Fox made one last examination of the map, one last mental examination of the probabilities and the certainties. Then he turned from the map-board, relaxed and faintly-smiling.

"Then I think gentlemen, that we may now dismiss the night's banditry from our minds and leave them clear for the main battle. Last night, the enemy won a number of minor engagements. Tonight, we shall only win one – but it will sweep the British back to the Nile!"

Some eight hours after this demonstration of military expertise on the part of the Commanding Officer of the Afrika Korps, the three men who between them held a loose joint command of the nearest representatives of his enemies, lay on the last crest of the Jebel Ahkdar, before it sloped away southwards into the desert. They were listening to a report brought in by the ever-efficient Sa'ad Ali. As the liquid sentences ended and Rutledge translated, Lieutenant Perowne's eyebrows rose and he glanced curiously from Rutledge to the Arab boy and back again.

"You mean that he actually saw the Jerries clear out, sir?"

Rutledge nodded.

"Every man jack, according to him," he answered. "There are only about twenty Italians left there under an officer, apparently in complete control. Seems almost too good to be true, doesn't it?"

Perowne shrugged.

"We had bad luck on the way in – maybe now it's changed."

He rolled over on his stomach and lifted the glasses to his eyes again, staring out over the hill-top towards El Machli.

"No damn good!" he said, dropping the glasses. "Heat haze and mirage – can't see a thing!"

"Do you think it could be a trap?" asked McCarran from beyond Rutledge. Despite the fact that Perowne was the most junior officer present, there was no doubt that he was in real control at the moment: he glanced across at McCarran, then stared at the ground directly in front of him, then examined the backs of his hands.

"Look!" he said, his voice suddenly light and unemotional again. "Maybe it is a trap – I don't know! Neither, I suggest, do you – nor anyone else up here. But whether it's a trap or not, we've got to take El Machli tonight – and if it's only held by twenty Wops, then it'll be that much easier."

He rose lithely to his feet and stood looking down at the other two. "I'm going to tell my chaps now – and yours, – and Sergeant Orr and I will work out how we're going to do it."

He hesitated a second, then looked at Rutledge.

"I wonder sir, if you would be kind enough to take charge of the Bren, and give covering fire if anything goes wrong. It'd release one of the signallers to come in with us."

Gravely, Rutledge accepted the hint and agreed to it.

"Certainly, Mr. Perowne. Will I have a Number Two?"

As Perowne's eyes crossed towards McCarran, the latter spoke.

"I'd like to go in with you, old chap, if I may," he said quickly. Perowne looked at him steadily for a moment.

"You'll be with me, not Sergeant Orr," he said, and left the statement in the air, questioning its acceptance.

"O.K.", said McCarran wryly. "I'll do as I'm told."

Perowne nodded, then swung around and dropped quickly down the back of the hill towards the small wadi where the rest of the band were sleeping after the previous night's march.

"I wonder what it is about that young man that makes me feel as though I'm back at school, Robert?" asked Rutledge.

"It's probably his accent as much as anything," grunted Mc-Carran. "That and his air of weary patience as he explains to us civilians the best way to avoid hindering the real soldiers."

"Would you like him as a friend, Robert?"

"Him?" The word burst from McCarran like a cork from a bottle on a hot day. "Good God, we haven't a single thing in common! We'd drive each other nuts if we had to spend a week in each other's company. And it'd have to be forced on us: I'm quite sure he wouldn't submit without a struggle."

"That wasn't quite the question, Robert," said Rutledge gently. "Would you like to be able to claim him as a friend of yours?"

McCarran wiped some of the sweat from his face and in his mind compared his own fat dumpiness with Perowne's tautness, his own sweat-ridden, clumsy, earth-bound divagations with the cool, efficient purpose which seemed to invest the other man's entire life.

"He's a lucky bastard," he said enviously – and Rutledge accepted the statement as answer to his question. Shortly after-wards, they followed Perowne down to the wadi.

The night was black, baking and breathlessly hot when you moved – chilled at the edges immediately a halt was called. They moved in single file across the open desert towards the fort and surrounding encampment of El Machli. McCarran was just behind Perowne, then Fusilier O'Reilly, Trooper 043 Jones of the S.A.S., and Sergeant Drummond. After Drummond came Ser-geant Orr and the Corporal and Trooper who would go off with him when the party split: Rutledge lay behind the Bren some dis-tance back, his heart rebelling against the consolation offered by his lucid mind: that this was the best place for a man of his age, and that in any case, his immediate responsibilities were high. El Machli lay three hundred yards in front.

Before the war, El Machli had been a single, desert fort – in a spectacular but efficient Beau Geste tradition, built at a road junction and around a well both to deny the water to resurgent Bedouin tribesmen as well as to form a traffic control point. But with the war of open movement which had been waged all around it, during the last two years, it had soon developed other uses in relation to the position of the front line: now it was in temporary favour as a routing point and as an advanced base for stores and fuel. More space was needed to store the fuel, more to house the men to guard the stores, more stores to feed the men to guard the . . . and so on.

The original fort was soon inadequate in every way, dumps of stores and huts sprang up outside the front wall, and in default of a regulation, double barbed-wire fence (the rock was too hard to take the posts), sangars were built to squat at the corners and Dannert coils writhed between them. Normally, sentries patrolled constantly inside the Dannert and Spandaus were permanently manned in the sangars, but with the withdrawal of the German complement, it was not absolutely certain how the Italian Commandant had disposed his forces. Certainly the majority were inside the fort and there were probably observers on the parapets and a man behind the machine-gun in the high, central watchtower: whether there were any in the wired space before the main gate was unknown.

It would be up to Sergeant Orr and his men to find out – and liquidate what opposition they found.

Perowne halted and half-turned and McCarran stopped himself just in time to avoid bumping into him: soundlessly from out of the night behind them, Sergeant Orr appeared, Corporal Reg Pointer and his invariable assistant upon these occasions, Trooper F. St. John ('Duke') Mallory. They melted off to the right at a signal from Perowne, and the rest of the section seemed unconsciously to pivot on McCarran, Perowne dropping back to his right, the others coming up on his left until McCarran suddenly realised that he was still standing while all the others had sunk silently to the ground.

As he started hastily to drop to at least a crouch, a hand came up from his right and gripped the link between strap and Tommygun barrel: as a result, there was no clink as McCarran's bulk came to rest. He glanced apologetically along the arm from the hand which still held his gun-barrel and saw Perowne's etched profile against the night, looking away after the other three. The head came slowly around, mouth slightly open, eyes flickering over the ground between them and the nearest sangar, now only fifty yards away: then Perowne's eyes met McCarran's – they were bright, eager, and for the first time that McCarran had seen, vital.

As Perowne drew his hand from the gun, he grinned – unaffected, friendly, boyish. He peered along beyond McCarran at the others, winked as his eyes came back, then watched over towards the fort again, occasionally wetting his lips, his breathing slightly faster than usual.

Seeing all this, MacCarran became suddenly unafraid: his skin contracted away from the sweat-sodden clothing and allowed the hot discomfort of fear to escape, he settled back more comfortably and stared ahead. Then he began to wonder what would happen next – remembered, and as he lifted his wrist to examine his watch, he saw that Perowne was already staring at his. Perowne glanced up, grinned again, then with his eyes on his watch, silently mouthed 'Six . . . five . . . four . . . three . . . two . . . As his lips formed the W for one, the shot rang out.

Major Rutledge was both punctual and accurate, for the single bullet from the Bren smacked against the front wall of the fort just to the left of the gate. Three minutes later, another shot rang out – from a point further away along the foothills, and once again came the smack as it flattened itself against the sandstone walls.

"See anything yet?" whispered McCarran.

Perowne shook his head, but on McCarran's left, 043 Jones pointed excitedly into the jumble of shadows behind the Dannert.

"Look man, by the hut there," and as though to confirm his sibillant directive, a shot rang out from just in front of them, its flash momentarily outlining black, amorphous shapes of dumps near the wire.

It now became obvious that there was at least a prowler guard loose in the forecourt, for either through common sense or merely officiousness, a sharp voice angrily reprimanded the nervous riflemen for wasting ammunition on an Arab sniper.

"The slippery swine will have gone before you've got your rifle up to your shoulder, dolt!" shouted the voice – and warming to its task, continued. "When you've been out here long enough to lose the taste of your mother's milk, idiot, you'll know not to give your position away and waste ammunition at the same time! Next time wait until you're told to fire by someone like myself who's been out here long enough to know what it's all about!"

Officiousness obviously – certainly not common sense.

Perowne dropped forward, waved his arm, and flat on their bellies the patrol wormed their way between small rocks towards the wire. They were within ten yards of it when Rutledge fired again – from even further off along the foothills – and beyond the wire they could see the rather stunted form of the sentry who had fired, while off between some huts a movement betrayed the position of the officious and self-proclaimed desert-worthy N.C.O.

As McCarran wondered rather feverishly whether the trick had worked sufficiently to reveal the whole of the prowler guard, another figure tiptoed quietly down the other side of the wire and joined Shorty, standing beside him as they both stared out towards the foothills.

There was a quick grasp on McCarran's forearm, Perowne waved to 043 Jones and Fusilier O'Reilly beyond, and as those two slipped off to the left with Sergeant Drummond, Perowne led McCarran away to the right. Dust filled McCarran's mouth; his arms and back ached and his clothing was soaked again.

"Is he sure, yet . . . or is he just gambling?" he worried to himself as he strove to keep up with the jerking boots a yard in front of his eyes. The coils of Dannert went by – just ahead was the low, circular wall of the sangar.

Perowne halted, lay listening: with a quick movement he beckoned McCarran up alongside him so they lay together, their heads five yards short of the sangar wall, staring at the darkness just above it, for a sign of movement. Silently, Perowne handed McCarran his Tommy-gun, fiddled at his waist for a second, then slid forward like a snake: steel glistened in his right hand. He paused for a second at the base of the wall and seemed to gather himself into a ball, then elongated upwards in a completion of the same movement and slid over the top of the sangar wall.

To McCarran the world was suddenly frozen into deathless immobility. Eternity ticked by: then Perowne's hand appeared above the sangar-top and McCarran breathed out. He took his own Tommy-gun in one hand and Perowne's in the other and reached the sangar with an efficiency born and brought to perfection by immediate necessity.

"Better keep low," breathed Perowne as McCarran flopped down into the sangar beside him. "The silly sod might start coming back – though he'll not get far. Look!"

As they peered inwards into the forecourt, three shadows moved purposefully across from the side wire towards the far edge where at least two – and by now probably three – of the prowler guard were congregated. One of the shadows was recognisably Sergeant Orr.

"Come on," breathed Perowne, and they slid along the bottom of the oval-shaped sangar, past the concrete-based stand for the Spandau (the gun itself had gone with its owners) and into the shadows of a dump of Jerricans. Perowne rose to his feet and moved ahead into the twisting maze between dumps and huts, seeming to know his way by instinct, communicating confidence all the time to McCarran close behind.

There was a series of sudden muffled sounds from the centre of the forecourt – too jumbled to be interpreted but ending in a stifled gasp of pain and fear, then silence. Perowne stepped out of the shadow of a hut and Sergeant Orr materialised in front of him: neither seemed surprised at the sudden appearance of the other, but no word was spoken. Thumbs up and a wave indicated the immediate past and immediate future, and the whole line now moved predatorily down upon the two unsuspecting sentries.

With excellent timing, another shot rang out from the foothills, whined shrilly over their heads and concentrated the attention of the quarry who murmured between themselves. McCarran could see them both now. They were about twenty-five yards away and separated from him by a sprawling sea of lorry-tyres. Sergeant Orr was already threading between the black petrified waves and McCarran caught a glimpse of two more silent figures away to the right nearer the fort: Corporal Pointer and 'Duke' Mallory. Perowne moved across in front of him, down toward the wire they had just crossed, but motioned him to remain where he was, while Perowne himself took up a position from which he could watch but then made no move nearer to the centre of action.

Pointer and 'Duke' moved closer down towards the unsuspecting sentries; ten yards now separated them – five yards. Then Sergeant Orr moving in from another angle, failed to see a lone tyre on the black-shadowed ground, trod on it and it tipped up and caught his other foot as he jumped clear. The noise caused the sentries to spin around, Corporal Pointer leapt for the nearer one with 'Duke' Mallory two feet behind him to catch the falling rifle, and the second sentry – Shorty – saw Sergeant Orr emerge from the tyre dump like an avenging doom. With a shrill scream of fear Shorty fled down the wire to the nearest sangar, meaning to escape from terror into the open desert.

His scream sliced through the night and in its quivering echoes went the best hope for a surprise attack on the main fort. Perowne yelled an order, Sergeant Orr whirled around – leaving Shorty to his fate – and with McCarran in the lead due to a surprisingly quick reaction, all three men raced back through the dump towards the solid main gate.

In the meantime, Shorty had reached his sangar, his hopes rocketed at the realisation that pursuit was not close on his heels, then sank like a plummet at unidentifiable gratings near by. The noises came from just outside the wire.

"Amico, amico," whispered Shorty in dire panic. "Amico mio – Engleeshman amico. Amico Engleeshman!" and he leaned beseechingly out over the low sangar wall.

"I'm not English, really," said 043 Jones as he stabbed scientifically upwards from the ground. "I'm from Abergynolwyn."

He held the knife firm with one hand while the other gripped Shorty's throat like a vice. When all movement had stopped, he twisted away and let Shorty fall, withdrawing the knife at the same time, wiping it on the Italian tunic.

"In Wales," he added in amiable explanation; then stepped over the wall into the sangar and followed O'Reilly and Drummond who were already racing through the dump towards the main gate after the others.

Despite his weight McCarran was still leading, for he had been nearest to the front wall of the fort when Perowne had shouted, and his mind had moved with the same speed and towards the same realisation as the others': they must get into the fort somehow before the defenders were completely organised. The ground thudded back under his feet as he charged up the centre passage of the dump and he could hear Perowne well behind him and Sergeant Orr coming in on his left flank. Ahead, the wall of the fort loomed black and solid and from behind it came growing uproar: then two red flames stabbed down at him from high on the parapet and something buzzed viciously by his ear – but he hardly noticed it for some heaven-sent Italian idiot was opening the main gate, presumably in order to help the defunct prowler guard.

The gate had opened about three feet before anguished screams persuaded the man behind it of his immediate danger, but there was a split second before it began to close and in that second McCarran saw what he must do: he dropped his Tommy-gun and screamed at the top of his voice, flinging his arms above his head but not checking his pace. The man behind the door, unnerved, hesitated and was lost. He recovered, tried to slam the gate, but when the gap was down to six inches there came a Tommy-gun burst from behind McCarran – which passed close enough to him to pluck at his shirt – and the man behind the door screamed and fell away. His nearest compatriots flung themselves forward and the gap closed further, but as the door touched the frame Robert McCarran, unarmed, launched himself like a self-contained battering-ram at the metal-studded surface.

He felt it cold and inexorable at the moment of impact and his shoulder for one frightful second seemed to start disintegration within his skin: then the door gave, bursting open and spilling him forward into the centre of a group of vociferous little men, four of whom went down like ninepins (he found himself about to apologise to them), the rest scattering across an open courtyard – but shot down before they could reach sanctuary by Sergeant Orr, crouched in awful efficiency just inside the gateway.

Perowne, racing up with Drummond, a wildly-enthusiastic O'Reilly and 043 Jones singing hymns at the top of his voice, swerved across the courtyard towards a lighted doorway, flinging grenades through it as he ran. He swerved again towards windows along the wall and before the grenades exploded panic-stricken figures were tumbling out through them, their arms in anguished surrender above their heads.

Sergeant Orr's bombs burst viciously behind the windows on the other side of the courtyard, the machine-gun in the central-tower stopped its apparently ineffective nagging, but red tracer still ricochetted off the tower-face at impossible angles: Major Rutledge had an astounding eye for a man of his age and was naturally loathe to leave a target which he had satisfactorily pin-pointed.

Robert McCarran rolled over and sat up: four feet away from him another figure did exactly the same, revealing stiff epaulettes with brassy stars, revealing also the fact that he still held a Beretta Automatic in his right hand.

"You'd better give that to me," said McCarran – and such is the *hubris* of victory that the Tenente meekly did as he was told. They sat side by side for a few more moments and watched.

Suddenly the night was quiet: the defeated huddled together, the victors snarling separately around them, threatening, preda-tory. Then a window was flung open and Sergeant Orr shouted down into the courtyard.

"There's none here but the daid, sir. Y' have all that's left doon there!"

"O.K. Where's the officer? Dove Tenente?"

The little man beside McCarran looked anxiously up at him, and rather protectively, Robert answered for him.

"He's over here, old chap," he shouted, getting rather awk-wardly to his feet, for he suddenly became conscious that his shoulder ached abominably – though not so much as it did a second later when his hand was being enthusiastically pumped by Perowne – totally disregarding the plaintive subject of his last enquiry.

"Christ Bob, that was bloody good! Thank God we had you with us – we'd never have got in otherwise! Would we Sergeant Orr?"

"Not a hope, Sir" agreed Orr who had come down, then more soberly to McCarran. "Y' did vairy well, sir. Vairy well, indaid! 'Tis a good job y' – uh – carry the weight y'do – otherwise we'd never ha' got in!"

It was some time afterwards that McCarran remembered the

Tommy-gun burst which had held the balance for his own on-slaught, and later, when he went out to regain the weapon he had dropped in his charge, he walked around the forecourt from place to place trying to work out the relative position of gate, himself, Orr and Perowne, at the moment of firing. Given the most advantageous circumstances, it was a incredibly expert piece of shooting: it had also required a cold and ruthlessly logical brain to take a gamble at such long odds – odds moreover which included McCarran's life and limb as a mere makeweight.

The conclusion depressed him, coming as it did immediately after the total exhilaration of being accepted – apparently – as a man among men. When Rutledge eventually arrived, sweating wearily under the weight of the Bren, McCarran enticed the older man up on to the fort parapet with tales of a cooling breeze and in due course, related to him the events of the evening.

"You must accept the fact, Robert," said Rutledge at the end of the recital, "that to be successful in war these days, a man must exercise some degree of voluntary schizophrenia. He must be able to maintain a genuine affection for his men or his brother-officers in barracks, but feel no scruple to bargain their lives for military advantage in action: psychic integration is a peacetime luxury. By the way," he added, pointing from the parapet away away to the east-ward," – what do you make of that?"

The horizon was fitfully lit with rosy light, and the dull thump of artillery came to them, seemingly through the soles of their feet. McCarran watched it disinterestedly for a moment, then with growing alarm.

"Are we early?" he asked, " – or has friend Rommel jumped the gun?"

There was no answer from Rutledge, who stared grimly at the flickering frame to an increasingly wide horizon.

"It'd explain the withdrawal of the Jerries from this place, anyway," said McCarran – with some relief in his voice.

"I wonder," muttered Rutledge. "I wonder!"

Chapter 15

THERE was a tiny, objective fraction of Alan's mind in which he could still speculate upon the forces which kept him on his feet: but the rest of his mind, his brain, his spirit, his body, was occupied by a dull block-like resistance to the exhaustion which piled leaden weights upon his shoulders and hung them from his waist, in an apparent effort to drive him vertically down into the rocky earth over which they were climbing. He had never before been so utterly drained of life – or the wish for life, for although the physical strains and stresses of the last forty-eight hours had been high, Alan knew that the basic reason for his condition was mental.

He envied Lewis and Jim, climbing on through the night ahead of him, for their problems were simple, physical and clear to them: they wanted as an immediate objective to reach El Machli – and after that, Kuffra or Siwa, and then the ensuing security of Cairo. But Alan did not know what he wanted, for he knew that all those places were for him at least, merely staging posts on the road to a disaster which might well be worse than one which could overtake him now, here in the Jebel.

All his physical instincts dragged him one way. One part of his mind rejected the idea of capture, rocketed away from any mental picture of death in ambush or hurtling down upon him from scouring fighter 'planes: but another part of his mind reasoned coldly that this might prove the most satisfactory solution.

No. That was not quite true – and for a moment he lifted his eyes from the sun-baked and scarified rock crawling back under his leaden feet, to look at Jim's plodding, dogged figure outlined against the sky, and the thought of the genuinely easiest and simplest solution rose Satanically to the surface of his mind. It was a part of his mind, however, with which he had no wish to associate. "Lockyer," he told himself angrily. "You are the most complete and utter bloody bastard I've ever had the misfortune to come across!"

"Yes, I know," replied the Devil smoothly. "We knew all about that months ago – but what about it? After all, it would really be for Jim's own good – now wouldn't it?"

Wearily, Alan addressed himself once more to the physical tasks of moving through the night. He had been over this point again and again in his mind, and if he didn't know exactly what he wanted to do, he at least knew what solution he must reject if he was to retain any vestige of his lately acquired self-respect. He prayed that he would have the strength to continue to reject it as the crisis approached. The trouble was that it was already approaching – from a distance and at a lingering pace: but a steady one.

The angle of the ground under foot eased slightly, then came level. Jim was waiting for him, face white and strained in the darkness but still able to manage a smile.

"How's it going, Alan?" he whispered. "Can't be much further now – let's have your Tommy-gun. I can manage it – honest, I can."

"Oh, Christ!" thought Alan, then pushed everything to the back of his mind, slipped his Tommy-gun gratefully from his shoulder and handed it with a grin to Jim.

"Let's have your belt then, chum. Fair's fair."

"I can manage," said Jim, delighted at this first sign for days of the old companionship, but Alan insisted and draped Jim's belt over the shoulder from which he had just removed the Tommy-gun. The combined weight of water-bottle, Colt and ammunition clips was not far short of that of the gun anyway, but the change in weight distribution gave an illusion of relief.

They both looked across at the eastern horizon, heard the boom of artillery as the pounding of their own hearts eased, then without a word, they crossed the hill-top and started down the other side.

Jim nudged Alan and nodded ahead.

"Queer the way he's gone back, isn't it?"

Lewis's silhouette, ungainly again, awkward with tension, lurched from side to side further on down the slope. His relaxation and friendliness had slowly ebbed during the daylight wait in the cistern – which they had regained soon after the dawn following the raid. As the heat had risen, a million flies had invaded their sanctuary and forbidden sleep, which would in any case have been sporadic due to the continued slow patrol of searching aircraft just above their heads. The inevitable speculations which these aroused contributed fully to an atmosphere already charged with bubbling antagonisms.

By the time dusk fell and they could set out on the first night's march, Lewis was back in the state of taut hostility from which the activity, and success of action had temporarily released him. It had, however, one slight advantage – for Alan.

"I don't care whether Lockyer thinks he knows the way or not, Corporal," stated Lewis coldly. "I shall lead. You follow. Lockyer brings up the rear!"

And in the state to which internal and external stress had reduced Alan, this was probably as well, for whatever Lewis's other faults, he led them through that first night's march in a manner which Alan could hardly have bettered, doing it moreover, by the coldly logical rule of thumb methods which are the only solution for the vast majority of us, but which so few of us master.

They had covered nearly twenty-two miles during that night and for the following day lay up under sparse cover on a small hill-top, which allowed them to watch all approaches but upon which the sun beat from a sky like brass, reducing them to a stupor in which the only realities were dull pain and consuming thirst. When the sun had at last grudgingly ceased its torture and some of its heat had drained away, they had partially recovered and in a cracked, hate-filled voice, Lewis had ground out his instructions.

"We keep the same order. Keep closed up – watch the skylines. When I think we're within sight of El Machli, we'll stop and wait for daylight. We're not going in in the dark."

It was not only breath, strength or saliva for his vocal apparatus that seemed to be missing, but also the humanity to talk to those who shared his peril, his late triumph and his present adversity: both Jim and Alan wondered what circumstances would be necessary to release him again from his psychological prison – and if anything short of cataclysm would do it permanently. It seemed unlikely.

Now Lewis waited on the far side of a broken wadi. Another hill rose beyond him.

"You two *must* keep closer behind me," he snapped as they came up. "I thought I made that clear before we started. El Machli is about four miles on and this is the last line of hills. We should see the place from the top when daylight comes, so we'll stop up there until then. Follow me!"

Once more the horns of Alan's dilemma presented themselves. Every muscle and sinew in his body welcomed the news that a respite from exertion was near, but he knew that once the first raw edge of exhaustion had been blunted, his mind would soon force back his less physical – but no less acute – problem to the forefront of his consciousness. And he was almost more exhausted by trying to find a solution to that than by climbing these endless bloody hills.

"Not much further, Alan," urged Jim. "By this afternoon we might well be on our way to Kuffra – or perhaps Siwa, eh? There might," he added wistfully, twisting the knife, " – be some mail."

And totally unconscious of the effect of his words, Jim led the way on up the hill.

Grimly, Alan watched him go, feeling the wave of sick apprehension rising up through him once more, his mind cringing away from the abrupt re-appearance of the problem from which it had just been enjoying its first release for days.

There'll be mail all right, Jim – he thought bitterly – I can see bitch's writing now!

As he started wearily to climb upwards, the words repeated themselves monotonously in his mind, in time with his footsteps. Dear Alan, Dear Alan, Dear Alan, Dear Alan – the treadmill of the damned.

There'll be mail all right, Jim – he repeated to himself, breaking the ring – but it'll be Dear Jim, Dear Jim, Dear Jim, Dear Jim – and I suppose I'll have to stand by and watch you take it, like I watched Bert Craggs being killed and Nick Barrett – and that poor little devil Sparrow in the sea. And that'll be another horror I can chalk up to my eternal damnation, and spend my life remembering.

Jim paused for a moment above him, turned, grinned whitely, then started off again.

I'd be willing to accept damnation at that – thought Alan, with tears of exhaustion, frustration and anger streaking miserably down his face – if only I could stop you getting that letter.

"Well, now – " murmured the Tempter. " – what about . . ."

"Oh, —— off!" said Alan.

At the top of the hill, Lewis was waiting for them, they slipped off their rucksacks and dropped to the ground, automatically checking their arms in the dark, then peering into the darkness over the hill-crest. The desert spread out below them, illimitable in the moonless night. If El Machli was out there – and there was no reason to doubt Lewis's word or navigation – it was as yet invisible: in any case their eyes and thoughts went automatically to the growling, blood-shot eastern horizon.

"Two hours to dawn," grunted Lewis. "Your watch I believe, Lockyer?"

"No, sir," said Jim quickly, intending to do stag for both of them. "It's mine!"

Alan and Lewis both spoke at once.

"No it's not, Jim . . ."

"If I remember rightly, Corporal – and I'm sure I do – you were

131

on watch before we started out tonight. It is therefore Lockyer's watch. Wake me in an hour's time Lockyer ; and you get some sleep too, Corporal. Don't waste your time chinwagging – there'll be time for all that later."

One of the most objectionable things about Lewis of course, was that he was invariably right: Jim grinned across hopelessly, rolled over, settled himself in a hollow, and went to sleep like a tired puppy. Alan watched him sadly, then turned and stared out into the night, once more alone with his thoughts. For a moment he postponed the endless twisting and turnings, and allowed memory to provide once more, the material cause: by now, he knew it by heart, and its tawdry, shallow, ungrammatical haste evoked the physical image of its author.

'Dear Alan,' (read the letter)

You might at least have written and answered my letters but as I no your much too high and mighty to worry about me and what you've done to me so I think its time I started to stand up a bit for myself. Last week an officer friend of mine took me up to London and I specially asked him to take me through Ruislip where I know you live. No wonder your so high and mighty if you can live in a place like that and with all your money I think a dirty shame that you will not do anything for me and for your own son who as you know very well is not Jims.

So I have made up my mind what to do and it is this. Old Mother Midwinter down the road will look after the baby for me but she'll want paying for it of course and I don't see why I should when you and your Mother and dad have got all that money so I think you should give me three pounds a week to pay Mother Midwinter so I shall be free to go out like other girls do with my friends.

Unless you do pay me this money then I shall have to write to Jim and tell him the truth and that the baby is not his and then he will see what a fine friend he has, always writing about you in his letters. It is now Friday and these foreign posts aren't all that long these days because I looked it up in the stamp book, so I am giving you a certain time to do it, because I know you will try to dodge out of it by putting it off and I am not going to have it. You will get this letter next week and unless I here from you by Friday in a fortnight's time then I will write to Jim and tell him everything.

Yours respec.
Cora.

The letter was undated, but the postmark read unidentifiably in

March. 'Friday in a fortnight's time' would therefore have been in the middle of April at the latest – and Alan had collected the letter from the wrecked aircraft on May 19th.

There would undoubtedly be mail for Jim. At last.

Whether it would be at Siwa or at Kuffra, or right back at Cairo, was uncertain – but somewhere that letter was lying for Jim to collect, and it did not need much imagination on Alan's part to envisage the terms of brutal insensitivity in which its message would be couched.

He looked across at Jim's sleeping, shadowed form, the young face relaxed now and pillowed on the rucksack, the craftsman's hands lying palely across stock and barrel of the Tommy-gun.

The Tempter arose again in Alan's mind and he was too tired to thrust him violently away.

"All right!" said Alan tiredly. "For God's sake – all right! Maybe it would be better if I did kill him myself – but we've a long way to go yet and perhaps Jerry'll do it for me."

He looked at Jim again and dully pondered the question. What would be best for Jim – death or disillusion?

But the strain of the last forty-eight hours had been given opportunity to impose its impact by the relaxation which Alan had allowed to take place between himself and Jim, and as his mind left the immediate present and explored backwards in time, the curtain crept immutably down. Soon Alan too, was fast asleep. Occasionally, as the hours passed and dawn came, one of the other two would stir as though some force of guilt or conscience was dragging their minds to the surface – and then relax and sleep again, but Alan was so drugged by both physical and mental exhaustion that he was practically unconscious: he never moved.

Until they all awoke – suddenly, frighteningly – on the edge of battle.

Chapter 16

AN hour before dawn had broken, Perowne had gone up into the central watch-tower of the fort and flashed a code-signal back towards the Jebel Ahkdar and then westwards along the approach by which the L.R.D.G. trucks would come in. He flashed only a single letter – but this would be enough to tell those who were expecting it that El Machli was in our hands, while to those not expecting it, it would mean precisely nothing. He then remained in the tower.

Ten minutes after daylight had shown the colour of the foot-hills, five men rose from a fold in the ground just this side of them and walked confidentally across towards the fort. Sergeant Orr on the parapet first identified them through his binoculars, and shouted across to Perowne.

"Mr. MacLeod, sir – and four."

"Who's missing?" asked Perowne and after another brief scrutiny, Sergeant Orr shouted again.

"Hm," thought Perowne. "Could be worse!" and salved his sense of loss of a good man with the consolation that if Corporal Braddock had been taken prisoner and not killed, at least the Germans would get nothing out of him – except a load of trouble. *If* he had not been killed.

When the five men came in, Lieutenant MacLeod joined Perowne in the tower and the two men swapped experiences: MacLeod's party had destroyed three Messerschmidts and either ten or eleven Stukas on Ftaiah airfield.

"Bit of a mix-up at the end," explained MacLeod. "Braddock's party ran into trouble and we had to clear out, but I expect the I-blokes will be able to tell us the score: pity about Braddock though – don't know what happened to him. Where's all the rest of your chaps?"

Shortly, Perowne told him of the shooting-down of the trans-port 'plane, and when he had finished there was silence for a while.

"Ah well," said MacLeod. "More room for us on the trucks, I suppose. It's a bastard's way of looking at it – but what else can you do?"

"Nothing," said Perowne. "Nothing at all. Look, here come the trucks."

Lurching over uneven ground, but steadily, three unarmoured

30 cwt. Chevrolet trucks climbed out of a hollow and weaved their way between the dips and bumps of the desert lying to the west until they reached the edge of the flat plate which held El Machli in the centre. Then they picked up speed and raced towards the fort.

"Only three?" asked MacLoed. "There won't be so much room after all. I wonder what trouble they've run into?"

They were soon to find out.

"Got to get loaded up and out of here as quick as we can!" shouted the Captain in charge, as the leading truck pulled up in a cloud of dust in the centre of the fort. "Rommel attacked us last night and the other patrol's been ordered back to Kuffra to provide transport to evacuate the place. We've got to get down there before they clear out or we'll be stranded."

Perowne looked across at Rutledge, and then at the last of the three trucks as it roared in through the gateway.

"There are still two parties to come in from the hills, Captain," said Rutledge firmly. "They should be in soon: we must wait for them."

The Captain stared hard at Rutledge, then looked quickly around the courtyard.

"Let's get loaded up in the meantime, anyway, sir," he said. "We can decide how long we'll wait when we're ready to go."

Already the rucksacks and packs of the parashots and those members of Rutledge's group who were present were being lifted up into the trucks, and the men stood around talking and smoking, occasionally shouting up to the men on the parapet.

"Three more coming in, sir," shouted Sergeant Orr, now up in the tower with the Italian Breda machine-gun.

"Is it any of our chaps?" McCarran yelled up to him, but Orr shook his head after a brief look through the glasses. "Never seen 'em before sir!"

In the courtyard, Rutledge looked around at the members of his own group and wondered how long he could delay the exodus in the hope that the missing faces would appear. From the attitude of the L.R.D.G. Captain, it wouldn't be long – even now, in order to save time, he was sending out one of the trucks to collect the newcomers.

"Bit short on trucks, are you not?" O'Reilly asked an L.R.D.G. driver.

"Patrol's been split," was the answer. "Half went on up the Trig to Msus. One of ours broke down last night and we came on without it."

The sun was gaining strength, the heat beating in from the western wall of the fort. Corporal Pointer, up on the parapet, turned back and shouted down into the courtyard that the new-comers had been picked up by the truck which was now on its way back: then he turned and strolled along the side parapet. Halfway along he stopped, shaded his eyes and stared out across the desert.

"Hey, Jock," he called up to Sergeant Orr. "What the 'ell's that out there?"

There was an urgency in his voice which stilled the chatter in the courtyard and sent Perowne racing for the steps, leading up to the parapet. Before he'd reached the top, however, he knew the answer.

"Panzers!" yelled Sergeant Orr. "Thick wi' Jerry Infantry! We're boxed!"

Well out of range of any of the light weapons inside the fort, six Mark II Panzers cruised slowly up over the lip of the plate, diverged and came on across it from the south. Grey-clad forms clustered on the pre-historic backs, writhing out of the way of the long-snouted guns as they slowly swung, keeping the fort in their sights. As the space between the diverging troops widened, some of the infantry dropped off, and then a troop-carrier came up over the lip, disgorging a grey flood, them moved back again. contemptuously, over the lip.

The L.R.D.G. Captain was already out in the forecourt, waving away the returning truck, the second went nosing back out through the gateway, charged down the centre of the dump and swung westwards after the first, drivers flogging the engines, men aboard stripping covers from the mounted machine-guns, check-ing small-arms, clinging on to the sides of the trucks for dear life in a welter of bumping and bouncing equipment. As the third swung around in the courtyard, the Captain ran back through the gate and looked up at the figures of Pointer, 'Duke' Mallory, Perowne and McCarran still up on the parapet, frozen into immobility as they watched the careering trucks.

"If you jokers are coming," he snarled. "Come now!"

But even as he spoke the words, a tight knot of infantry out on the plain fanned out, there was a spurt of yellow flame and a mortar bomb started its slow, inexorable climb: in the tower, maddened by inaction, Orr threw up the sights of the Breda and fired a long burst out towards the re-grouping figures. Immed-iately, two tank guns cracked on the eastern side, one shell smashed into the wall of the tower just below the gun post and one howled flatly away across the desert, but the first gun cracked again and the Breda and Sergeant Orr were reduced to a tangled, bloody mess.

And in the sky above, the mortar-bomb had hung for a second and then started its plunge: as Perowne turned to answer the L.R.D.G. Captain, it crashed down among the stacked Jerricans in the forecourt and bursting, plastered the front wall of the fort with petrol and jagged metal. The gate, however, was open and through it hurtled a disintegrating Jerrican, dripping like thrown bath sponge, to smash squarely into the radiator of the last Chevrolet and flood the remainder of its contents over the hot engine.

The driver jumped clear, the petrol flamed, and the men on the body of the truck leapt clear. As they did so, a second mortar-bomb dropped out of the sky and burst violently in the courtyard itself.

Out on the plain, the western Panzer-troop were racing across to cut off the plunging trucks. To the watchers on the parapet it was obvious that the second one was doomed, but there was a slim chance for the first one – the one which had gone out to pick up the incoming party. The driver was getting the best out of a powerful engine and he had not succumbed to panic, steering across the open plain in a long sweep which would keep him moving directly across the field of fire of the gunner in the nearest tank, never along it. Twice the gun cracked, twice the shell-burst blossomed among the low foothills; then abruptly, the tank stopped, the long barrel swung well ahead of the racing truck – and the world waited. Unfortunately, the truck had now passed in front of the tank and the driver could no longer watch the German tactics, while the racket of the engine drowned the shouts of those in the back.

On raced the Chevrolet towards the lip of the plain beyond which it might find sanctuary – on it raced towards the channel in the sights of the tank-gun. Then the tank hiccoughed in the recoil, flame stabbed from the barrel, the truck seemed to disintegrate, one side peeling outwards, the whole chassis lurching over and over until it passed the point of balance, skidded on its side for a few yards with its cargo spewing out in a tragic trail, then rolled on over with its wheels spinning madly in the air. As it slid to a final halt, it burst into flames.

Back towards the fort, the second truck had stopped, its bonnet scarred and jagged, the driver slumped behind the wheel – killed by a burst of machine-gun fire from almost dead ahead and at point-blank range. The man beside him had been wounded but managed to grab the wheel and keep the truck under control until it came to a halt. Grey-clad infantry ran over towards it, climbed over it, disarmed the men aboard (Sergeant Drummond was one of them, and 043 Jones), drove the truck slowly away towards the troop-carrier.

On each side of the fort, the tanks ranged themselves in line abreast and moved purposefully inwards, their guns covering the figures on the parapet.

The trap closed.

On the parapet, Perowne watched the approaching tanks, looked across at the waiting infantry on the south and the blazing petrol dump in the courtyard which effectively blocked a possible escape back into the Jebel. There were five of them left alive – the four who had been on the parapet and Major Rutledge who at the moment of the explosion of the mortar-bomb in the courtyard had been running up the central staircase to see if Sergeant Orr was still within the scope of mortal help. Two of those in the courtyard had not been killed outright, but blast in that enclosed space had wrought such internal havoc that they had died within ten minutes: to look inwards from the parapet was to view a charnel-house.

"Can you afford to be taken prisoner, sir?" he asked.

Rutledge considered the question.

"I don't think it would be fair for you to take that into consideration, Mr. Perowne. You four can – er – live to fight another day. I had better make my own arrangements."

There was a pause while each wondered what might be entailed in that rather oblique suggestion, then Corporal Pointer came alive with the quick wits of his breed.

" 'Ere, sir," he said. "Give us papers and your identity tickets. Quick!"

With the few scraps of pasteboard which proved Major Rutledge's military existence, Pointer vanished down into the courtyard and returned with more papers and his hands bloodstained.

"You're Captain Masters, now sir, of the L.R.D.G. – an' fer Gawd's sake don't forget it! Better 'ang the old shirt out, sir," he said to Perowne. "Them tanks is too close to miss – and they might get impatient. We can't get out o' this lot – but we can out o' the cage."

He turned to the lean, slightly gangling figure of his friend.

"I take it, Duke," he said, " – that you speaks the old Deutsch like a native?"

"As a matter of fact, Reg," answered 'Duke' sorrowfully. "I'm afraid I don't. Not a word!"

"Bloody 'ell!" snorted Pointer in tones of deep disgust. "I thought you was supposed to be edjucated! Lot of 'elp you are in times of trouble. Ah well – " he said, looking grimly down over the parapet. "No doubt them bastards 'll be able to make themselves understood!"

PART FOUR

Chapter 17

IT had been the crack of the tank guns firing at Sergeant Orr followed almost immediately by the explosion of the first mortar-bomb amongst the Jerricans, which had awakened the three on the hill-crest. The unfolding catastrophe of the next few minutes was sufficient to push any thoughts of recrimination into the background and appalled, they watched the battle develop. They were nearly three miles to the North-east of the fortress itself, but although by the time the ring of German infantry closed around and actually entered El Machli, the heat haze was shimmering everything into delirium, the opening phases of the battle and the actual fighting had been clearly visible: the wrecked and burnt-out L.R.D.G. truck lay, in fact, on the lip of the plate just below them, less than a mile away.

Alan's first reaction had been purely instinctive – a cringing down against the earth as the unmistakeable howl of a falling mortar-bomb came faintly across to revive memories of Dunkirk – followed first by relief that he was not in the fort, then by growing alarm at the predicament which would face them when, inevitably, El Machli returned to German command. Immediate peril forced thoughts of Cora from his mind: pure self-preservation drove his brain, fresh again after its first real sleep for over a week.

"Two trucks?" he thought to himself. "Where the hell are the rest?" – and although his eyes followed the action and his brain registered its progress, this was the problem which lay all the time at the bottom of his mind, like an Alka-Seltzer tablet at the bottom of a glass of water – slowly bubbling, slowly coming to pieces.

Jim's feelings were of compassion and grim resignation, stirred towards action when the truck was wrecked.

"Let's get down there," he said. "Some of those chaps in the back of the truck might still be alive – might need first aid."

"Stay where you are, Corporal," snapped Lewis. "What good could we do? If they are still alive, then the enemy can look after them better than we can."

He stared savagely out over the scene, his eyes sucking in the sorry details.

"You must never have friends in wartime!" he suddenly hissed –

140

and there was something fanatical about his intensity. "Never, never, never!" – and with each insistence smashed his fist into the rock.

Jim stared at him in shocked amazement for a second, then relaxed faintly and turned away.

"Not so much friends," he said. "They're our chaps. British."

"That doesn't matter!" Lewis almost screamed the words. "There is no room for sentiment or affection if you're fighting a war. No room at all!" – and his words hung, unanswered, in the air as he stared defiantly at Jim's and Alan's carefully presented profiles, which showed Jim's mouth disapproving, Alan's slightly smiling.

As though baulked of opposition, Lewis's eyes returned to the details below – the smoking truck, the blazing petrol dump, the outlines behind it – and the ring of tanks and infantry slowly closing around the fort. Sweat ran down Lewis's face and dripped from the sharp-pointed chin and from the end of his nose. A sudden mirage showed a distorted figure standing on a platform, dispiritedly waving a piece of cloth: then the mirage elongated and vanished, and the trap of the nearest tank – the only one still clearly visible, was thrown back and the head and shoulders of its commander appeared. The tank moved off towards the fort, gradually losing its shape in the dust and heat-haze.

The battle was over.

There was silence on the hill-crest for a few moments, then simultaneously, both Alan and Jim turned and looked at Lewis, waiting for him to speak. It was a position which Lewis had obviously not visualised during the time he had been watching the conflict below, in fact he seemed to have given no thought to the immediate future at all: as a result, he had no suggestion to make nor orders to give, and fell into the error of blurting out the first thing that came to his head.

"I should put you on a charge, Lockyer," he snapped. "You slept while on duty!"

"If I hadn't" answered Alan levelly, " – we'd be down there. There's nothing to stop you going on down if you want to renounce the advantages of my dereliction of duty!"

He was suddenly feeling sure of himself again, the old certainty was returning, the ability to plan. Lewis felt the assurance and was impressed by it despite himself, but before he could recover and bark an answer to Alan's impudence, Jim interrupted.

"Look!" he said suddenly, pointing down toward the burnt-out truck.

Something – one of the dark shapes strewn back from the scar on the desert which ended in the black and smoking ruin – was moving. Through glasses they saw the shape move closer in towards the truck, obviously crawling on hand and knees, occasionally stopping by or detouring towards other crumpled tragic shapes on the way. Some yards from the wreck, the figure managed to struggle to its feet, swaying uncertainly, but after a few moments and an obvious effort, managed to walk steadily forward to encircle the truck.

"Who is he?" asked Alan, "Can you tell, Jim?"

"Too far away," grunted Jim. "He's just a moving blob to me."

"What does it matter anyway?" broke in Lewis – and some of his anger seemed to have evaporated. "If he's got any sense he'll turn back and give himself up at the fort – he doesn't know we're here and a man by himself – "

"We can soon put that right!" began Jim and struggled to his feet.

"Hold it Jim," interrupted Alan. "I want to see where he'll head first" – and there was something in Alan's voice which compelled attention.

Jim sat down again, looking at Alan curiously. Lewis frowned and stared through the glasses.

"He'll either go back and give himself up – if he's got any sense – or else he'll break back into the Jebel. In which case we can intercept him down there" – and Lewis pointed sideways with his glasses towards a jumble of foothills to their right.

"Ah!" said Alan. "But will he?"

And he lowered his glasses and watched the tiny speck below eagerly as it moved again around the truck and its debris. The expectant look was back in Alan's eyes, the half-smile, the confidence.

"Ah!" he said softly, and raised the glasses again, for the figure had left the truck and was moving steadily away towards the lip of the plate – but not towards them. It reached the edge of the foothills, paused for a moment, then disappeared behind a lift in the ground, came out behind it and moved purposefully on.

"Bloody fool!" grunted Lewis. "Where the hell does he think that'll get him?"

"He thinks it will get him to the rest of the L.R.D.G. transport – wherever that is!" said Alan with certainty. "And we'd better get down and catch him up."

He looked sharply at Lewis and saw – or perhaps only sensed – some of the irresolution which slopped fitfully behind the tight-held facade.

"I don't want to walk home – even if you do!" said Alan, and before Lewis's carefully built-up personality could explode into anger at this impertinence, Alan laid the ground-bait. "There are only two trucks down there, sir, and there can't be more than two or three in the fort because there's not room. Where are the rest?"

He pointed down towards the moving dot among the foothills.

"He's going to find 'em. Come on!"

He jumped to his feet, picked up his Tommy-gun and rucksack, and with a quick jerk of his head brought Jim to his feet. Lewis still lay, caught between a reasoning which his excellent brain could not fault and a position of subordination which his neurotic complexes would not accept.

"Do you think if I fired a burst it would attract his attention, sir?" asked Jim, with just the right degree of respect.

"Not yet – the enemy might hear it as well! Wait till we get down nearer to him!"

And Lewis was on his feet, leading away across the hill-top and down the other side.

Behind his back, Alan grinned across at Jim and winked – and the snatch at his conscience was remote and slight for there was work to be done: Cora and her machinations faded to the back of his mind. With Jim behind him, he scrambled along the hillside after Lewis, quite content not to lead for the moment and in complete agreement with the tactics Lewis was using.

"He's an intelligent bastard," he conceded to himself as he watched Lewis keeping parallel with the moving dot and above it, not yielding to the temptation to plunge down into the broken ground through which the quarry was threading his way, but in which he could quickly be lost.

They moved like this for nearly an hour until they were wet with sweat on the exposed hillside, and beginning to tire.

"Why the hell doesn't he ever look up?" swore Alan, staring down at the tiny moving figure which trudged implacably on, never resting, never turning.

"He's watching the tyre tracks," suggested Jim. "I reckon we could try a burst now – the Jerries are probably too busy to take any notice even if they heard it."

The same thought apparently struck Lewis, for he paused now, then led on up to a small outcrop upon which he climbed and stood, poised against the skyline. He waited until Alan and Jim had joined him.

"Get ready to wave everything you've got when he looks around," he said, then waited again while they stripped off their camouflage smocks.

"Right!" he said when they were ready – and fired a quick burst into the air.

The figure below trudged unheedingly on, without a check.

"Blast!" said Lewis. "Too far away!"

"Could we get down nearer?" asked Jim, but both Lewis and Alan shook their heads, for the ground immediately below dropped steeply and at the bottom they would still be almost the same distance from the quarry – who would now be out of sight. Moreover, they would themselves be almost indistinguishable from the dun-coloured background of the hillside should the man look around.

"We'd better all fire a burst together," said Lewis.

"Watch the ammo!" interjected Alan, staring curiously down at the still-plodding figure. There was something disconcerting about that implacable progress – and anyway Alan thought that the first burst should have been heard, for they were separated by less than a mile. However, they stood together, Tommy-guns raised, and produced a sgort, thunderous crash through half a magazine each.

Below the man trudged purposefully on, his eyes on the ground, his course unwavering.

"Blast!" thought Alan.

"Poor devil!" thought Jim.

"Concussion!" said Lewis.

And they stared perplexedly down at the man who might – or might not – provide for them the means of escape.

"Could you put a shot into the ground in front of him, Jim?" asked Alan. "That'd make him look around."

"Not with a Tommy-gun – at this range."

Alan's eyes went over the ground between them and the course the man would be probably taking for the next hour. From the foot of the hill, small, broken wadis and undulations spread far out towards the horizon, smoothing off into more level desert just before it disappeared into the heat-haze. The man's course was between the wadis and presumably a track was visible to him, though from above there was no sign of one, despite the fact that the whole scene was spread like a sand-table. Jim must be right – he was following tyre-tracks.

"There's only one way to catch him that I can see. You stay up here and guide us sir, and Jim and I will go down and try to head him off. We'll be able to see you up here all the time and you can direct us over to the right or left until we're in sight of him."

Lewis looked quickly up at the two of them, then frowned down at the scene below. He had already been manoeuvred into one course not entirely of his own choosing and although, once again, he could pick no logical fault in Alan's suggestion, he was damned if he was going to be ordered about by this young pup who obviously thought he was just as good as Lewis himself. He cast about in his mind for a reason at least to amend the plan, if not to change it entirely.

"After which, I suppose – " he said nastily, " – you two just push on ahead with this chap whoever he is – and I follow on as best I may."

There was a stunned silence while Alan and Jim stared back at him, but before either of them could speak, Lewis caught at another idea.

"There seems to me no reason at all for us to split up. We can ignore that fellow entirely, now I come to think of it – the only reason I didn't think of it before was because of this unnecessary idea of yours, Lockyer, that we should make contact with him. He's following a track, isn't he? All we have to do is to proceed due south from here and we'll hit that track. Then we can follow him along it."

"And suppose we hit other tracks first, sir?" pointed out Alan. "He's following a track which he knows to be right. We might hit German or Italian tracks first – or even some which the L.R.D.G. made weeks ago – and we won't know whether they're the right ones or not. They may lead us straight back to Slonta."

There was far too much truth in this for Lewis to deny, but before he baulked – as he would have done – at a complete retraction, Jim spoke up.

"Why don't you two go off and catch him, sir?" he asked. "I'll stay up here and guide you."

Lewis stared at the ground, shame goading his rising anger, his intelligence curbing it.

"Right!" he spat out, and without giving the others a chance to comment further, he started off down the hillside.

"I'll shoot that bastard before we get home, Jim," muttered Alan as he made to follow him, then paused again and dropped his smock and rucksack at Jim's feet. "I'll come back and meet you, chum. Bring those halfway and I'll carry yours afterwards."

He caught up Lewis at the foot of the slope and they set off across the first of the rocky, jagged wadis. As they climbed its far side, Alan looked back up at the figure on the spur above him, now pointing away to the right, and waved back cheerfully: he had managed to bury the future.

After a short while Lewis, who had taken in the facts of Alan's lack of burden with a rather pointed silence, accepted the wisdom of the idea and stripped off his smock, dumping it with his ruck-sack under a boulder.

"Leave it fairly visible, sir," said Alan with deliberate and rather polished malice. "Jim and I will collect it and bring it over. There'll be no need for you to come back."

And was rewarded by the crimson flush which crept up the back of the other's neck as he led off again, between hillocks and across wadis, moving easier now with just his Tommy-gun in his hands and the weight of Colt and water-bottle hanging from his belt.

Neither Lewis nor Alan had need to speak for some time, nor much breath to spare for it anyway – but always Jim's arm pointed away to the right and it began to seem incredible that they had not already passed well beyond the track the man was following. Their fingers bled from pulling themselves up the broken wadis, their feet burnt, their sinews ached.

"Where the hell is this bloody man?" asked Alan eventually, as he straightened up after a muscle-tearing scramble from the bed of a dried-out water-course, and wiped the sweat from his eyes.

"There!" said Lewis, suddenly pointing – and Alan turned his head just in time to see the quarry disappear behind yet another hillock. They were now close enough to make out head and shoulders but not close enough to recognize the man as anyone they knew.

"Could be one of the L.R.D.G. blokes, of course," thought Alan as they plunged after him again, aiming to intercept him on the other side of the hillock. "Probably be best if he is, too."

They ran quickly along a narrow, winding valley between more undulations, then up to cross a low col connecting two of them. Lewis was ahead and half-way up, when Alan caught his foot in a snag and was brought painfully to his knees. He heard Lewis's triumphant yell as he went over the top, followed by a click of a Tommy-gun bolt. As Alan pulled himself up to the col, Lewis fired, sending up spurts of dust well in front of the man – who was now less than a hundred yards away but had still apparently, heard nothing of his pursuit.

The effect of this burst, however, was immediate, for the man dived sideways into the cover of a boulder, his rifle coming down from his shoulder and into his hands with a facility which spoke of long training.

"Look out!" yelled Alan, his ever-active nerves shrieking out their warning – but Lewis was already charging forward, shouting at the man and waving, but still holding his Tommy-gun in the

Assault Position as carefully taught by instructors at battle-school and OCTU.

If he heard Alan's shout, he never acted upon it: there was a crack from behind the boulder, a flash – and Lewis seemed to check in his headlong rush, spin away sideways, pitch forward and roll over on to his back. He must have been dead before he hit the ground for he never moved, but as Alan stared unbelievingly at the ever-appalling sight of sudden death, the rifle cracked again and something snatched viciously at the woollen cap-comforter he still wore on his head.

Danger and tragedy are too vast in their effect to be appreciated so soon as the minor irritations; as Alan rolled over and over down the back of the slope, his Tommy-gun sliding away, his hands outspread to find and hold on to something to check his painful progress, his dominant emotion was of irritation and annoyance which did not really reach up even to the level of anger. "This – " he said, " – is just plain, bloody silly!"

He picked himself up at the bottom of the slope, recovered his Tommy-gun, remembering to wave up to the diminutive figure on the high spur, and looked up at the line of the col again and tried to work out what he should do.

What would he do if he were in the other man's position?

An unanswerable question, for he didn't know the entire explanation of the man's actions to date. He had presumably taken cover because he thought he was being attacked, but surely Lewis – despite his probable appearance of charging hostility – had been shouting loud enough for the man to recognise the English tongue, even if not until after he had fired the fatal shot? In which case why did he fire at Alan?

Was he still suffering from the effects of being flung from a capsizing lorry at high speed? If he'd hit his head at some medically crucial point, the results could be anything from permanent insanity or temporary amnesia.

"Oh no, it couldn't," Alan told himself curtly. "If he was plain nuts he wouldn't have followed the track so purposefully and if it was amnesia he wouldn't have started out in the first place: he knows what he's up to all right!"

He thought of the split-second reactions in the scene he had just witnessed and for a second he pictured it all again and heard Lewis's shout before he fired. He drew the only apparent conclusion and examined it. Then with a dry mouth and a pumping heart, he moved quickly away along the line of the valley until he came to a break on his left through which he crawled, keeping very low but making no particular effort to move quietly.

"I must be right," he told himself. "It can't be anything else!" But his mouth remained dry.

He crossed a low hillock flat on his belly, climbed through a wadi, and at the top found the tracks of lorries. He looked at them and wondered whether he had the courage to support his reasoning, eventually finding a compromise by leaving his Tommy-gun by the side of the tracks, drawing his Colt and walking forward with it held in his left hand behind his back – out of sight of anyone he might meet.

His heart thumped like a drum and he felt sick: but he walked on – his eyes fixed on the scene directly ahead. He went around one corner, then another. Ahead lay an outcrop and around the other side of that must be the rock from which the man fired while to the left lay Lewis's body. Alan reached the outcrop and leaned against it, gathering his courage.

"There's no other explanation," he told himself. "He'll probably realise you're British the moment he sees you – but if he doesn't, then the only hope'll be that he realises you're unarmed!" – and with considerably more cold-blooded courage than he had ever shown in his life before, he put the Colt down at the foot of the outcrop and stepped out into the middle of the track with his arms spread wide.

The immediate anti-climax brought with it a faint sense of the ridiculous, for there was no-one lying behind the easily recognisable boulder, but with sinking heart Alan realised that this only meant prolongation of his suspense: the man was somewhere – and had to be found.

He walked forward into the open, looked across passed Lewis's body and saw a khaki-clad figure working scientifically from cover to cover towards the col from which Alan had witnessed the death of Lewis. Lewis's body lay exactly as it had fallen, and with a sense of relief, Alan saw that it had not been examined: his theory still held.

Still keeping in the open and with his empty hands held well out from his body, he walked across towards the crouching figure. When he was five yards from it he augmented the crunch of his boots on gravel by a shout, but as he expected, there was no reaction.

There was in fact, no reaction at all until he actually placed his hand on the other's shoulder. Then the head and hands came round and Alan found himself looking into the blue, troubled eyes of Fusilier O'Reilly.

He was also looking almost straight down the barrel of that born infantryman's rifle and for a moment he thought that

O'Reilly's finger was going to work quicker than his brain. Then the rifle-butt dropped, the man stood up, still staring incredulously but with joyful recognition flaring in his eyes.

"Tes Lockyer!" he said, and then puzzlement darkened his face and he smashed his clenched fist hard into the side of his jaw, just below the jutting, out-spread ear. But his eyes never left Alan's face.

" 'Tes Lockyer," he repeated. " 'Es ut not?"

And Alan, whose conclusions had been correct, wasted no breath on words. He nodded.

Owing to some accident of falling and striking his head – or possibly of the explosion of the shell which had wrecked the L.R.D.G. truck – Fusilier O'Reilly was as deaf as a post.

Utterly, completely, stone deaf.

Chapter 18

TRUDGE, trudge, trudge, crunch, crunch, crunch and on they went over the never-ending gravel, up the water-course, down the wadi, between the hillocks, sometimes over the top of sanding dunes, in and out between low bushes and ever-scrawnier trees – always following the parallel patterns, listening for the sounds of an engine, praying that they would be in time.

Mostly they marched abreast – with O'Reilly in the middle continuously glancing at Jim or Alan to see whether they were talking, desperately afraid of missing something and rather pathetic in his boxed-in isolation. They took it in turns to carry O'Reilly's rifle for they had buried the Tommy-guns near Lewis's shallow grave and were travelling as light and as fast as they dared.

Why?

Because they must. Because they *must* catch that broken-down L.R.D.G. truck before it left! Left to go where? That didn't matter for although it might be coming along the track towards them and El Machli – it might not be.

And they must catch it – they must, they must, they must, they must. The words repeated themselves in Alan's mind with the crunch, crunch, crunch, crunch, of his boots on the gravel.

And his feet were beginning to hurt, too – that slight pressure on the inside of the right one, just behind the ball, which he had felt on the night's march from the cistern, had now resolved itself into a definite point of discomfort which would become pain when the leather sole wore thinner and the nail burst upwards through the lining.

But he had no time to stop now: they must get on, they must get on, they must get on! Left, right, left, right, left, right – by the book.

Not quite by the book.

They no longer marched upright for all three had developed a leaning-forward with the speed and the eagerness, which was being augmented now into a stoop by the beginnings of hunger and exhaustion. But for the moment, hope and fear kept physical weaknesses at bay.

For the moment.

But it was agony when they stopped.

And worse agony when they started again, although somehow they were always ready to move off when Jim's statutory ten minutes was up. Alan wondered whether he would have had the self-discipline to enforce a periodic rest if he'd been alone, and concluded that he wouldn't: the temptation to press on was so constant, so unremitting. The truck might be just around that corner there, or just over the top of that dune. It must be somewhere and it might be just ahead. If they rested, it might start up and go off, leaving them to die in the desert.

All right, perhaps it wouldn't – but you can't rest completely if you're frantic, and the sooner they found the truck and climbed aboard, the sooner the fear would leave his mind alone and he'd be able to rest properly.

"Right!" croaked Jim. "Ten minutes." – and without hesitation all three flung themselves down on to the burning sandstone and felt the pain ebb from their thighs and calves and the muscles reaching up from the small of their backs towards their shoulders, go slack with release.

Alan dragged his cap-comforter forward and crumpled it into a soft wad under his forehead and it was dark down there with the honey-coloured grit shadowed by his own head and no longer reflecting back into his eyes the hard incessant daylight glare. His feet throbbed. Sweat trickled out from under his arms and ran down across the curve of his chest until it reached the cloth of his shirt, and he put his right hand down and unbuckled his belt, dragging the hard block of his Colt out from under his thigh.

Then he put his arm outwards from his body again and eventually found a place where his hand could lie without pain on the burning ground. His mind had retreated now, dazed by light, stunned by fear, exhausted by hope – like his body, too weary to do anything but accept the present relief. A too warm point of irritation on the sole of his foot warned him of the pain to come, but he must ignore it and let his body suck what strength it could from peaceful ease.

His mind too must rest – he mustn't think.

So he lay inert, and let the worry, the tension, the guilt – and the fear – mount up in the recesses of his mind.

Beside him, lay O'Reilly.

Tes yr own fault entirely an' yu' know it well. If y'd not led such a wicked an' unholy life then this wouldn't hev happened at all, an' y'd ha' still bin ebble t' hear God's Creatures and sounds o' birds singin' an' men's voices an' women's too, wi' their nagglin' sometimes and their softness, an' whin they wrap their arms and legs around yu' an' draw the nature out o' yu' at both ends ut once.

Ye've only y'rself t' blame, an' don' go tryin' t' put the fault on t' others. Or on t' y'r luck – or on t' the Heavinly Father Himself or mebbe he'll strike yu blind too, wi' this sun always shinin' straight in y'r eyes – thut Father O'Malley alwus sed wus open an' innocent an' concealed a powerfu' lot o' sin an' forgetfulness.

An' he wus right.

Yu've no justification t' whine, Michael O'Reilly – or snivellin' now – whin yu' wouldn't go to the Holy Mass wi' the sun shinin' an' you hearin' everything that went on aroun', and the clink o' bottles an' the cool smell o' beer an' the sawdust an' the barman pullin' up the drink an' it gurglin' in the pot like a sweet stream over the rocks.

Ye've brought it on y'rself wi' y'r own forgetfulness an' sinful ways – so don't go sqawkin' now ye've bin hurt.

Though mebbe a couple o' Hail Marys wouldn't do any harm now, would they?

Y'r a back-slidin' louse O'Reilly, wi' no guts.

Ah, but they wouldn't now, would they?

Mebbe they wouldn't. All right then, let's try.

Hail Mary full o' Grace, the Lord is wi' Thee Blessed art Thou among women.

An' there yu' heathen hooligan – yu' can't go any further can yu' now? You an' y'r Hail Marys that yu' can't remember.

Hail Mary full o' Grace, the Lord is wi' Thee Blessed art Thou among women.

Well, then. Now whut?

A lot a good that'll do yu', Michael Sean O'Rourke O'Reilly – an' it's no less than yu' deserve, forgettin' the good words yu' were taught as a young laddeen.

Hail Mary full o' Grace, the Lord is wi' Thee, Blessed art Thou among women. Hail Mary full o' Grace, the Lord is wi' Thee, Blessed art Thou among women, Hail Mary. The Lord is wi' Thee, Blessed art Thou among women, Hail Mary full o' Grace.

The Lord is wi' Thee.

Blessed art Thou among women.

Blessed art Thou.

Blessed . . .

Blessed . . .

Blessed.

And slowly gathered into the protective arms of childhood faith, Fusilier O'Reilly fell asleep.

Jim lay against the hard sandstone and wondered how much

more of this they could all take. Somehow, he could force himself to keep up with the others, and knowing that his training had been as good as any in the world – for this or any other type of soldiering, he would not fail so long as he could guard against and suppress his own weaknesses. O'Reilly seemed in good shape – he should be: he came from a good Regiment, and Jim would under no circumstances allow himself to crack before a Fusilier, so this was something which should somehow give him, Jim, additional strength.

But would they both be able to keep up with Alan? And if not, would it be right for them to hold him back?

It most probably would be right to hold him back to a certain extent, for Alan still needed guarding. It was always the same with these brilliant ones: they had a gift for seeing a lot further than ordinary chaps like himself, but with their eyes on distant horizons they had a tendency to fall over their own feet unless watched. And helped.

Which was, after all, Jim's job.

And now for the immediate future–he supposed Alan did know what he was up to? This pressing need to rush forward – was it necessary? Well, yes – Alan's reasons were so simple and apparent that Jim had thought of them too, and was faintly disappointed when Alan did not produce some obviously more lucid and brilliant plan to get them home.

So they must press on.

But properly – with proper rest intervals: so Jim looked at his watch and saw that there were still ninety seconds to go before time was up, and he allowed himself to pass these in luxury, thinking of Cora and the baby.

Five seconds before the sweep hand came vertical, he rolled over and sat up, squinting again against the sharp sunlight.

"Right!" he croaked. "On our way!" – and he leaned over and prodded O'Reilly.

They marched on into the heat of the day until it began to stupefy them, then without discussion, the ten-minute break was allowed to stretch on and on towards an indeterminate moment of physical recovery. There was no way of fixing when this moment would be likely to arrive, for now even lying down in this remorseless heat seemed as fatiguing as marching had been previously. There was no shade except that which they could make themselves, and they could either lie face down and withstand the blast of the furnaces which then built themselves up between the sand and the contours of nose, lips and hollow of cheek, or they could turn over and submit their eyes once again to the sear of the sun.

Whichever way, there was no rest – either mental or physical, and Alan wondered fearfully when he would have that essential peace of brain and body for the complete picture of their position to form itself in his mind. The present trouble was that they were pursuing a course which had been arrived at, logically perhaps – but under a stress of circumstances which had kept him both mentally and emotionally occupied.

He had thought; he had felt – and he had not relaxed. Therefore he had not soared upwards until he could see everything and pluck the correct solution of their troubles with certainty from the revelation. In the cave before Guidano Corba, or on the hill-crest above El Machli, he had seen everyone's position and could see how and why they would act in the way they did.

But not know.

Now, he neither knew where the L.R.D.G. truck had broken down, where the rest of the patrol were, or what physical conditions surrounded them: therefore he couldn't tell how the men in command, or the drivers, would react.

And he was far too tired and worried to leave his mind alone, and let the missing factors fall into it, and take up their places in the picture: he was like a small boy who can't open the box to let out the last pieces of his jigsaw puzzle.

He wasn't even certain that there were any more pieces.

He only knew that he was not satisfied.

So he worried.

And that closed and exhausted his mind, even more.

The time passed. The sun leaned reluctantly over towards the west as though it too, had been affected by its own enormous labours and was feeling weak with the effort which had sucked every drop of moisture from the world around and crushed every speck of life down into the dust.

Some of the pain and heat eased itself out of the sky: it became possible to breathe without pain, to lie in peace.

Jim stirred and sat up.

"Come on," he whispered. "We must go on now."

Crunch, crunch, crunch. Crunch. crunch, crunch. Crunch, crunch, crunch.

The beat had changed: it was slower now and irregular, and not all its uncertainty came from the fading light. The ground was still hard, but flatter in general though uneven for bruised feet in worn leather. The tracks were more difficult to follow, for with the wider horizons, the alternative routes were many and when the tracks became faint it was no longer easy to judge from which direction the trucks must have come.

"It's no good, Jim," said Alan, when darkness at last brought a blessed relief to the body but more difficulty to the task. "We can't see the tracks easily now and we're wasting too much time and effort looking for them. For God's sake let's try to get some sleep. If we don't find the truck in the morning, we must go back into the hills."

Jim looked carefully around, staring away into the darkness.

"Up there then," he said, pointing to a low rise which seemed to constitute the highest point in the vicinity. "You and I will have to share watch, Alan. O'Reilly would never hear the engine if a truck went by."

But when this solution was made clear to him, Fusilier O'Reilly refused to have any part of it.

"Oi can stand up and walk aroun' all the time, can Oi not?" he asked defiantly. "An' ef they go by, at all, Oi'll see 'em. Oi'll do me stag with both of yu' – an' t' make sure Oi'll start off now. Now get yu' heads down, both o' yu'."

So Alan slept for two hours, woke in his turn and watched the empty desert, occupying some of the time by stripping, shaking the sand from his clothes and brushing it from his naked body. Then he walked softly and tenderly around in his bare feet until the cold drove him back into his clothes: he was still tired and he ached, but during that hour he managed to keep his mind free from worry, and deliberately avoided thought on any deeper problems than the condition of his boots and the amount of water left in his bottle.

The result was that he slept soundly from three o'clock until five and awoke clear-headed and refreshed. Half an hour later, he woke up Jim.

"We must leave the tracks and go due south," he explained. "By yesterday mid-day, the chaps on the truck which got left behind must have realised that something had gone wrong at El Machli – otherwise the others would have been back. They had two alternatives – either to go back down the Trig el Adb to meet up with the other half of the patrol who went to Msus, or snake around south of El Machli and try to find out what happened there. My guess is that that's what they did – went to El Machli."

Jim peered up at him through the early dawn half-light, and frowned.

"Seems to me more likely that they'd stay at their rendezvous if they were in any doubt," he said, pulling on his boots. "But I dare say you're right."

He looked across at the still-sleeping O'Reilly.

"We're going to have a hell of a job explaining to him why we're leaving the tracks."

In the event it proved absolutely impossible to explain to O'Reilly, but this did not affect the issue for after some minutes trying to break through the barrier of his deafness, the Irishman suddenly grinned, shrugged his shoulders and said "Well, 'tes no cause for argument anyway. Off wi' yu' an' Oi'll follow, for 'tes luck an' the will o' God 'll get us home, now – an' yu' can be just as right or wrong as Oi am!"

By full dawn they were on their way, limping over rough but level ground as their feet wore protestingly back into the battered shape of their boots and the muscles of their thighs complained against this renewal of effort.

It was nearly an hour afterwards that they saw the truck.

It was travelling due south and parallel to them and it was immediately evident that Jim had been right and Alan wrong in the diagnosis of how the truck commander would react. What was equally certain was that if they had waited until dawn and then followed the tracks, the truck would have been away on its southward journey long before they reached it: whatever had prompted Alan to move had saved their lives, although his reasoning had then taken them in the wrong direction.

Saved their lives?

The truck was moving rapidly away towards the south and unless someone looked around soon it'd be out of sight.

Fortunately Jim was carrying the rifle, and while Alan shouted and screamed and O'Reilly fired his Colt into the air, Jim dropped flat, and coolly and scientifically estimated the range, then made himself comfortable.

"For Christ's sake, Jim," yelled Alan. "They'll be gone!"

"Shut up, Alan," replied Jim curtly and dropped his head forward over the stock.

The rifle cracked and before the sound had died from the warming air, the bolt slocked out and back again.

"Two fingers laift an' y'r a hairsbreadth low!" shouted O'Reilly. "Yu must ha' pulled – but sight high!"

Again the rifle cracked, again the reload like a reflex but Alan was jumping up and down waving his shirt, and the truck seemed to be slowing.

"Get out of the bloody way, Alan," shouted Jim, shocked by the tension into most unusual language, and by annoyance too for Alan had lost control and rushed forward towards the truck, straight across Jim's sights.

But the truck had stopped, a man in the back was undoubtedly examining them through binoculars and as Jim got to his feet, another jumped down from the passenger seat and also raised glasses to his eyes. Alan was still running forward, but the two regular soldiers stood side by side and watched him, and looked past him towards the truck. The Irishman was grinning widely – with both relief and genuine amusement; Jim looked grim.

"Ah, boyo, he's all right!" said O'Reilly, slapping Jim on the back. "He's young yet – but he's learnin' fast. He'll not make a soldier – but one day he'll make a man!"

The truck circled and drove towards them across the flat, uneven desert.

"Who was the joker who put that shot across the bonnet?" asked a thickset, bearded New Zealander beside the driver, as the truck drew up in front of them.

"I was," answered Jim, vainly looking for some sign of rank.

"Well next time, be a bit more bloody careful," replied the Kiwi. "You damn near took off the end of my moustache! Who are you, anyway?"

Chapter 19

THE engine roared, the fat tyre span like a catherine-wheel and like its tail sand sprayed out from under it in a ten-yard long arc. Then the tyre found and bit on the steel channels, the truck lurched forward like a drowning man reaching for the bank, they all flung themselves frantically at its yellow, plunging sides and pushed and heaved to send it just that extra yard past the end of the channel, that extra foot nearer the far edge of this clinging, treacherous, infernal sand.

The channel whipped away behind them, the side of the truck dipped, the bonnet rose and swung away, the back wheels span again and sank to the hubs.

"Hold it!" they screamed vainly against the hollow din.

The sand flew, the back settled deeper, the engine stalled.

" —— it!" they said in the ensuing silence, and turned back to fetch the shovels, the sand-channels, the crowbars. Behind the truck, the smooth surface of the sand had been convulsed along a band four yards wide and two hundred yards long, telling the story of seven hours of sweat and profanity.

"God help us if a shifti-kite comes over," thought Alan during one of his few lucid, uncommitted moments that day, but the heat haze which made their condition so painful had at least given them some slight protection as well: they had not heard the searching 'planes above the tumult of their own enormous exertions – but the 'planes had been there, and only the pulsing mirage had saved the truck and its cargo.

As Alan leaned down to pick up a crowbar, he shook his head and waited – but now no drops of sweat fell, for he was bone dry. Earlier in the day, some hundred and fifty yards back, he had similarly bent to pick up the crowbar, seen the glistening drop fall and form a dark circle on the brown steel, then vanish completely within a second: he had almost expected to see a puff of steam.

He straightened and dragged the bar along to the truck to begin once again his present allotted duty in the routine task. The bar was thrust horizontally between the back axle and the sand until its point was some two feet in front of the axle: then Alan dug his way underneath until he could wedge a flat stone under the point to spread the load when it came.

On the other side of the differential, the bearded Kiwi – Ryman – was similarly occupied, while Jim and O'Reilly dug out the sand in front of each wheel and, the L.R.D.G. fitter, Corporal Vickery, and the driver, brought up the sand channels. Each time, the operation took at least fifteen minutes to complete – sometimes twice as long if the truck had gone too deep on one side.

Every hour, they exchanged duties.

In the grave beneath the truck, Alan jammed the stone in under the end of the bar, made sure its top surface was reasonably level, packed sand back under its near edge, then wriggled painfully and wretchedly back and out into the sun again. It was killing work and he had never felt so filthy.

He was sealed into his body with sand.

There was not one single orifice or pore, fold of flesh or joint of limb, which was not blocked or lined with grit: it filled his ears and nose, turned reluctantly to sludge between his teeth, grated under his eyelids, and split the skin between and beneath his toes. He was caked with it – and there was no point yet in even trying to brush it off, for hours of this searing misery still lay ahead.

Jim and O'Reilly climbed up out of the trenches they had dug leading back down to the front face of the black tyres, and Vickery and the driver dragged forward the channels and forced them deep along the bottoms of the trenches. Then they straightened up, and without a word, the driver climbed back into his seat, the others took up their positions.

Jim faced Alan across the back end of Alan's crowbar, Ryman and O'Reilly paired on Ryman's, Vickery waited on the near side of the truck. The starter whirled, the engine fired: the four men at the back stooped and gripped the steel bars. Then the clutch went in, the truck shuddered, the off-side rear wheel span and Alan and Jim were enveloped in a stinging, yellow cloud.

"Now!" yelled Ryman – and they all lifted frantically on the shuddering bars to lever the truck that important fraction forward.

Inch by inch their hands rose, note by note the engine whined up the scale, the sand stung sharper, the hot rubber shrieked and stank, then found the edge of the channels and the truck leaped forward. They dropped the bars and flung themselves against the back of the truck, grinding their shoulders under the steel framing, their hands gripping the top of the tailboard, their arms rigid, their leg muscles bulging, their boots driving deep into the sand under them as they sought almost to lift the plunging, heaving truck forward and out of this sea of hot agony.

Then the engine note soared again, the wheels span, the bonnet swung up.

"Hold it!" they yelled.

159

The engine stalled.

They were ten yards further on.

They turned and went back for the channels, the shovels, the crowbars.

It had been like this since first light.

They had waited all the previous day close to the northern edge of the wide strip known as the Trig el Abd, in a small wadi which gave only the cover afforded by its irregular shape. When, by evening, no other trucks had come in from the direction of Msus, the New Zealander Ryman announced that they must cross the Trig that night and try to get as far south as they could before dawn.

"If orders have come through to evacuate Kuffra," he said, "those jokers down there won't leave anything for Rommel or the Wops to use – or for us. What they can't take with 'em, they'll burn all right – and its a long, long walk from Kuffra back to the Nile."

"Couldn't we make for Siwa?" asked Jim.

"You can if you like," answered Ryman. "You could do it, too, I reckon – about ten day's march if yu' feet'll stand it. But our orders are to get back to Kuffra – and that's where we're going."

"We'll come with you," said Alan quickly. "Siwa sounds a long way off."

"Too right! You might not hitch another lift like yu' did this morning!"

So they had started out as soon as the light had gone, crossed the Trig without incident and when later, the moon rose, made very good time down towards the edge of the Great Sand Sea, which they had intended to skirt to the westward. Then less than an hour before dawn, the truck had suddenly lost momentum, the wheels had churned and the near side dipped alarmingly. Alan, dozing in the back among the rucksacks and camouflage nets, had woken to a distinct impression of being on a sinking ship, an impression heightened when he was engulfed in unrolled netting.

"Out all!" shouted Ryman briefly. "Stuck!"

And what the three from Rutledge's party didn't know about the technique of 'unsticking' trucks, they soon learned. The only error of judgment of which the New Zealander could be accused, was that it might conceivably have been safer for them had they retraced their route for a matter of eight miles to the nearest cover behind them, then spent possibly the whole of the next night trying to find a way around this long but narrow strip of soft sand.

"We may not find it then," he argued when the suggestion was raised. "Then we'd be twenty-four hours or more behind schedule. Let's have a crack at getting across now – it may not be as bad as it looks."

Unfortunately, it was every bit as bad as it looked – and maybe a bit worse. Dawn came and passed, and by the grace of the protecting Powers, no enemy air patrols came their way until the heat haze had blanketed the area with its waves of distortion, by which time the truck was nearly thirty yards on into the sand strip.

Now it was late afternoon, and to all of them it seemed that for their entire lives they had fought and heaved and cursed and dug in that yellow sea of frustration. They were drained of strength, but anger kept them going – an unrelenting rage kindled by the dull, unreasoning obstinacy of the soft desert.

The starter whirred, the engine fired, the wheel span. Again they heaved at the crowbars and flung themselves at the lurching truck. Again the stinging spray, the strain, the stalled engine.

"Sweet Mother o' God," said Ryman, long past profanity. "Not much further – and it's cooler now!"

They fetched in the tools again.

The end of their labours was somewhat nearer than they thought, for they had been crossing what was virtually a long crack in the rocky substrata of the desert which had in time filled to the brim with drifted sand. In the middle the sand had been some eighteen feet deep, but the fault shelved up steeply from the bottom then shallowed off to either side. Twenty yards and two stages further took them to a line where the soft sand was only twenty inches deep, and when next they dropped the crowbars and flung themselves against the truck, it kept moving away from them – occasionally skidding away sideways it was true, and sometimes the rear wheel span again, but the truck never stopped altogether and eventually went forward without their efforts, first pulling them – cheering hoarsely – then leaving them behind, with hope and anguish and frantic satisfaction warring together in their minds.

Then it reached the visible edge of the sand and ran on to hard rock, and they all staggered on after it across the last of the sand – leaving the crowbars and the shovels where they lay – so that they could slap its sides and kick its wheels, and laugh and curse around the symbol of their gigantic effort.

The release of spirit was too much for the maintenance of hard common sense.

"To hell with the expense!" croaked Ryman. "Brew up!" – and not even Jim was cautious enough to demur – so that when the 'planes came, they were caught well out in the open with no sign of cover nearer than the horizon.

The Stukas formed part of a squadron which Rommel had deliberately ignored in his order of battle for that day, employing them on routine sweeps to keep his lines of communication clear instead of over the battle area. When they returned to base for re-fuelling the squadron pilots had endured some caustic denigration from those who had been more perilously engaged – and their resultant annoyance was not mollified when it became obvious that any dangers threatening Rommel's lines of communication were being most efficiently dealt with by ground forces.

When, therefore, through the gradually lifting heat-haze, they made out the flickering outlines of a truck below them, instead of dismissing it as just another deserted and probably burnt-out wreck, they swooped down to investigate.

But if there was no cover beneath which the truck could hide, there was at least plenty of room in which it could manoeuvre and Corporal Vickery and the driver, who had been checking over the engine, acted with commendable unison: at the first sound of engines as the Stukas came roaring down at them out of the sun, they slammed down the bonnet and leapt for the seats. O'Reilly was standing in the truck body ferreting through the chaos to which the cargo had been reduced to find the tea and sugar, and although he heard nothing, he felt the jerk as the bonnet came down and looked around in time to see the 'planes sweeping in low, white globules dropping from the leading edge of the wings.

With a hoarse roar and all the surging emotion of his race, he leapt for the mounted gun and as the starter whirred and the engine fired, he ripped off the gun-covers. The 'planes screamed by, the machine-gun bullets ploughing the sand each side of the truck, and as they climbed to circle back, the truck leapt forward and raced off across the desert, throwing O'Reilly down among the tangled nets and tumbling rucksacks.

As he fought his way clear of them and back towards the gun, Corporal Vickery pulled himself over the back of the front seats into the truck-body with him.

"Get rid of that petrol!" he shouted – and by example made his point: as the truck swung and circled and the Stukas came in again, Vickery and O'Reilly fought to unstrap the reserve jerricans and fling them out on to the sand. Then the 'planes came in again, one from the rear, one from each side, the props almost feathering in the attempt to keep down the air-speed. The truck jinked to the right, the 'plane from the left swooped in: the truck jinked left, the 'plane climbed again and the one from the rear dived steeply to drop its bomb five yards in front of the truck bonnet. Sand, rock and shrapnel erupted from the desert and as the truck lurched blindly through it all out on the far side, the right-hand 'plane dropped like a hawk and delivered the death-blow: its bomb landed about eighteen inches behind the driver's seat.

The 'planes circled again, the pilots watching the flames, the smoke, the occasional spurt of exploding ammunition: then they flew across the desert towards three black spots moving spasmodically towards the holocaust. For a moment, the senior pilot considered trying a little practice on the midget, moving targets but was deterred both by the technical difficulties and by the dangers of such low-level intricacies. Besides, there was a much simpler way: he picked up his microphone and addressed his command.

"Verschwende deine Kugeln nicht und lass die vor Durst sterben!"

They climbed and roared off back towards their base.

Below, the moral effects of the catastrophe and the physical effects of the day's exertions made themselves felt. All three suddenly stopped running, Alan slumped first to his knees, then flat on his stomach, the other two limped slowly on towards the now black and smoking wreck: it was possible to make out the body of the driver and there was something in the back which might well have once been a living head and torso – nothing else was identifiable.

"Why the hell couldn't they have come *before* we crossed that bloody sand?" whispered Ryman bitterly.

Jim made no reply but stepped in nearer to the wreck. A yard from it, he was beaten back by the waves of heat, so he looked back over the desert towards the nearest of the jettisoned jerricans, limped over to it and forced open the plug. Then he carefully reclipped it, moved on to the next and did the same. Ryman watched him dully for a time, then limped over to the still prostrate form of Alan and crouched down beside him. He shook Alan's shoulder.

"Had the brew-can been filled?" he asked.

Alan raised his head in sudden desperate realisation, shook it, then rolled over and sat up.

"No," he said dully. "I was mixing the petrol into the sand, O'Reilly was looking for the tea, and Jim was cleaning out the dixie. I'm pretty certain he hadn't filled it."

They both looked across at the still-smoking heap, then at the plodding figure moving between the jerricans.

"He won't find any water in them," said Ryman. "They're petrol, all right."

He looked around at the empty scene, then up at the clear, cooling sky.

"It's going to be a long walk," he muttered.

They sat together in silence until Jim reached and examined the last jerrican, then left it and came slowly across towards them.

"Any hope of water still in the truck tanks?" he asked briefly, squatting down with them.

"Always hope," replied Ryman. "But not much."

"How far to Siwa?" asked Jim.

"Two hundred miles – maybe two fifty."

"Ten days?"

"More like twelve."

"Without water."

They sat in silence, listening to the cracks and sudden whines of the cooling metal.

"We could go back to the Jebel," offered Alan eventually, putting into words what they were all, in fact, thinking.

"Let's see if there's anything to help among that lot first," said Ryman. "Even if there's not, we could still try to reach Siwa. One of our jokers walked for nine days once, back to Kuffra. He was still on his feet when they found him."

"Nine days," thought Alan. "Ten days for us – perhaps twelve. Under this sky!"

Jim got up and walked across to the wreck again, but the heat still pulsed out from it and the metal would have blistered the skin.

"Now's the time to rest," said Ryman. "It's cool now and we're all dead beat. I'm going to get rid of some of this sand I'm carryin' round, then get my head down. If I can remember my prayers, I reckon I'll say 'em."

It was advice to follow. For fifteen minutes Alan shook sand from his hair and clothes like castor sugar from a shaker, and brushed layers of it from his skin. Then he lay down and pillowed his head on his boots, staring up into the purpling sky. For a short time, his mind worried at his problems, until physical exhaustion saved him and he fell asleep: his last conscious thought was that after getting out of France, he was damned if he was going to be taken prisoner now – despite the facile solution which such a fate seemed to offer.

When he woke up, Ryman and Jim were already turning over the charred remains of the netting, rucksacks and assorted paraphernalia which had made up the cargo of the truck. Every now and then flames would shoot up as air reached smoldering fabric, and there were distorted but nightmarish shapes laid apart on the sand.

But the water tanks had split, and their precious contents had been sucked away by the heat or drunk by the thirsty sand below – when with sinking hearts they forced open the taps, nothing dropped from the spouts other than charred remnants of the washers. They searched grimly and silently through the tangled mess, and one by one the remains of the water-bottles came to light, in each case with seams gaping where the contents had boiled in the heart of the fire, and burst the thin metal. At last there was no more hope.

"What about the engine?" asked Alan suddenly. "There's water in the radiator, isn't there?"

Ryman laughed like a watchdog's single bark.

"There was before the rubber hosings burnt through," he said bitterly. "Look at that!"

The sheet metal of the bonnet had warped up like a saucer and through the yawning gaps could be seen the blackened cylinder-head, the bare distribution wires, the top of the radiator and the metal pipe jutting down from the top of the radiator grill, its inch-wide mouth surrounded by a black ring of sticky, stinking, charred rubber. Ryman seized the edge of the buckled bonnet and pulled it back, filling the night with the jangle and rasp of sheet-metal. He looked bitterly at the split battery, the charred bakelite covers, the filters choked with black stuff, and as his nose and mouth filled with the bitter acrid stench, he swore steadily and monotonously.

Then suddenly his voice stopped and there was a quality in the silence which followed which rooted both Jim and Alan to the ground. Ryman's hand came up and he wiped his mouth, then very quietly and steadily, he said, "Jim. Empty one of those jerricans and fetch it in, will you?"

His voice held so strong a warning against hope that without a word, both Alan and Jim turned and walked over towards the nearest jerrican and emptied it, both intent on cultivating an unusual pessimism, but as the last of the petrol gurgled out on to the staining sand, their eyes met. They turned again and ran back towards the truck.

"Now don't flap!" snapped Ryman as they came up. "There's not a hope really, but we might try it. Some joker's replaced the rubber hosing at the bottom with metal sheathed stuff, and it doesn't look as though the fire got to it. We'll have to wait anyhow, until the petrol's dried out of that can."

They took it in turn for a while to blow into the can to try to dry it out, then at Alan's suggestion they collected fine running sand from the edge of the sand pocket, half filled the jerrican with it, shook it around inside then emptied it, carefully watching the colour of the sand. The last to come out was slightly brown and damp, but the smell of petrol from the spout of the can was considerably reduced.

"Wrap it in some of that smoldering netting," said Ryman, and for an endless five minutes, they sat around the drying can, deliberately keeping their minds devoid of anything except the probability of a return to the Jebel.

"Right!" croaked Ryman, and they carried it over to the truck and carefully propped it under the radiator so that the small, yawning mouth was below the radiator tap. Ryman turned the tap.

Nothing happened.

"Possibly sludge," said Ryman unemotionally. "There's a wrench in what's left of the tool-box."

While Jim and Alan fumbled for the wrench, Ryman ripped a single strand of wire from the bared distribution leads. He took the wrench, reached down and began slowly twisting off the tap, and when it was half way out of its seating he crawled under the engine and put one end of the strand into the jerrican mouth, still holding the wire in his left hand as he unscrewed the tap with his right.

As the tap came clear, he jabbed into the seating with the free end of the wire: thick, brown mud oozed reluctantly through the metal circle and started to slide along the wire. Impatiently, he scooped it away with the fingers of his free hand, still probing with the wire held in his left.

Then Jim and Alan, silent and unbreathing, heard his soft, incredulous whisper.

"Thank Christ!"

Water tinkled musically into the jerrican.

Chapter 20

By dawn they had covered nearly seven miles and the rhythm of march had worked its way well into their limbs and their minds: the only breaks came at the hourly rests which Jim had persuaded even the reluctant Ryman were necessary. After each break, the one who had been walking unburdened during the previous stage would take the rear end of the stretcher upon which they carried the half-full jerrican. It was not a stretcher really – it was two pieces of blackened angle iron which had formed the frame of one of the truck sides, with the jerrican lashed between them in the middle, but the assembly was carried by two of them in the same manner as stretcher-bearers carried their equally precious burdens.

Then the sun lifted itself above the eastern sand and they knew that their ordeal was about to begin. The edges of the angle-iron bit into Alan's hands as he carried the forward shafts, the taste of petrol and oil still lingered rankly on his tongue and between his teeth, but Ryman, well out in front, trudged sturdily along and some of the New Zealander's undaunted certainty of purpose communicated itself to Alan.

And Jim carried the rear end of the stretcher, his step the regimental length, his rhythm exact.

"We'll make it all right," Alan told himself. "It's a bloody long way, but we've got enough water if we take it carefully."

Two hours later however, it needed a good memory and a lot of faith to keep going: the water they had drunk before setting out had been sucked out through their skin, and their eyes were stinging with the glare. Alan was at the rear of the stretcher now and the metal was fast becoming too hot to hold, while the water which looked such a paltry amount when considered as the life force for ten days for three men, took such toll of his strength and imposed such torture on his shoulder and arm muscles that at times he had already caught himself wondering if it was worth the effort.

Ryman marched doggedly on between the front shafts, but surely his head was a little lower, his step not quite so certain?

Alan brought up his own head, caught sight of Jim well ahead and nothing but the shimmering haze beyond him. But the direction was right – soon they must hit the edge of the Sand Sea; some two hundred miles eastward along its northern edge, lay Siwa.

Deliberately, Alan surveyed the assets they possessed, individually and collectively. They were all young and they were all fit: they had nearly two and a half gallons of water between them, which would allow a ration of at least half a pint each per day – not much, but enough – and although they had no food, the thought of death from hunger did not seem very real. In fact death from any cause did not seem near, and Alan took some satisfaction from the thought that it was not fear which kept it from his mind, neither was it entirely hope.

"Hold it chum," grunted Ryman from in front.

Surprised, Alan stopped and lowered his end of the stretcher. Ryman stood up, massaged his stomach and belched.

"That's better," he said, blowing out his cheeks.

They picked up the stretcher and started off again, but they had to stop once more before the rest period came around and the same thing took place. By the time the next stage was complete, with Alan in front of the stretcher and Jim behind – it was becoming evident that something was wrong, for Ryman marched continuously with his fingers massaging his belly, and a long, overwarm probe which promised to start burning soon was exploring Alan's gut just behind his solar plexus. Jim too, occasionally grunted with stomach pains. The odds were shortening.

Then about midday, they saw through the heat haze the half-sinister, half-familiar outlines of a deserted fifteen hundred-weight truck, and in the shade beneath it they found a temporary shelter from the blistering, maddening sun.

As they lay panting in the meagre shade, each one dug his fingers into the soft muscle below the belt-line.

"Do you think the water's definitely bad?" asked Alan, eventually.

"Search me," grunted Ryman. "It's been boiled enough times in that radiator, God knows. It must be some muck that got into the engine-jacket, or something in the jerrican with the petrol – maybe they had cylinder-lubricant in it which didn't dry out completely."

"Let's see if there's any water left in this engine," suggested Jim, but there wasn't, for the fifteen hundred-weight had obviously been there a long time, probably since the time of Wavell's first offensive.

"There's a hundred reasons," said Ryman, when Alan wondered how it came to be there. "On our patrols we come across trucks dotted about all over the desert – some left by the Wops, some by ourselves. When the big retreats start, chaps just drive until they run out of juice or get shot up. Then they either hitch a lift if they're in convoy, or start walking or blow their brains out if they're alone. Mostly they blow their brains out."

They lay beneath the floor of the fifteen-hundredweight until nearly five o'clock when the sun, if not relenting in its impartial anger, had at least begun its dip towards the horizon. With rest, the pains seemed to have eased, the internal pressures dispersed.

"Are we going to drink now?" asked Alan, conscious of his swelling throat.

"Let's get as far as we can," suggested Ryman. "We don't know what's going to happen next time we drink that stuff. Anyway it's best to wait until the cool of the evening."

Gradually the fierce enmity of the day dispersed, the air cleared, the blue waves of the mirage disappeared and some of the weight of breathing went with it. Alan could walk upright again, still harnessed by his arms to the angle-iron – the hour's freedom was so short, the two hour's spell so unending. He could feel the nail working up again in his boot, for although he had managed to beat it flat with a tyre lever before they started off that morning, there had been no pliers to rip the offending spike completely out. But there was still the essential problem of the water.

Would it poison them?

Or would it save their lives?

As the ball of the sun touched the world behind them, Ryman put down the front end of the stretcher.

"Well," he croaked. "What do we do?"

Alan looked at Jim and then back to the New Zealander.

"Christ!" he thought, "If we look like this now, what are we going to be like in twelve day's time?"

Aloud, he said "Let's just wet our mouths now. We can carry on for another stage or two before we stop and get our heads down. If we drink then, perhaps it won't affect us so much lying down."

Once again the biting steel, the weight on the arms, but Alan was faintly conscious now of a new kind of satisfaction: his had been the choice – and a difficult and unpleasant one. It was Alan too, who later in the night called and insisted upon a long halt – against the continual, nagging pressure to get on at all costs. While strain began to weaken the others, Alan found strength.

They each drank, slowly and luxuriously, a half pint of the tepid oily liquid which they had brought with them, filtered with hope through a piece of Alan's shirt into the blackened metal mug which Ryman had carried all day hanging from his belt. Then, surprisingly, they slept, their muscles easing out from the taut knots into which effort had tied them, exhaustion drugging their minds before doubts and worries could nag them away from sleep.

But Alan awoke to the sound of retching, and when he rolled over to go to Ryman's help, pain twisted his bowels and wrung the strength from them. Ten minutes later, the worst of the pains had subsided and all three lay weakly on the ground, despair reaching icily towards their hearts.

"Come on," whispered Alan at last. "We must only wet our mouths from now on."

Without a word, they rose to their feet and struggled on, the dark blue fading from the sky, the glare coming up over the forward horizon.

At daylight, Alan was alone in front, Jim and Ryman carrying the stretcher, and at first Alan thought that the blinding light of the sun in front of him was already breaking down his sight. There was a black shape somewhere at the bottom of his vision, but when he tried to look at it, white, red and yellow spears slid through his brain. He stopped, knelt down, shaded his eyes and looked again. Then the sun shifted infinitesimally and he saw the shape clearly. It was a figure dressed in khaki, lying on the ground – and Alan had seen enough of death by now to know that this one had reached and passed his limit.

When they reached the spot, the story was clear enough – and one which struck only too close home. There were no badges of rank on arm or shoulder and identity discs revealed the rank as Driver, but one shot had been fired from the revolver and Alan wondered wryly whether the boy would have 'acquired' the weapop if he could have foreseen the use to which he would eventually put it.

"Can't have happened very long ago," croaked Ryman. "Last night maybe."

"Wouldn't we have heard the shot?" asked Alan.

Ryman picked up the gun, pulled back the hammer and fired into the dunes. The noise was surprisingly soft.

"It's automatics that make the row," said Jim, " – and this is only .38 anyway. We'd have heard a forty-five."

Alan looked down at the immature face on the sand. The bones were fine, but the chin was sharp and the mouth soft: what beard there was, was fair and fluffy, and there was no swelling around the throat.

"He wasn't half so thirsty as we are," said Alan softly. "Where's his truck?"

They found it less than an hour later and at first sight the only thing that was wrong with it was that the petrol tanks were bone dry. It was a Bedford three-tonner.

"Panic and bloody ignorance," said Ryman caustically. "It kills more men out here than the eighty-eights."

"Here's the work ticket," said Alan from the driver's seat. "Where did he come from? Doesn't say. Last entry on the fourth."

His eyes suddenly narrowed and he looked down at Jim standing by the door. As the same thought struck both of them, Ryman reached the bonnet and flung it back.

There was no need for anyone to ask – the angle of the radiator-tap was sufficient and there was not a drop of water left in the engine; the young driver, having lost himself in the desert, had remained with his vehicle in the hope that someone would find him before the time came when all the water was gone. Then – and only then – had he set out to save himself – and the silence and loneliness of the desert had broken his will long before his body had reached the end of its resources.

They leaned against the side of the truck, in the shadow – and for a long time in silence.

"Nine days at least," said Alan, breaking it. " – And that water's poison, to all intents and purposes."

Ryman and Jim looked at him, waiting for the suggestions.

"We could put it in the radiator," said Alan softly.

Ryman grunted.

"Is there anything else wrong with the lorry other than lack of petrol?" asked Alan.

"Not that I can see," croaked Ryman.

He looked bitterly at the looming truck, the filler cap dangling mockingly at the end of its chain.

"God damn it," he exploded. "We can't go all the way back and fetch the petrol."

"You can't," agreed Alan. "Your guts seem to be taking it worse than Jim's or mine. You had dysentry some time?"

Tight-mouthed, Ryman glared at him.

"Anywhere a Pommie goes," he grunted, " – so can a Kiwi." Alan grinned.

"That's not the point, chum," he said. "Two *must* go – all the way. You stay here and rest, then come to meet us. We'll need your help by then – you'll probably have to carry the petrol *and* us."

In the silence that followed, Alan felt a new certainty of mind, a realisation of the change in values which had taken place in him. Ryman would agree.

"It's all of twenty miles back," said the New Zealander. "Do you think you can make it?"

"We can make it there all right," answered Alan. "Can't we Jim? Whether we make it back here'll probably depend more on you than on us – we'll try to bring back two jerricans."

Before they left, Alan again flattened the nail in his boot, and they searched for and found the driver's water-bottle.

"I suppose there'll be enough left to stop the engine boiling?" he asked, as it was filled from the reeking jerrican.

"Doubt it," said Ryman. "We'll have to stop every few miles to let the engine cool – but it'll be better than walking. I'll start out to meet you tomorrow morning."

When they passed the dead driver again, the heat was building up and they took his socks and shirt with a swift, unfeeling ruthlessness, but there was neither time nor energy to spare for burial: they hurried onwards into the heat haze. They marched side by side, but without a word spoken and a strength to the bond between them which it had never had before – but wryly, Alan thought of the shock which soon it must bear.

"If it's only the friendship which breaks," thought Alan, " – the price'll be cheap. It's Jim I'm worried about."

But the problem did not loom so large now – for most of the picture was filled with heat and thirst and the thought of the weight of nine gallons of petrol. And soon the thought of the weight of the petrol faded and only heat and thirst remained, for there was no shade at midday when they were going back over footprints made the previous evening, and the wreck of the fifteen hundred-weight lay two hours ahead. The sun struck down, hammering through the tops of their skulls and pile-driving at the bones at the base of their necks: for minutes on end they forced themselves along with their eyes virtually shut, opening them to mere slits to keep themselves on the line of footprints.

After a while, they began to fall – and each time it took a little longer to get up until each realised that whatever happened he must keep the other on his feet. Things went a little easier after that, and at last they reached the deserted truck and crawled into the dark furnace beneath it just before the sun started to slide down the sky.

"We must re-time this lot," thought Alan as he floated on the edge of consciousness. "The sun will kill us tomorrow if we try to walk through it, carrying the petrol."

They recovered as darkness shielded the land, and after wetting their tongues and throat, crept out from under the fifteen hundred-weight and went on again. Tiredness now and lack of food began to make itself felt, and Alan's legs below his knees were rubbery, almost numb: he found that the best manner of progress was to lean forward slightly, then force his feet to keep up with him.

Every hour they would rest for ten minutes, but each time the effort to begin again was greater. An hour before dawn, they stumbled over the edge of the horizon which held the burnt-out Chevrolet, and as light grew they saw the black dots of the jerri-cans.

"Now the trouble really starts," thought Allan.

By the time the sun was well up, they had collected two of the cans, topped them up completely from another and were lying in the skeletal shade of the wreck.

"We're not moving from here until this evening," Alan had said, but they were both conscious – not only of the passing of time – but also of Ryman struggling through the heat of the day towards them. Anxiety and faint guilt troubled both of them, and sleep would not come.

Moodily, Alan got to his feet and limped idly around the blackened shambles: on the far side lay an indented disc – the bare remains of the spare wheel. Alan looked down at it for a moment, passed his hands across his cracked lips and tried both to think clearly and not to hope too much: from the centre of the disc sprang a long cup which presumably took the end of the half-shaft. He picked up the wheel, climbed over the ribs of the truck-body and tried to fit it on to the top of the gun-mounting: but it was no good, for nothing was the right shape, the right length, or the right diameter. He sat on the frame work, trying to think what to do.

"The tyres are still on the front wheels," said Jim suddenly, from under his feet.

"Have we got a jack?" asked Alan carefully.

"I don't know! Maybe. What do we want a jack for?"

"Must have a jack to take off the wheels," said Alan, his eyes travelling from heap to heap of blackened rubbish in the hope of seeing something recognisable. The light was beginning to hurt his eyes again.

"Alan?"

"Yes?"

"What do we want to take the wheels off for?"

The metal of the gun-mounting was almost too hot to hold, but he gripped it tightly.

"Christ!" he prayed. "Not that! Not Jim!"

He tried to think what to say, how to grapple with delirium in addition to everything else.

"I reckon we can take the whole front axle off *with* the wheels,

Alan. No need to take the wheels off separately. What's the matter?"

"Nothing!" said Alan, as he jumped down. "Just a thought!"

They went through the remains of the cargo, finding spanners, screwdrivers with no handles but still usable, pliers, a hammer. Then they got down underneath the front axle and examined the frame and chassis above them.

"Do you know anything about lorries, Jim?" asked Alan.

"Not really, no."

"Well, then – let's just undo everything in sight and see what happens!"

It was neither as difficult nor as dangerous as it sounded, for luckily this particular truck was not fitted with four-wheel drive so they had only the spring shackles, shock absorbers and steering-rods to disconnect. As all L.R.D.G. vehicles were kept in continual maintenance there were no rusted-in nuts or stripped threads to deal with: after an hour's work, they scrambled out from underneath and looked at each other.

"Unless there's something we don't know about, we ought to be able to pull the whole lot out now," said Alan.

They had found a wire towing-rope among the rubbish and this they twisted around the axle close to the nearside wheel. Nothing moved at first, but then Alan remembered the crowbars: inch by inch, Jim pulling on the rope Alan levering behind the wheel, the whole assembly began pivoting forward. Then it passed the point of balance, the blackened chassis started to swing sideways and Alan jumped free.

With a crash and clanging of sheet metal, the engine and body dropped and the axle and front wheels leaped forward and bounced away, narrowly missing Jim who had flung himself sideways just in time. An hour later, all the petrol which had been flung from the truck – contained now in four jerricans – was in position on sand-channels which had been in turn, lashed to the axle. A crowbar formed a shaft: it was a good job, but they were yet to learn its cost.

"I reckon we've earned our rest, Jim."

They built a shelter from the sun with the remains of the tailboard and leaned the empty jerricans against it to fill the gaps. Then they crawled thankfully underneath and prayed for sleep and some respite from the torments of thirst. There was no water left in the bottle now, and their tongues seemed to have absorbed it all like a sponge, leaving none to ease their cracked and aching throats.

When Alan came back to consciousness, he lay still for a little while, wondering what was wrong. He had become so accustomed to dull pain and throbbing head and joints that he had difficulty in identifying the locality of this new discomfort: then he looked at Jim and guessed the truth. Jim's mouth was slightly open and between the cracked lips Alan could see the end of a swollen, purpling tongue. His own was the same, his mouth almost filled with dry, choking leather. By an effort, he could withdraw his tongue sufficiently to close his lips.

Outside, the heat was going, the blue, saving night gliding across the sky – but Alan knew that this was their last chance. Another day would kill them or unhinge their minds. He shook Jim into wakefulness, pointed to the improvised trolley and then at their own mouths. They took their places on each side of the crowbar which had been lashed in places as a shaft, picked it up and dragged themselves forward into the night.

They stumbled a lot at first, and the crowbar was awkward to grasp and pull, but gradually the rhythm came to help them, the dull monotony crept into their minds as a soothing anaesthetic: the world was reduced to a black, arid circle, and a weight to drag on through all of life, eternally, inevitably.

They took no rests, but marched ahead almost blindly. Sometimes it seemed to Alan that he must have slept as he marched, for landmarks occasionally registered themselves in his mind when he had no memory of those they must have passed before. Not that the landmarks were many or striking – a rock like a man wearing a cloak, a depression in the ground with straggling bushes which might have been a water-course five weeks before. Slowly the world went back under his feet.

He had no memory of meeting Ryman again either, but when they reached and passed the deserted fifteen hundredweight, Ryman was already with them and had been for some time – pushing at the rear of the trolley. Then just before dawn, a faint breeze sprang up and incredibly, it bore moisture in its soft caress which eased his tongue and he could suddenly speak.

"Not much further, Jim," he croaked, and Jim nodded back and tried to grin while Ryman grunted encouragingly from the back.

They passed the naked, swollen body at dawn and reached the lorry before the sun tore its way clear of the horizon – and by not allowing any pause in effort, they unloaded the jerricans and poured the contents of two of them into the tank.

"Battery!" thought Alan dully to himself. "It can't be flat."

175

It was – but it was not dead. It would not turn the starter but Ryman had fully expected that and allowed for it in his calculations: he filled the float chamber by hand, made sure that the carburetter-pistons weren't stuck, then put the starting handle in place and looked at Alan.

"O.K." whispered Alan. "You get up in the seat. I'll turn it."

He looked dully at the steel bar in his hand and wondered whether they were to live or die – the next few minutes would surely tell them. He looked up at the driving seat and saw Ryman lift his hand.

"God!" prayed Alan, and flung himself down on the handle.

It dropped, jerked at the bottom of the swing and as he pulled it up again, he felt the jump of the compression. Over the top and down again, up, up, over the top and down again – and panic began to rise in his mind.

Then at his last despairing pull up, there was a sharp explosion from the rear of the lorry and the engine roared. The handle came loose in his hand and he stood swaying against the vibrating bonnet with Jim feebly slapping his shoulder and trying to shout something at him. He grinned, handed Jim the handle and tried to walk around to the back of the lorry, but his legs were all rubber now and the world was tilting up and he had difficulty in holding it off.

Vaguely, he was conscious of being dragged along the ground, then slowly pushed up into the body of the lorry. He heard the tailboard swing up and felt the hard floor jerk under him and start to move: then blackness came over him and he fell away from the heat and the horror.

Chapter 21

PARTIAL consciousness came back to him at times during the day – he felt his body jerk against the hard flooring when the lorry stopped and started again, he realised at some point that Jim was stretched out beside him and from somewhere in the dim recesses of his memory came the tag ' – and in death they were not divided'. But he knew that there was something that must be done before he died – even if Jim came with him – for he felt a deep and imperative need to have done with the past and make a clean, fresh start, somewhere, somehow, even in death.

Then he went back into the shadows again and beat with weak hands on steel walls which ran with beads of molten fire. The beads dribbled over his finger-tips, ran over the backs of his hands and along his arms to reach his shoulders and form a tight ring around his neck. Slowly the ring closed. He fought against it, tugging at the ring, thrusting with his feet against the void.

Then suddenly, he started moving upwards – like a diver striking for the surface – and he came up unbelievingly to a cool, pale-blue twilight and his face was wet and his mouth was full of water which dribbled down his chin because his throat was still locked against it. As he grabbed for the neck of the goatskin, it went away from him and a voice said "Take it easy, now, take it easy."

He lay on the hard floor and looked up at the stars, wondering if he had the courage to move and maybe break the dream. Then Jim coughed and choked beside him and he rolled over to help: Ryman crouched above them both, holding Jim's head with one hand and the bladder of the skin under his arm as he poured water from the neck with the other. Jim's hands came up and again Ryman said "Take it easy, now. Take it easy."

Ryman let Jim's head fall back again and looked across at Alan.

"Sit up against the side," he ordered. His voice was easy now, rough still, but not a croak – and his face was not quite so hollow.

He helped Alan up into position, then took the blackened enamel mug and filled it half full of water.

"Look Alan," he said carefully. "I got to work a bit more on Jim. If I give you this mug, will you promise to sip it only? You know it'll kill you if you drink it straight down?"

Alan nodded weakly.

"Sure," he whispered.

"O.K., then. I'll trust you."

If I drink it down it'll kill me, said Alan to himself, it'll kill me. And I can't die yet, Not yet.

The water passed his lips and was cool on his tongue, and as it ran back over it there was suddenly room now in his mouth where there'd been none before. He felt the water cool and healing in the back of his throat and it lay there for a second and then was gone; he sucked a mouthful but stopped it going down just in time, fighting against a screaming need, rolling the water around inside his mouth, letting it soak in. Then there was still some left in his mouth and it slid smoothly down past the back of his tongue and lay behind the upturned V his ribs made where they divided, and he carefully put the mug down on the floor of the lorry until the water in his stomach had gone.

Then he drank again; then again – and again, and then the mug was empty. Much later, he and Jim eased themselves off the floor of the lorry and went to sleep on soft sand – and Ryman was there all the time helping them.

But he wouldn't give them any more water.

*　　*　　*　　*

It was dark when Ryman woke them up, and he made them get to their feet and try to walk around before he would tell them much. Then he let them lean against the side of the lorry and stood facing them.

"Look," he said harshly. "We're all three pretty weak still – but we're not home, and if we're not damn careful we're going to be taken prisoner or shot or God knows what."

They stared unbelievingly back at him.

"Have you got that?" he asked. "We can still be taken prisoner. We can still be shot."

Alan rubbed his face in his hands and concentrated.

"Where are we?" he asked.

"We're in a wadi about eight miles south of Jarabub," said Ryman – "and the Wops are in Jarabub."

Alan stood away from the lorry now and felt his weight come on his knees and on his feet: the rubbery feeling in his legs was still there, but going.

"Where did the water come from?" he asked.

"A wog fetched it for me," answered Ryman. "One of the Senussis who live in the village – but he was dead scared and any more we want we've to get ourselves."

"How far are we from Siwa?" asked Jim.

"Best part of seventy miles – and we've only got petrol left for twenty."

Alan swayed from side to side on his feet, trying them out, getting his balance back: he was feeling light-headed.

"Have we got any more water?" he asked.

"No. I put the rest in the engine because when we do move, maybe we'll want to move fast."

There was silence and Alan's head swam until he forced it clear.

"Fifty miles still to go after we run out of petrol?"

"Yep!" Ryman held up the goatskin and the driver's water-bottle. "We've got to have both these full or we're not going to make it. We haven't made up yet for the water we sweated out, and as soon as we start walking our guts'll let us know it. That trek back for the petrol damn near killed you two, and yesterday did the same for me – it was a bastard driving this crate along with a boiling rad and no-one to help me swear at it. That's why I headed up this way – I knew we'd never make Siwa without a drink."

Alan sat down and started to take off his boots.

"It's all right," he mumbled. "I've got a bloody awful nail here."

He sat in silence for a while, his fingers feeling for the spike, his mind working.

"O.K.", he said at last. "Can you and I go into Jarabub, leaving Jim as close outside as we dare – in the lorry with the engine running?"

"It won't be very close – and he'd better switch off the engine. We can't waste petrol."

"Why can't I come in with you Alan? We're used to working together."

Alan looked at Jim, his face serious in the darkness. There was a long pause.

Then Alan said softly, wonderingly, "I don't know, Jim. But I've got a feeling you'd better stay outside."

*   *   *   *

Alan and Ryman lay in the irrigation trench at the bottom of a small plantation.

"Might as well be back at Giovanni Corba," thought Alan objectively. He held the revolver in his right hand, the water-bottle in his left, and Ryman had the goatskin.

"I can't see a sentry or a guard anywhere," whispered the New Zealander.

"Perhaps they've only got one out in the whole village," answered Alan. "Why should they have any more? They're not expecting an attack – what is there here that we'd want? I'm surprised they've got any troops here at all."

"They've got 'em all right. Came in a day or so back. Couldn't make out all that the Wog said, but he did say there were plenty."

They peered over the edge of the ditch, trying to see where danger might lay – but nothing moved.

"Come on," said Alan. "We must get moving."

They crept along between irregular date-groves, reached the low wall of a sandstone outhouse and found themselves in a narrow, foetid alleyway. Ryman touched Alan's arm and pointed to an alcove in the wall further along. From it they could look across part of an open square, with the well in the middle and a new, modern-looking building just beyond it.

"That's where the Headquarters'll be," whispered Ryman, " – and most of the troops. It's part of an observatory the Wops built before the war."

As they watched, a shadow moved slowly across beyond the well, rather jerkily, but upright and oddly disturbing. A long rifle spiked the night above his head. As the shadow went on out of the field of vision, Ryman crossed to the other side of the alley-way and slid along the wall until he was just short of the corner. He stared across towards the observatory, then carefully peeped around the corner: then he slowly withdrew his head and beckoned Alan alongside.

"As far as I can see, there's only this sentry," he whispered, "He'll be coming along this side soon. I'll grab him as he goes by, you deal with his rifle and then go for the water."

Ryman's forehead was wet and there were dark ridges between his eyes and the upper edge of his beard: for a moment he reminded Alan of Lewis before the raid.

They waited and then heard soft, uncertain steps coming along the side of the square towards them: as the sentry stepped into sight, Ryman's hands clamped on the back of his neck and across his mouth and Alan grabbed at the rifle. The sentry seemed almost to jump in towards them to the mouth of the alleyway and the only sound he made was a muffled wail – then his rifle came free of the struggle, Alan heard Ryman's fist cracking bone, he put the rifle down on the ground, snatched up the goatskin and water-bottle and raced across the square towards the well.

He dropped into the shadow of the low wall which surrounded it, slid his hand over the top and felt for the surface of the water, finding it almost at his finger-tips.

" —— it," he said, and threw caution to the winds. He leaned over the parapet and thrust both the water-bottle and the goat-skin below the surface, hearing the air gurgling out of both, feeling his back naked and immensely vulnerable.

But Ryman had the sentry's rifle and also the revolver and he must have dealt with the sentry by now for there was no sound. The air bubbled out, the water gurgled in – and no other sound disturbed the night: sweat ran across Alan's face, for if he lifted his head to look for danger, he lifted the containers too. He hung over the parapet, head down, tip-toes touching the ground.

But Ryman didn't come to help.

Alan's back was breaking but the water-bottle was full and the goatskin bulging and heavy beneath the water, but still bubbling. Then the bubbling stopped and he levered himself back and up, scraping elbows and knees on the stone, still waiting for the shouts and the bullets, still waiting for Ryman. Then he was down in the shadow of the wall again, corking the bottle, stopping the neck of the goatskin.

He looked carefully around.

No sign of movement anywhere, wet patches on the ground beside him, gleaming hands, cool and moist. He sucked them, then rose and went back over the parapet again, scooping water up from the surface in his hands and sucking it down cold and clear into his stomach.

He remembered just in time and stopped, pulled himself back, picked up the goatskin and water-bottle and ran back to the alley way. Ryman was crouched, shaking, over the still, slight form of the sentry.

"The bastards," he sobbed. "They shouldn't bring kids like this into war! Look, he can't be more than about fourteen – that's the same age as my kid at home. And I killed him! Me!"

He cradled the slight, unmoving form in his arms, trying to hold the head firmly on the broken neck – the fragile bones which had snapped beneath his fist. On the child's collar was the metal badge of the Fascist Youth.

Alan felt his heart move with pity – then hardened it.

"He'd probably have been a right little sod if you'd been a prisoner," he said brutally. "Pull yourself together and let's get out of here."

"It's not their fault," hissed Ryman, "Not at that age – it can't be. He's the same age as my boy at home."

There was all of the desert, the strain, the thirst of the last few days in Ryman's voice, and now was added the separation from home and the beloved child: Alan felt the New Zealander's rage and misery like a tangible force and it silenced him.

And in the silence, the door of the observatory was flung open and a man's voice, authoritative and brutal, shouted from the threshold.

"Bastiani! Ecco! Bastiani! Dove . . . ?"

With a grunt of savage rage, Ryman flung himself past Alan, out of the mouth of the alleyway and around into the square.

"You're the bastard who killed him, really," he shouted as he ran. "Not me!" And the revolver spat wildly in his hand.

But the distance was too great: Alan, taken by surprise, had hardly time to regain his feet when there was a shout and a burst of fire from the doorway, the whine of ricochets, and searing agony ripped up his right leg from knee to thigh. As he dropped to the ground he caught a glimpse of the scene in the square – Ryman flung back in death across the parapet, a huddle of frightened boys beyond the doorway, the figure of the officer, sliding down against the doorpost, his hands clutched to his belly, the sub-machine gun clattering on to the stone steps. Ryman's hand still held the smoking revolver.

For a few moments Alan lay watching, his brain stunned by the suddenness of the action, acceptant of the apparent certainty of his own capture: then he realised that no other adult had as yet appeared and the scene in the doorway was one of mounting hysteria.

He collected the water-bottle and goatskin and tried to stand up. Eventually he managed it and, fending himself off with one hand from the wall of the alleyway, made his way slowly and painfully as far as the sandstone outhouse. He was leaving a clear and unmistakeable trail, but by wedging the water-bottle under his left arm and holding the goatskin in his left hand, he could grasp and hold together the gaping flesh of his leg with his right.

The blood started to coagulate, closing in around the stone chippings embedded in the muscle. He knew that it was only a matter of time before loss of blood would weaken him to collapsing-point, and he must cover as much ground as possible before then: he pushed himself away from the wall and lurched from tree to tree along the grove, staggering over a plank bridge across the irrigation ditch.

Behind him, he could hear the rising pandemonium of frightened, youthful panic, and it gave him hope, for he knew he had no time to waste on cover or subterfuge. He ground his teeth together against the pain, prayed for strength, and forced himself along over the uneven ground. As he went past remembered point after another, the pain began to dull, and his head became wonderfully clear.

As his mind reached the shaded area between clarity and delirium, Jim rose from a shadowed pocket in the ground and ran towards him.

"It's all right, Alan. I brought the lorry in closer when I heard the firing. Not much further now."

Chapter 22

FOR a few minutes after the sun rose it was possible to lie in comfort, and there was some release from pain although his leg still throbbed. His teeth stopped chattering, the ice in his bones thawed out but soon the heat would start, the flies would come back and the space under the floor of the lorry in which he had frozen during the night, would become a slow, daytime furnace.

It had been bad enough yesterday when he had still had company, for Jim had remained with him all day after driving from Jarabub until the fuel had run out. Fortunately Jim had been able to run the lorry into a narrow wadi with the last few cupfuls of petrol – and then had cut a few straggling bushes to break the outline of the truck. He had moved Alan into the most comfortable position, crawled in after him and lay beside him during the whole of the day, occasionally wetting a piece of the driver's shirt and wiping Alan's face.

"You ought to get some sleep, Jim," Alan had protested weakly. "Remember you've still got fifty miles to walk to Siwa."

"O.K., Alan, I've been sleeping, really I have. How's the leg?"

The leg was bad then and likely to get worse today – and the next day, and the next and the next and the next, until there were no more days.

Alan sighed and looked up at the sand-shot boards above him. They were blank, uniform, and reminiscent of a coffin, and the thought was in his mind that that indeed was the last purpose which they would serve – but now, in the face of death he should surely be able to feel some release from the burden of guilt which he had carried around with him for over a year?

Jim now knew everything.

Alan had told him during the brief twilight before he had set out on the trip to Siwa, and when at last – whitefaced and completely wordless, Jim had stumbled away into the darkness, Alan had felt overwhelmingly that he would never see his friend again. It had needed all Alan's determination to hold Jim back at twilight in order to soften the shock which lay in wait for him either at Siwa or some other base – but it had to be done, for Alan's sake almost as much as Jim's.

There had been in Alan's mind a hope that it would in the end prove worse for him than for his friend, but when the time had come and he had put out his hand and said – "Wait a minute,

Jim. I've got something to tell you before you go." – then he had known that Jim would bear the deeper hurt. The slow paling of Jim's face beneath the grime and the burn had confirmed it – the disbelief, the shock, the realisation of betrayal, then the beginning of the slow, bitter anger.

At the end, Jim had taken the water-bottle, crawled out from under the truck – and gone. Without a word. Without a backward glance. Without even a curse.

* * * *

And now Alan lay and wondered what could be the advantage which had been gained by himself. Somehow he knew that in risking and quite probably sacrificing himself in order to protect Jim against the full force of Cora's unfeeling selfishness, he too had benefited.

At first he had reasoned that if Jim did take his revenge by leaving him to die of thirst and pain under the truck, then at least he, Alan, would die with a clear conscience, but as the night had worn on and the tumult of emotions had died down, he perceived that this was not so. Cora and he had betrayed Jim – and merely telling Jim did not wipe the slate clean, even under those circumstances and with that motive.

Yet he remained aware of some inner adjustment of mind which benefited him. Despite his throbbing leg and aching bones, despite the ever-growing clarity of the predicament in which his confession had placed him and the fate which thus almost certainly awaited him, Alan felt that at last he had acted correctly and that the virtue which would certainly be its own and sole reward, was also a source of strength.

The flies buzzed under the truck, the smell of hot metal and rubber grew, and faintly, disgustingly, came also the first hint of corruption: he took a mouthful of water from the goatskin, rinsing it slowly around inside his mouth before swallowing it. Then he faced the long torture which lay immediately ahead, and tried to blank off his mind against the present realities.

As the heat rose, so did the pain and the thirst. The surface of his mind bubbled and all was confusion above, but deep down a new strength awaited such time as it could best be employed. For hours he drifted towards delirium but always something kept him from reaching into the doubtful sanctuary of unreality: he lost himself in troubled dreams but never touched insanity.

Then the sun went down and coolness brought relief. He found that he could think again, and inevitably he thought first of the future – and having shortly exhausted its barren simplicity, turned to the past.

It was not a pretty or even an unobjectionable picture, he concluded, but as he remembered the thoughts which had moved him and the impulses and conditions which had forced him to act, he thought that he would trace throughout it all, a certain inevitability. Given *his* heredity, *his* environment, *his* physical circumstances, it was difficult to see how – with his nature – he could have acted differently.

'With his nature' – herein lay the secret, the fault, the weaknesses. And now some of the weaknesses had been strengthened: therein lay his present benefit.

Imperceptibly, his thoughts shifted to the future again – to the future as it could have been. Now there were no subconscious pressures to force him away from the main engagements, no desires to lose himself in triviality. No wars would be won by road-watches or nuisance raids in the night, no life lived in proud isolation or the exploitation of solitary talent.

He must return somehow to the comradeship of regimental life which he had tasted so briefly in France, he must shape his life to join in the main stream of humanity. If his talents were really of worth, then he would eventually be chosen as a leader in some capacity or other, but he must wait until chosen, and accept the war – and the world – as it came.

The night was cool and his leg a dull, inert burden which only pained when he moved it: as his mind examined and accepted a new philosophy, his growing physical weakness drifted him inexorably towards sleep, and then, as poison accumulated in his leg – towards coma.

He did not wake when daylight came again.

And in the afternoon, the searching jeeps found him.

Available Now!

THE DRUMS OF APRIL

CHARLES MERGANDAHL

The superb *Drums of April* by Charles Mergandahl is a powerful novel which unfolds dramatically against the bloody and glorious background of the American revolution. Here brought vividly to life is Paul Revere's famous ride, the battles of Lexington and Concord, and the rousing charge at Bunker Hill! Striding through the story are such heroes of history as George Washington and the dashing General Johnny Burgoyne, side by side with the author's own characters including the sensuous Annie Blake, the mysterious Abby Cato and the staunch Major Gillis. This novel, Mergandahl's last, confirms and enhances the high reputation which this major writer established in *The Bramble Bush*.

TANDEM BOOKS

3/6

Available Now!

REVENGE AT SEA

BARRIE PITT

On November 1st, 1914, Graf von Spee's squadron on
the prowl off the west coast of South America caught
and smashed the British naval force at Coronel in
Chile, in the first dramatic naval battle of the war.
"Annihilate the Enemy!" was the message flashed from
Admiralty. On December 8th the avenging fleet located
the German Squadron and in a decisive action known
as the Battle of the Falkland Islands, utterly vanquished
the foe and turned ignominious defeat into glorious
victory!

Barrie Pitt, the distinguished war historian, brings all
the excitement, impact and suspense to the re-creation
of these two great sea battles. Illustrated. First published
under the title Coronel and Falkland.

TANDEM BOOKS

3/6